D0191986

THE HOUSE OF WOLFE

A BORDER NOIR

JAMES CARLOS BLAKE

NO EXIT PRESS

First published in 2015 by No Exit Press,
an imprint of Oldcastle Books Ltd,
PO Box 394, Harpenden,
Herts, AL5 1XJ, UK

noexit.co.uk
@noexitpress
© James Carlos Blake 2015

The right of James Carlos Blake to be identified as the author of this work has been asserted in accordance with the Copyright, Designs and Patents Act 1988.

All rights reserved. No part of this book may be reproduced, stored in or introduced into a retrieval system, or transmitted, in any form or by any means (electronic, mechanical, photocopying, recording or otherwise) without the written permission of the publishers.

Any person who does any unauthorised act in relation to this publication may be liable to criminal prosecution and civil claims for damages.

A CIP catalogue record for this book is available from the British Library.

This is a work of fiction. Names, characters, places, and incidents either are the product of the author's imagination or are used fictitiously, and any resemblance to actual persons, living or dead, businesses, companies, events or locales is entirely coincidental.

ISBN
978-1-84344-559-3 (Print)
978-1-84344-560-9 (Epub)
978-1-84344-561-6 (Kindle)
978-1-84344-562-3 (Pdf)

2 4 6 8 10 9 7 5 3 1

Printed in Great Britain by Clays Ltd, St Ives plc

THE HOUSE OF WOLFE

LANCASHIRE COUNTY LIBRARY
3011813213435 8

Other Works
By James Carlos Blake

Novels
The Rules of Wolfe
Country of the Bad Wolfes
The Killings of Stanley Ketchel
Handsome Harry
Under the Skin
A World of Thieves
Wildwood Boys
Red Grass River
In the Rogue Blood
The Friends of Pancho Villa
The Pistoleer

Collection
Borderlands

In memory of my grandmother

MAMÁ CONCHA

a peerless teller of tales

LANCASHIRE COUNTY LIBRARY	
3011813213435 8	
Askews & Holts	24-Jul-2015
AF THR	£8.99
NPO	

Though your house be built of the hardest stone, it is only as strong as the creed of they who reside within.

—Anonymous

Yes, character is destiny, and yet everything is chance.

—Philip Roth

We are each the only world we're going to get.

—Jim Harrison, *New and Selected Poems*

To be free is to do as you wish until somebody stops you.

—A Mexican outlook of long standing

WOLFE LANDING, TEXAS

RUDY

It's been a slower Sunday than most in the Doghouse, only a half dozen of us still here—not counting the cantina's resident tomcats, one-eyed orange Captain Kiddo and all-black Sugar Ray, who are dozing on the ledge above the back bar. I'm playing dollar-a-hand blackjack at the bar with my cousins Charlie Fortune and Eddie Gato, and behind the counter with Charlie, Lila the barmaid is doing the dealing. My brother Frank and the Professor are sharing a pitcher at a side table. It started raining around midday and it's still coming down, light but steady. The temperature's dropped through the afternoon but the front door's still open, as well as the windows under the propped-out hurricane shutters. Everybody's wearing flannel or sweats except for Charlie, who's in a sleeveless T-shirt proclaiming, "An Armed Society Is a Polite Society." He's the reason the windows are open. It's his joint and he likes it cool, which for him doesn't cross over to cold till it hits the freeze mark. The air's heavy with the smells of the river and muddy vegetation, and there's a loud, steady runoff from the roof gutters into the rain barrels. All in all, a pleasant January evening in the Texas delta. A night on which the last thing you'd expect is hazard.

There's not much likelihood of even some passing stranger dropping in, since Wolfe Landing isn't on the way to anywhere else. We're out in the boonies, midway between Brownsville and the mouth of the

Rio Grande, on sixty acres in the middle of the last palm groves on the river, a lush little forest, actually, with a good share of hardwoods hung with Spanish moss. Outside the grove, it's almost all scrubland and mud flats between Brownsville and the Gulf of Mexico. Wolfe Landing has been a duly chartered town since 1911, and is named after our founding ancestors, but with a population of only sixty-six and nothing but dirt lanes except for tar-and-gravel Main Street, we're really no more than a hamlet. Whenever we speak of "town," we mean Brownsville. You could pass by on the road to Boca Chica Beach and never know we're here except for the little roadside sign reading "Wolfe Landing, 1 mile," with an arrow pointing down the sandy lane that winds through the scrub and into the palms. Even at night you can't see the Landing's lights for the trees. Once in a blue moon somebody will swing down here just out of curiosity, but otherwise nobody visits except on Saturday evenings to enjoy the Doghouse supper specials—seafood gumbo or barbecue ribs, take your pick—and most of those visitors are Brownsville regulars. Charlie loves to cook and likes to draw a crowd to the cantina once a week, never mind that those Saturday nights almost always involve at least one fistfight, which is anyhow generally viewed as part of the entertainment. But woe to him who pulls a knife in a fight. And very serious woe to whoever introduces a gun.

Charlie wins a sixth straight hand and grins big as he rakes the three bucks over to his pile.

Eddie says he has to wonder if somebody he will leave unnamed is slipping winners to her boss.

Lila smiles sweetly and gives him the finger.

"Eloquent," Eddie says, and heads off to the men's room. Halfway there he looks back and gives her a wink and she returns it. They've been an item around here for the past couple of months. Charlie doesn't miss the winks, either, and he rolls his eyes at me.

"Siboney" comes to an end on the replica Wurlitzer, and Frank goes over and punches in a moody CD set of Sinatra that goes well with a night like this. You've never seen such a diverse array on a juke as Charlie has in this one. Everything from Hank Williams to Xavier Cugat to the Rolling Stones, but about half the selections are big band standards. There's occasional complaint about all the Glenn Miller and Artie Shaw, but Charlie just shrugs and says nobody has to listen to it. His bar, his music. No sober patron ever argues the matter. He's an imposing figure, Charlie. The only Wolfe known to have achieved six feet in height, he's majorly muscled but supple and quick as a snake. His buzz-cut hair and close-cropped beard and the white scar through an eyebrow all add to the effect. He's ten years older than Frank and twice that much older than Eddie, and we're all in good shape too, but none of us would stand a chance against him one-on-one. Maybe not even two-on-one.

Lila uncaps another Negra Modelo for him and Shiner Bock for me and asks if we want to play a hand while we wait for Eddie.

Charlie looks at me. "What say, Rudy Max?"

I say why not, and Lila starts shuffling the cards.

Eddie and I got back earlier today from running a load down to Boca Doble on the Tamaulipas coast last night, and as usual on the day after a run, I'm feeling pretty good. Most deliveries go off without a hitch, but you never know. Every time you go out on one you have to be very much on your toes, and even if you don't run into any trouble you're pumped on adrenaline the whole while. This time it was three cases of M-4s, three of Belgium FALs, three cases of ammo for each type of rifle, a carton of clear-cover Beta C-Mags, and a Dragunov sniper rifle equipped with the works. An altogether very pricey load.

It's what we do, we Wolfes. Besides the law firm and the South Texas Realty Company and the Delta Instruments and Graphics store, besides Wolfe Marine & Salvage and the three shrimp boats and the charter boat, besides all of the family's legitimate and prosperous businesses in Cameron County, what we do is deal in guns. Mostly through the Landing and mostly into Mexico. Been doing it for a hundred years. We have a wide and dependable supply network and can get almost any kind of firearm in almost any quantity. We do business with a variety of customers, but our biggest buyer is an organization called Los Jaguaros, which happens to be the Mexican side of our own family, almost all of whom live in Mexico City. They're descended from the same paternal line and hence also named Wolfe. Many in the family have long referred to the lot of us as the House of Wolfe, an apt designation I've always liked. Guns aren't the only thing we smuggle, and smuggling is but one of our illicit enterprises, which we refer to collectively as the shade trade. Charlie's the head of its operations and answers only to the patriarchs of the Texas side of the family, the Three Uncles, who are the chief partners in the Wolfe Associates law firm and among the most highly esteemed trial lawyers in the state. What we don't smuggle is drugs, and very rarely people. Not only are drugs a commodity of which we disapprove, but also the trade attracts too many folk of irrational mentality and rash disposition. As for smuggling people, it's something of a rule with us not to transport anything that can talk, though every now and then we'll make an exception. We also do quite well in the business of identity documents, from the expertly forged to the officially issued. We can provide you with an entirely documented identity and life record from birth to the present day. Big seller, that package, and selling better all the time. In a world of increasing facility for bureaucracies to turn us into numbers and computerized data packets, it's only natural that a resentful and increasing bunch of us are feeding the machines lots of conflicting numbers and false data. You have to beat them at their own game.

But our principal calling has always been gunrunning. Highly illegal, yes, but the way we see it, there are certain natural rights that transcend statute law, and the foremost of them is the right of self-defense. Without the right to defend yourself—and the right to possess the means to do it—all other supposed rights are so much hot air. There's more than a little truth to the old saying that neither God nor the Constitution made men equal, Colonel Colt did. Ergo, as we used to say in debate class, any law that denies you the means to defend yourself against others armed with those same means is an unjust law and undeserving of compliance, albeit noncompliance makes you a criminal by definition. There are of course any number of people of intelligence and good conscience who disagree with our view, and that's fine. We Wolfes are great believers in free choice and free expression. If you're content to trust the state to protect your law-abiding self in all situations, be our guest and best of luck. But if you want the means to defend your own ass, as is your natural right, then step right up and be our client. And if some client should want to buy a gun or even a few caseloads of them from us for uses beyond that of self-defense, well, that's his business. We don't permit anyone to tell us our business, nor do we wish to tell anyone his. The same goes for moral outlooks. Don't tread on us and we won't on you. We're a tolerant, liberty-loving bunch, we Wolfes.

Lila deals me a jack down, then one faceup, and I tell her I'm good.

With an eight atop his hole card, Charlie says, "Show me the magic."

Lila flips him a trey and he laughs and turns over a king to win again and sweeps up the two bucks.

Calls for a card on eighteen and makes the twenty-one. What're the odds? I tell him only fools and drunks call for a card on eighteen, and the only reason he's winning is absolute sheer blind goddamn luck, because he sure as hell doesn't know how to play the game.

"Luck blind as a bat," Charlie says with a smile, and gives Lila a wink.

She laughs and says to me, "He's not called Charlie Fortune for nothing." Actually, Fortune was his momma's maiden name.

Then they both look off toward the front door and lose their smiles.

I turn on my stool as somebody with a Mex accent commands, "Hands on your head! *Everybody!*"

A pair of dudes in black ski masks and wet clothes, one medium high, one short, both holding cut-down pumps. Nobody heard them drive up under the sounds of the juke and the runoff into the rain barrels.

We do as he says. Sitting as I am, though, half-turned toward them, I get a glimpse of Eddie Gato at the entrance to the little restroom foyer in a front corner of the room and out of the dudes' line of vision. Then he's gone.

"Órale!" the shorty says to Frank and the Professor. "Asses to the bar."

They do it, getting up from the table slowly and carefully, keeping their hands on their heads, and come over and sit on stools behind mine.

A sawed-off shotgun is a seriously authoritative weapon, especially indoors. These are an Ithaca and a Remington, but both of them older models, and even from where I'm sitting I can see that neither of the cut barrels is well dressed. Whoever these guys are, they're amateurs and wide-eyed edgy, which makes them all the more dangerous. I figure they're not looking to square a grievance with anybody here or they'd have popped him already. It has to be a heist. In all my years in the Landing there's never before been a robbery try. I doubt these guys are locals or they'd know who we are, and nobody who knows us would try a stunt like this. Maybe they heard something in town about the terrific Saturday suppers at this raggedy joint out in Nowheresville and decided a Sunday night was a perfect time to hit it since the weekend cash wouldn't go to the bank until Monday. Who knows? Could be they were just cruising by on the beach road and spotted the arrow sign and decided to take potluck.

"Apaga esa pinche música!" the shorty says.

The other one does as ordered and goes to the juke, reaches behind it, and pulls the plug on Sinatra's melancholic croon about learning the blues.

The nearest of my guns is a .44 magnum Redhawk revolver in my truck, which is parked practically at the front door but might as well be in Egypt. I don't think Frank's carrying, either. Lila is never armed on the job, and as far as I know, the Professor's never touched a gun. But Charlie usually keeps a piece behind the bar, and the question of the moment is whether he'll try pulling it in the face of two sawed-offs that can nail us all before he can put both guys down. I'm guessing he'll give them the money and let them get out the door, then see what we can do. Even if they make it out of the Landing, we can run them down soon enough and teach them the error of their ways. We can find anybody.

Yet there's still Eddie. I think he left his pistol in the truck too, but maybe he's got it and is hunkered in the foyer with something in mind. No telling with him. Could be Charlie's thinking the same thing.

The shorty comes closer to the bar, holding the Ithaca in Charlie's face. "You the boss man, Tarzan?"

Charlie says he is, and the guy says, "Where's the safe, fucker, and no bullshit. I *know* there's a safe."

Charlie points an elbow toward a door in the rear. "Back there," he says. "Office."

Shorty keeps his piece on Charlie and starts backing up toward the end of the counter to go around it. "Wáchelos," he says to his partner, who sidesteps toward the bar to keep closer watch on all of us.

Just as Shorty's backing up past the other guy, Eddie Gato comes through the front door, his arms extended in front of him with his Browning nine in one hand and my Redhawk in the other and each gun pointed at a masked head. The same noise cover that worked for them lets him come up behind them without being heard, and he's close enough to spit on them when he says in a normal tone, "Con permiso."

They flinch and start to turn, the shotgun muzzles angling away from us, and—all in less than two seconds—I drop to the floor and Frank tackles the Professor off his stool and Lila lets a squeak as Charlie yanks her down behind the bar and there are almost simultaneous blastings of handguns and a cut-off and then clatters and thumps on the floor.

My ears are ringing as I look up and see Eddie lean over one of the laid-out robbers, set the Browning muzzle inches from his heart, and . . . *bam* . . . shoot him again. Then he pushes the other one over on his back and does the same to him.

Always make sure. Longtime rule.

Lila and the Professor have witnessed more than a few fights in the Doghouse, but I'm not sure either of them has ever seen anybody killed before. Some of the tan has gone out of Lila's face. She says she's all right, she just needs a drink, and she pours herself a stiff one. The Professor accepts one, too, looking a little ashy himself.

The cats have vanished but it's unlikely the shots have alarmed any of the residents. Gunfire isn't uncommon in the Landing. The shooting range behind the Republic Arms gets almost daily use, and it's no rarity to hear somebody taking target practice along the river or at one of the resacas, and every so often there's a shooting contest behind the Doghouse, even at night. Just the same, Frank goes out to see if anyone's been roused to curiosity, but he reports no sign of it. Except for his and mine and Charlie's houses, all the Landing's residences stand at a distance from the Doghouse, and it could be nobody even heard the gunfire, not with the houses closed up against the rain.

I retrieve the Redhawk from Eddie and eject the spent shells while he chugs down the beer I had on the bar. Then he starts on the rest of Charlie's brew as he tells us how he got to the restroom foyer and saw what was going on and whipped back around into the men's room and went out the window and over to the truck for the guns. He'd fired two fast rounds from each gun at the bases of their skulls, going for the brain stems to cut motor function and reflex trigger pulls, but he wasn't used to the Redhawk, and its first shot obviously missed the medulla because the guy jerked the trigger in the microsecond before the second bullet cut his lights. The buckshot charge peppered the far wall and shattered two of the glass-framed posters hung on it. One of them, which Lila made, reads, "Resist Much, Obey Little" directly above a hand-scrawled "I mean *all* you sonofabitches! Uncle Walt." The other is a large blowup of Natalie Portman lying naked on a big towel on a plank floor and staring lustily at the viewer, a trio of buckshot holes in one gorgeous thigh right next to an inscription reading, "To Charlie Baby, the world's greatest plowman, from his most grateful furrow. Yours forever and *ever*, Nattie." Our cousin Jackie Marie made it for Charlie for his fortieth birthday three years ago. She lost a bunch of bets that he wouldn't hang it on the wall.

Charlie swigs from a fresh Negra and lets Eddie finish his account, then chastises him for taking such a reckless chance that could've got some of us killed.

"I got an M-4 with auto select under here," Charlie says, tapping the bar counter. "I could've put the whole magazine in the two of them before they cleared the parking lot."

But his heart's not in the reproach and we all know it, because he'd have done the same thing in Eddie's shoes. Besides, Eddie's mode was first-rate. The casual "excuse me" in Spanish didn't spook them into blasting away but distracted them just enough for us to hit the deck before the barrage went off.

Eddie says it *was* a risky thing to do and he knows it, and yeah, we could've nailed them outside or hunted them down afterward. Still, he was afraid they might shoot us any second for whatever dumbfuck reason, or even by accident, so he had to chance it.

Charlie seems about to rebut that argument, but then shrugs and lets it go.

The ruin a magnum hollow-point can make of a human head is impressive. Except for the blood that's sopping through the ski masks, we're able to contain most of the mess inside the hoods as we pull them up carefully to look at the faces. Neither guy is anybody we know. They're both carrying wallets. One has a Texas driver's license with a Laredo address, the other a Mexican license. Maybe the names are real, maybe not. Makes no difference. Both wallets hold pictures of women, lottery tickets, paper pesos, a few dollars.

Although we're in the legal clear in putting down a pair of armed robbers, Charlie sees no reason to report the matter to the sheriff's office in town. We all agree. Why go through the bother, the questions, the paperwork? We anyway don't like being in the news in connection with a violent incident. We have political and media friends in town who at times help us avoid that sort of publicity, but we prefer not to use them except in extreme cases.

Lila accepts the Professor's offer to help clean up. Tomorrow she'll get somebody to repaint the shot-up wall and reframe the posters. The rest of us put on our rain ponchos and pick up the bodies and shotguns and haul them out the back door.

It's still drizzling and the night's gone colder. The river's barely visible under the dense cloud cover and the risen mist. I bring my truck around and we load the bodies into the back and strip them to undershorts and masks, leaving the masks on because I don't want any more blood than necessary on the truck bed. We put the clothes and shoes and wallets into a plastic trash bag and add a couple of big rocks and tie it off and I cut a few slits in it with a jackknife. Then Eddie takes the bag and the two cut-offs over to the dock and flings it all into the river.

Charlie gets in the cab with me, and Frank and Eddie climb into the bed, and I drive slowly down a narrow track that snakes into the deeper regions of the grove. This is the darkest part of the Landing even on the brightest day, and tonight it's so gloomy we can't see anything but what the headlights show. The wipers swipe hard at the tree drippings. We can see vague orange lights in the windows of Charlie's piling house as we go by but can't make out its shape.

We arrive at a small clearing next to a resaca, which in this part of Texas is what they call an oxbow. There are resacas all over the lower Rio Grande, and the palm grove around the Landing has no fewer than a dozen of all sizes. This one's called Resaca Mala and is the biggest and most remote in the grove. It's shaped like a boomerang and we're near its lower tip and there's no simpler way to get to any part of it than the one we've just come on. The air's heavier here, the smells riper. The banks are thick with cattail reeds and brush except for a few clearings like this one. I turn off the engine but leave the headlights blazing out over the black water and glaring against a wall of cattails on the opposite bank.

Charlie and I get out and go around to the back of the truck, and Eddie lets the gate down and we get the bodies out. The only sounds are of us and the massive ringings of frogs.

I grip the bigger guy by the wrists and Charlie gets him by the ankles and we carry him over to the bank and set him down. I take the hood off him, knot it around a fist-sized rock and toss it in the water, and rinse the blood off my hands. Then we pick him up again and Charlie says, "On three." We get a good momentum on him with the first two swings and on the third one loft him through the air and he splashes down more than ten feet out, then bobs up spread-eagled in the ripples and floats off a little farther. The frogs have gone mute.

Frank and Eddie sling the other guy into the water. Even though he's smaller he doesn't sail quite as far as the one we tossed, but Frank's had a creaky shoulder for a few years now.

The water settles around the floating bodies, and Charlie says, "Cut the lights."

I go to the truck and switch off the headlights and the world goes black as blindness.

We stand motionless and I hear nothing but my own breath. Then the reeds start rustling in different parts of the banks. There are small splashings. Then louder ones. Then the water erupts into a loud and frantic agitation of swashings mixed with hoarse guttural grunts.

"Lights," Charlie says.

I switch them on and starkly expose the mad churnings of a mob of alligators tearing the bodies apart. Some of them are ten-footers, and Charlie's seen some around here bigger than that. This resaca has had gators in it since our family settled here in the nineteenth century. They've always served us well.

"Damn," Eddie says.

"Yeah," Charlie says. "Let's go."

The water's still in a thrashing fury as we get in the truck and head back to the Doghouse.

In the morning there won't be so much as a bone or a bootlace to be found.

Now it's after one o'clock and the four of us are still in the Doghouse. An Irish string band is plunking on the juke. The floor's cleaned up, and we've put the robbers' vehicle around back—a Ram pickup truck about ten years old. Tomorrow Jesus McGee will come over and check it out. He owns Riverside Motors and Garage over on Main, and he'll decide whether it's worth giving the pickup a new VIN, tag and title and selling it on this side of the river, or if it'd be better to peddle it "as is" to some Mex dealer in Matamoros.

Charlie had let everybody have one on the house when we got back from the resaca. The Professor gulped down his shot and thanked him and said he was going home. Lila asked if it'd be okay if she took off too and Charlie said sure, and she gave Eddie a little wave and left with the Professor. The other four of us have been nursing our drinks, but we've stretched out the pleasure of the evening's excitement long enough and we don't really mind getting run out when Charlie says, "Time, gentlemen. You don't have to go home but you can't stay here."

We're all heading for the front door when the old rotary wall phone at the end of the bar starts jangling.

That phone's been there since before I was born. Nineteen times out of twenty, a call on it is either from some Landing resident looking for some other one, or from somebody in Brownsville asking about the weekend supper specials. Neither's likely at this hour.

"The hell with whoever it is," Charlie says and goes to the door with the keys in his hand.

"Whomever," I say. I'm not really sure if I'm right, but nobody but Frank would know, and he and I like to get a rise out of Charlie by flaunting the benefits of our B.A.s in English. He gives me a look.

The phone keeps ringing.

"Maybe Lila forgot something," Eddie says, and goes over and picks up the receiver and says, "Yeah?" as if expecting Lila. Then he loses his smile and says, "Who wants him?"

"I ain't here, hang up," Charlie says, and gives me another look and silently mouths the word "ain't."

"Oh Christ . . . Sorry, sir, didn't recognize your voice," Eddie says. "Eddie, sir, Eddie Gato . . . Yessir, he's right here."

He covers the mouthpiece and holds the receiver out toward Charlie and says, "Harry Mack."

That gets everybody's attention. As the eldest of the Three Uncles, Harry McElroy Wolfe is the head of the Texas family. He's also Charlie's dad, and it's unheard of for him to call the Doghouse phone. Whenever he calls Charlie he calls his cell, and if Charlie's got it turned off, he just leaves a message. He's probably tried the cell already. That he's calling the cantina phone at one-thirty in the morning implies an extraordinary circumstance.

Charlie takes the phone and says, "Yes, sir?"

I've never heard Charlie address his father by any name but "sir," and whenever he refers to him in conversation it's always as we do—Harry Mack.

Charlie listens for more than a minute without saying anything other than "right" and "yessir" a couple of times. His face is unreadable.

"Yessir, we can," he says. "Just need to get clothes and passports. We'll be there in less than an hour."

Passports? I exchange looks with Frank and Eddie.

"Yessir, I do," Charlie says. "Of course. Yes, I agree. . . . We will, sir. Thank you."

He hooks the receiver back into its wall cradle and just stands there a minute with his hand still on the phone and his back to us.

Then he turns and says, "They've got Jessie."

I

1 — ESPANTO AND HUERTA

Mexico City on a chill Sunday evening. A pink trace of sundown behind the black mountains. An oblong silver moon overlooking the city's sparkling expanse and bright arterial streams of traffic. Black clouds swelling in the north.

A gray van exits a thoroughfare into the opulent residential district of Chapultepec and makes its way into a wooded hillside neighborhood. The van glides along winding arboreous streets of imposing residences fronted by high stone walls and wide driveways with iron-barred gates manned by uniformed attendants. Before long it is passing through several long blocks whose curbs are lined with chauffeur-attended vehicles bespeaking some sizable social event taking place.

The van rounds a corner and midway down the street it stops at the mouth of an alleyway. Three men in black suits exit the van and it drives away.

A police car wails in the distance. Now an ambulance.

The three men walk through the amber cast of the alleyway lampposts jutting above the walls to either side. Like the street walls these extend the full length of the block and are ten feet high and two feet thick, but unlike the street walls these are topped with cemented shards of broken glass and rolls of razor wire. The sprawling grounds within are patrolled by armed men and teams of dogs trained to attack in silence. Every estate's segment of the alley walls is unnumbered but fronted by a set of large garbage bins and has a solid iron gate with an inset peep window. The gates cannot be opened from the outside by any means short of explosives. Even the alleys of the city's most privileged quarters are roamed by feral dogs, however, and a pack of them fades into the farther shadows at the men's approach.

The men count the gates as they pass them. They are almost to the one they seek when a pair of headlights swings into the alley from behind them. A neighborhood security cruiser.

Two of the men sidle to opposite walls so that the garbage bins shield them from the headlights, and from under their coats take out pistols fitted with silencers. The third man stands in place in the full glare of the car's lights and watches their slow advance.

The cruiser stops a few yards short of him, its radio crackling through the rumble of the engine. The man standing in the light has a brush mustache and a short spike haircut. His shoes gleam. He turns the palms of his hands forward so the security men can see he holds no weapon.

He walks up to the car and looks at its identification number on the rear fender, then waits until the radio volume is reduced before he leans down to the open window and says softly, Business of Zeta. I advise that you depart at once, car Q30-99, and forget you have seen us.

He steps back from the car and crosses his arms, one hand under his jacket.

For a few seconds nobody moves and the only sound is of the patrol car's idling motor. Then the car begins to roll slowly in reverse. It backs up all the way to the end of the block and around the corner, then guns forward past the end of the alley and is gone.

The other two come up beside the spike-haired man. One of them blond and clean-shaven, the other mustached under a large hooked nose.

Business of Zeta, the hooknose says, imitating the low tone of the spike-haired man. Then laughs softly.

Hey man, soon enough be true, the blond one says.

They all chuckle and continue down the alley, passing two more gates, then stop at the next one. Dance music is audible from the other side of the wall.

"La Cumparsita," says the hooknose man, and executes a little tango step.

The spike-haired man draws a pistol from under his coat and gives the peep window two quick taps with the silencer attached to the muzzle.

The window rasps open and someone within inquires, "Quién es?"

"Espanto," says the spike-haired man.

The window slides shut and there is a dull clunk of a large door lock, and on well-oiled hinges the gate silently opens inward just enough to admit each man in turn.

They enter a wooded garden encompassing more than two acres. Night blooms sweeten the air. The high trees reflect the soft glow of Japanese lanterns posted at intervals along meandering stone walkways. At a distance is a swimming pool radiant blue with underwater lights, and just beyond it a blazing two-story mansion, its music much louder this side of the alley wall.

The man who admitted them is tall and sports a mustache and he too wears a black suit. On his assurance that the Dobermans have been removed from the premises for the night—the owner of the estate not wanting to risk that one of his guests might stroll into the garden and get mauled—Espanto reholsters his weapon. He nods at a large low building on the far side of the garden and says, Garage?

Yeah, the tall man says. Come this way. Less light.

Keeping to the darker shadows and skirting a circular fountain centered by a mermaid sculpture spouting water from her upturned mouth, the tall man leads the men to the garage. Its wide roll-up door is closed and all the windows shuttered. They enter through a side door.

The interior of the garage is bright with ceiling lights and contains ten cars parked side by side in a row that yet has room for several more. The floor is spotless. Parked nearest to the roll-up door are four black

Lincoln Town Cars. The other cars are all of different and expensive makes and models, and excepting a 1948 Tucker and a 1952 MGTD Roadster, none of them is more than three years old.

Now that they can all clearly see each other, Espanto introduces the two men with him to the tall man, whose name is Jaime Huerta. Espanto and Huerta have met once before, a few weeks ago at a park bench in the Alameda Central, where with another associate they clarified a few details of the plan for this evening. Huerta owns and manages Angeles de Guarda, a home security and bodyguard company, relatively small—seven male agents and two female office workers constitute his entire staff—but of excellent reputation. For the past four months he has served but one client, Francisco Belmonte, the owner of this estate, who employs Angeles de Guarda on a lavish and exclusive contract to provide round-the-clock protection for his home and family. Belmonte had fired his previous guard service when his wife caught its chief ogling their visiting teenage niece from the girl's second-floor bedroom window while she sunbathed topless in the pool courtyard below. He'd had his hard-on in his hand and wrapped in a pair of the girl's panties. In immediate need of another security firm, Belmonte accepted the recommendation of a friend who had twice employed Angeles de Guarda on brief assignments.

The two men with Espanto are Gallo and Rubio. Both of them are neatly barbered and they wear a suit well, the main reasons Espanto selected them to work with him tonight. Gallo's hooked nose and fierce black eyes give him an aspect of rooster, and Rubio, so called for his fair hair and skin, is the only man of them without mustache. He and Gallo position themselves to either side of the door through which they entered, Rubio at a window whose shutter he opens a crack to keep an eye on the pathways to the garage.

Espanto looks about and says, "Donde están?"

Over here, Huerta says, his Spanish tinged with the inflections of Puebla, his home state.

Espanto follows him past the cars and to the far end of the garage, where two men are sitting on the floor with their backs to the wall, their hands bound under their knees with plastic flex-cuffs, their mouths covered with duct tape. Each gag has a small hole poked in the center so the man can breathe through his mouth if his nose should get stopped up. They are employees of Angeles de Guarda whom Huerta had assigned to guard the garden tonight. They wear black suits, Mr. Belmonte ever insistent that his security people present a uniform but dapper professional appearance.

You did them up by yourself? Espanto says.

I had one do the other, Huerta says, then I did him, then I checked the first one to be sure he'd been done right.

The trussed men are glowering at Huerta.

Hey, guys, what the hell, Huerta says to them. I *said* I was sorry. Get over it. You see a chance like this, you take it, no? Don't tell me *you* wouldn't.

One of them tries to curse him through the tape gag.

Espanto checks his wristwatch. The drivers will be out here in about half an hour, right? he says. That'll leave two of your guys in the house. One in the ballroom, one on the front balcony.

Yeah, nothing's changed, Huerta says. They won't know what's happened till it's happened.

If the driver guys are late getting out here, Espanto says, we could have a problem. The pickup's at seven-thirty. I don't want my guys waiting out in the alley with their thumbs up their ass.

We been over this, man. They won't be late. I told them seven and they'll be here. Only thing not sure is when the after party bunch heads out. Supposed to be at eight, but, you know, fucking reception, no telling when they'll go out to the cars. I figure they'll hold to the schedule. The wedding and all, been partying for seven hours, and they still got this other thing. They'll want to get to it.

Espanto regards the cuffed men on the floor, their fierce staring at Huerta. Jesus, he says. These guys would like to skin you alive. Belmonte will too. You're gonna have to get lost really good.

Listen, friend, day after tomorrow not even God will be able to find me, Huerta says.

Espanto smiles. Really? Where you going?

Huerta gives him an arch look and swings a hand in a circle around the room, saying, That way. The minute I get my cut, I am *gone*, buddy, I am nowhere.

Espanto smiles and says, I believe it.

Here they come, Rubio calls from his window post.

He and Gallo extract their weapons, compact Glock 19s with silencers, the same as Espanto carries. They move a little farther from the garage side door, keeping their backs to the wall. Huerta stands near the front of a yellow Cadillac and raises his hands in an attitude of captivity. Espanto ducks behind the Caddy's other side.

The side door opens and three men enter the garage, all wearing black suits—the Angeles agents Huerta has assigned to drive the Town Cars. Two of the men are laughing over something the third has just said.

They halt at the sight of Huerta with his hands up.

Hey, chief, one says, what's—

Do what they say, boys, Huerta says.

Espanto stands up from behind the Caddy with his gun pointed at Huerta's head and says, "Manos arriba, chingados!"

Do it *now!* Rubio orders, announcing his presence behind them. Get them *up!*

Two of the men fling up their hands, but the third one, the biggest man in the room, his large head round and crew cut, starts to turn to look at Rubio, and Gallo rushes up behind him and clubs him hard on the crown with the silencer-weighted pistol barrel.

The man grunts and staggers forward with a hand to his head, then turns toward Gallo, who curses and goes at him and pistol-lashes him again, across the ear, snapping the man's head half around and sending him tottering sideways to bang against a car. But he remains upright, his hand trying to find its way into his jacket and to his gun.

Espanto points his pistol at him and says, Don't do it!

Infuriated that the man is still standing, Gallo snarls and lunges at him again, this time swinging the pistol like he's throwing it, and hits him just above an eye.

The man reels like a drunken dancer and falls backward, his head hitting the concrete floor with a hollow *bonk*. He lies unmoving, eyes closed. A small rivulet of blood runs from under his head. One ear looks like a mashed plum, and a red welt the size of a cheroot swells over his eye.

Jesus, Gallo says. Head like fucking rock.

He dead? Espanto says.

Gallo gets down on one knee and reaches into the big man's coat, withdraws a Ruger .380 and slides it over to Rubio, then puts two fingers to the man's neck to probe for a pulse.

The man's eyes snap open and he clamps one huge hand around the wrist of Gallo's gun hand and the other onto his throat and yanks his face down toward his bared teeth. Gallo braces his free arm on the man's chest, keeping their faces inches apart, feeling the man's hot exhalations, unable to draw breath nor even scream at the pain of the thumb jabbing hard into his Adam's apple as they struggle in a frenzy, legs flailing.

Huerta crouches beside them with an open switchblade and with a deft stroke cuts into the bicep of the arm choking Gallo. Blood jets and the big man yowls and the cut arm drops limp.

Gallo slumps to the floor, gagging, then labors up to his knees and starts to raise his pistol to hit the big man in the face, but Huerta shoves him back, saying, "Basta!" and Gallo falls on his ass, still beset by choked coughing. Rubio helps him to his feet, and Huerta points toward a corner and says, Bathroom, and Rubio leads him away.

The other two security men are wide-eyed and still have their hands up. They all hear Gallo hacking in the bathroom while Huerta tends to the big man. He cuts away his jacket and shirt sleeves to expose the wound streaming blood, uses a strip of shirt sleeve to fashion a tourniquet above the gash, then binds the wound with a cleaning rag and another strip of sleeve. He loosens the tourniquet and helps the man to sit up, then stand. The back of the big man's head is a sticky web of blood and he cradles his arm to his chest like a sick child.

You didn't have to *cut* me, he says.

You moron, Huerta says. You're lucky you didn't get your brains blown out.

I'm still bleeding, the man says. He looks near to tears.

You're okay. It'll hold till a doctor tends you.

Huerta pats the man's coat and extracts a wallet from an inside pocket and tosses it to Espanto, who adds it to a ragbag holding the other Angeles men's wallets. Their guns are in another bag.

Why you *doing* this, chief? the big man says in a voice plaintive as a child's.

Huerta ignores him.

Rubio returns from the bathroom and says that Gallo's okay and getting cleaned up. They put the three Angeles agents with the other two at the back wall of the garage. Huerta takes the bags of guns and wallets to the Town Car nearest the garage door and puts them under the front seats. He gets a handful of flex-cuffs and a roll of duct tape from the trunk and he and Espanto gag the three arrivals in the same way as the other two, then cuff all five of them with their hands at their backs.

Gallo reappears, having cleaned off his suit with damp paper towels. His neck shows small dark bruises but he has washed his face and combed his hair and looks presentable enough to carry on.

He gives the big man a hard look and calls him a son of a whore.

The big man stares back in glum silence.

Again holding to the shadows, Espanto and Huerta take the five Angeles men from the garage to the garden's rear gate. The music from the house is louder now, the voices and laughter. The north sky now starless for the massing rain clouds.

Espanto has warned the bound and gagged men that if they try anything stupid he will beat them unconscious with his pistol, but if they do exactly as they're told, they'll be fine. They will be taken to a house outside the city and there spend the night. In the morning they will be set free. We don't give a fuck what you do after that, Espanto told them.

When they get to the gate, Huerta extracts black blindfolds from his jacket pockets and applies one to each man. He senses a swelling of their fear and says, Don't worry, boys, this is just so you won't have to lie to anybody when you tell them you don't know where you were held. Remember, I'm the bad guy, not any of you. You guys are in the clear.

One of them mutters angrily but unintelligibly through his gag. Espanto smacks him on the head and tells him to keep quiet.

They've been waiting in the darkness only a few minutes, Espanto at the open peep window, when they hear the rumbling engine of a vehicle coming down the alley. It stops just outside the gate. Espanto opens it and he and Huerta move the men outside. Standing there with its engine idling is a gray van, two men in the front seats. A man of Oriental features pokes his head out of the driver's window and says, All aboard, gentlemen.

Espanto slides open the rear door and Huerta helps the blindfolded men to get in. The backseats have been removed. The man in the passenger side front seat tells them to lie down and stay that way until they're told to do otherwise.

Huerta slides the door closed and its lock clicks. Espanto slaps the roof and says, "Váyanse."

The van departs.

Should've been smoother, Espanto says as they go back through the gate. Hardhead bastard nearly fucked things up.

Could've been worse, Huerta says. We might've had to haul a body out here.

At twenty minutes to eight, they take the four Town Cars—Huerta driving the lead vehicle, then Espanto, Gallo, and Rubio—up the wide curving driveway, lined on both sides with the attended cars of special guests, and around to the front of the house and park one behind the other in the reserved stretch along the curb near the verandah steps. On the other side of the driveway is a large courtyard, its dense trees softly underlighted. The men get out of the cars and come around them to post themselves on the passenger sides, facing the house.

A few couples stand along the verandah railing, some of them silhouetted against the brilliant windows, holding each other close, murmuring, laughing low. From the ballroom come the jolly strains of a Strauss waltz.

At ten past eight, the small party they've been awaiting comes out of the house in a loud jabber and flows down the flight of steps to the Town Cars, and the waiting drivers open the doors to receive them.

2 — JESSIE

As the orchestra crescendos toward the conclusion of Strauss's "Voices of Spring," Jessica Juliet Wolfe whirls round and round in the arms of Aldo Belmonte. He's waltzing her toward the corner of the chandeliered ballroom where a row of tall potted palms blocks the room's view of the restroom foyer.

Jessie knows what he's up to and she's decided the thing to do is let him make his move and get it over with.

He spins her off the floor and behind the palms as the last notes sound and the ballroom bursts into applause for the orchestra. He brings her to a halt at the wall, a hand at her nape under hair of strawberry blonde, gazing in her eyes with a soulfulness so theatrical she nearly laughs. She surprises herself by not averting her mouth from his kiss, but isn't at all surprised to feel his hand slide down to her ass or the press of his hardness on her tummy. He tries to insinuate his tongue into her mouth but she locks her lips in a tight smile, then giggles at the feel of his tongue tip trying to breach the barrier.

He pulls his head back. Very cute, he says.

"Sorry, sailor," she says in English, pushing his hand away. "A cop of ass and a dry smooch is as far as it goes tonight."

"Tonight, huh?" He consults his Rolex. "Well, it'll be tomorrow in just a few hours." His English has a tinge of Spanish accent.

"Forget it, amigo," she says. "I told you."

He puts his hands on her hips and again presses his pelvis to her. "*This* old amigo of yours would really like to, ah, get together again."

"Jesus, Aldo. Suave as ever."

She squirms free of him and shakes straight her shoulder-length hair and runs her hands over her hips and bottom as if to smooth her gown but really just to tease him because he has it coming. The dress is a navy sheath of silk jersey, sleeveless and floor-length, identical to those of the other two bridesmaids, and she knows how fetchingly it holds to her butt. He comes toward her again and she moves out from behind the palms.

"C'mon, JJ, don't be—"

"Would you be a dear and get me a glass of white?"

"Now? We'll be leaving in a minute."

"Would you please?"

He sighs, but says, "Yeah, sure," and goes off to the bar as the orchestra begins a jazzy number.

Rayo Luna Wolfe emerges from the crowd along the near side of the dance floor, smiling as she heads toward Jessie with a green drink in hand. Jessie grins at her pixie-haired cousin's brazen strut and the way she pretends not to be aware of all the attention she draws as she passes. Her clingy black minidress dispels all question of whether she's wearing anything under it save maybe a thong.

"Hey, you sexy thing," Rayo says in English. "I thought you'd be gone to that other shindig by now."

"Pretty soon," Jessie says. She gives a pointed look at the obvious jut of Rayo's nipples against the dress. "And speaking of sexy things, it's not *that* chilly in here, kiddo. What's got them so worked up?"

Rayo looks down at herself, then leans closer and says, "It's this dress. They *love* the feel of silk. That and the looks I been getting from a certain dude."

"More than one dude, sweetie, take my word for it."

"No, mija, I mean a real stud. And you know what they say. Guys get horny at weddings."

"I thought that's what they say about women."

"That's what *guys* say they say about women."

"Well it's true enough of one woman I could name."

Rayo makes a face at her. "Actually, guys get horny if they're awake. And you? I saw you and Aldo go waltzing off into that little jungle."

Jessie rolls her eyes. "Christ, he won't quit."

"I been there, babe. Some guys, you do them in college, they think it gives them a lifetime ticket. *So* dickhead."

"What the hell *is* that?" Jessie asks, staring at Rayo's green drink.

"Not real sure. For a joke I asked the bar guy for absinthe. I mean who drinks absinthe, right? But the guy doesn't bat an eye and pours me this." She sips at it. "Yipes. I think it *is* absinthe."

Like much of the Mexican side of the Wolfe family—and most of the three hundred guests at this reception—Rayo is of mostly mestizo lineage, caramel skinned and black haired, a sharp contrast to Jessie, whose light red hair and cream complexion make her one of the fewer than three dozen racial standouts in attendance.

When Jessie was asked to be a bridesmaid, she was told she could bring a guest of her own to the wedding, and she naturally chose Rayo, whom she's known since they were both fifteen. Rayo was born and raised in Mexico City—like Jessie, an only child—and her mother had thought it a good idea for her to correspond with someone of their American kin in order to practice her English composition and maintain family ties, and she had suggested Jessica Juliet because they were the same age. So Rayo wrote to Jessie in English, who responded in Spanish to say she was happy to get her letter and liked the idea of being pen pals in each other's main language. They began swapping photos and descriptions of life in Brownsville and in Mexico City and were soon sharing confidences about family, school, personal aspirations, and of course boys. When Jessie invited Rayo to come visit the following summer, Rayo asked her parents, they said yes, and it was a memorable ten weeks. Jessie introduced her to friends and took her to raucous parties. They went sailing on the Gulf, rode horses, swam in resacas. They sometimes spent the day with her Uncle Charlie at Wolfe Landing, target shooting at the Republic Arms range. They had both been taught to shoot when they were kids, and Jessie was a good marksman, but Rayo was a deadeye and won most of their contests with both handgun and rifle. The girls shared favorite books and watched videos of favorite movies, talked and talked about boys and sex, subjects that at the same time fascinated them and induced howls of laughter. They'd each acquired an early confidence with boys but Rayo was the bolder. She had such an easy way of sassing them, of putting more sway in her stride when she knew they were checking her out, that Jessie was a little surprised to learn she too was still a virgin at sixteen. They had both, however, had their share of encounters with urgently naked erections, and they had each on occasion relieved one with her hand, and in a few instances of what-the-hell, with her mouth. They had also both known the reciprocal pleasure of a boy's tongue that through skill or blind luck found just the right spot—although they agreed the experience more often entailed a tedious endurance of sloppy lapping until the guy was glaze-faced and gasping and they'd pat him on the head and say something along the lines of, "Enough, baby, wow, really great." In the course of that summer they became to each other the sister both had always wanted. Their bond was tightened all the more on the July night they happily ceded their virginities to a pair of brothers named Mike and Joey McCall, on blankets spread on either side of a Boca Chica sand dune under a sky encrusted with stars and hung with a crescent moon at the far reach of the sea. A year later, when Jessie informed her that the McCall boys had been killed in a highway accident on the way back from spring break in Corpus Christi, Rayo wept with as much heartache as her cousin. After high school Jessie attended the University of Texas in Austin to major in journalism and minor in dance, while Rayo studied theater arts at the University of Miami and lettered in track, tennis, and swimming. In each of their college years they got together in New Orleans for Mardi Gras, where once in a Jackson Square bar an obnoxious fool would not desist in his pawing of Rayo until she floored him with an expert knee to the balls that drew cheers from onlookers. They attended each other's graduation, but later that same summer Rayo's parents were killed when the private plane bringing them back from a Havana vacation crashed in the Gulf. Bits of the aircraft were found, but no bodies recovered. Since then, Rayo has lived alone, as has Jessie, and they have remained each other's closest confidante. In addition to alternating annual visits, they rarely let a month go by without an hour-long phone talk to share the doings in their lives, and their weekly e-mails sometimes include an attachment of

Jessie's most recent newspaper feature or magazine article, or a video clip of Rayo's latest stunt work in some movie or TV show.

Jessie had long been aware of the arms-smuggling partnership between the two sides of the family, but it wasn't until her visit to Mexico City last year that she learned of Rayo's recent entry into the family's Jaguaro organization, though she also still works in film. Because Jessie has had nothing to do with the family's illicit dealings, Rayo had thought of not mentioning her own role in them, but as she explained it, "There has to be *somebody* I don't keep secrets from, and you're it, kid." Jessie was less shocked by the revelation of Rayo's membership in the Jaguaros than she was worried about the dangers of it. Rayo said she wished there *was* some danger to be concerned about, something to make the work more exciting, but she was never assigned to do anything riskier than keep an eye on somebody or serve as a diversion. "Mostly I'm the *girl*," she said. "You know, the go-to whenever they a need a nice ass to distract some guy's attention." She was willing to tell Jessie anything she might want to know about it, but said it was basically boring stuff and she herself would rather talk about other things. Jessie said she would too, and they hadn't spoken of the Jaguaros since.

"Ooh, there he is, míralo," Rayo says. "Over by the bandstand. Cigarette, Caesar hairstyle. Gregorio something-or-other. Goes to school in California. His father owns mines or something. Longtime friends of the Belmontes. Son muy ricos."

"*Everybody* here's real rich except you and me," Jessie says. She gives Rayo a mock knowing look. "Hunting for a well-heeled hubby, are we?"

"Oh, *please*." Rayo says. "Not well-heeled or any other kind, thank you. It's just this guy's got the look, you know? Like he can reeeally do it."

Jessie laughs. "You are *such* a slut. You'll never change."

"God, I hope not."

Jessie studies Gregorio—who looks like he can't be more than nineteen or twenty—standing with his hands in his pockets and addressing a group of young people at a table near the bandstand. Handsome devil. His smile and body language exuding great satisfaction with himself and the table's attention. He says something that prompts everyone's laughter, then looks over and smiles at Jessie and winks at Rayo. Who raises her glass slightly to him and winks back.

"I don't believe you," Jessie says.

Rayo affects a look of blank innocence.

Gregorio excuses himself from the group and comes over to the Wolfe women, smiling wide.

Good evening, ladies. I am Gregorio Marcosas Alemán.

Rayo introduces herself and then Jessie. Jessie says she's pleased to meet him and proffers a handshake. He kisses her hand and says, "Encantado, señorita," and asks her pardon for his lack of English. Then turns to Rayo and asks if he might have the honor of a dance.

Rayo says he may. She hands her drink to Jessie and accepts Gregorio's arm.

"I'm off in a minute," Jessie says. "Have fun and don't do anything I wouldn't."

"Contradicting yourself again," Rayo says as Gregorio squires her away. "First one back to my place is a hopeless skank."

Aldo returns with a glass of wine and with Jessie's shawl from the checkroom. He hands her the shawl and nods at her drink. "What's that? You wanted white."

"Try it," she says, and trades drinks with him. He tastes the absinthe and frowns.

"Good stuff, huh?" She smiles and sips at the wine.

"We gotta go," he says. "Trio just told me. Everybody's meeting at the front door." He takes the wine from her and puts both drinks on the tray of a passing waiter.

She lets him lead her by the hand and they wend their way through the throng, cutting through the dance floor, begging the pardons of persons they jostle. Then she sees the front doors up ahead and the waiting bridal party entourage.

Both bride and groom are from families of means. Francisco Belmonte, father of the groom, Demetrio—called Trio by friends and family—owns interests in heavy equipment and food canning and a major share in a television network, but his most gainful venture is Fuentes de Oro, a company that manufactures platforms for offshore oil drilling and has a number of international clients. His American wife is the daughter of a Hollywood film producer of good critical reputation. Oscar Sosa, father of Luz, the bride, heads a corporate entity that builds and manages luxury resorts in many parts of Mexico and Central America. He also owns a number of real estate companies specializing in the sales and leases of mountain retreats and seaside villas. It is common knowledge among the capital's social elite that Luz's mother descends from the Xavier-Morales family, whose lineage extends from the viceroy era. Both mothers are lean and lovely exemplars of social grace, the fathers tall handsome men, trim by way of gym regimens, their naturally dusky complexions darkened the more from golfing, sailing, big-game fishing.

Neither family, however, is given to ostentatious display of its wealth, and the wedding has been a relatively modest affair. One of the few excesses in the original wedding plan had been to have a dozen bridesmaids and groomsmen in the bridal party. But the bridal couple—sweethearts since they were seventeen-year-old classmates at a Cuernavaca academy—have a great many friends, and they feared offending those who couldn't be included in a bridal party even that large. So they decided on just three bridesmaids and groomsmen and all of them relatives except for Jessie, whom Luz Sosa insisted on including.

She and Jessie had met in a freshmen English course at the University of Texas at Austin. Luz was delighted to learn that Jessie had relatives living in Mexico City, though to this day the only Mexican Wolfe she has ever met is Rayo. Their friendship was rooted in their mutual writing ambitions—Jessie in journalism, Luz in fiction—and in their love of modern dance, and they took several writing and dance classes together. In their last two years in Austin they were roommates in an off-campus apartment. Luz's first book, a trio of novellas published in Mexico a year ago to uniformly good reviews and currently being translated for paperback publication in the United States, includes an acknowledgment of Jessica Juliet Wolfe's "invaluable critique" of the manuscript. Trio and his older brother Aldo, serving as his best man, and Luz's younger sister and matron of honor Linda, also earned their degrees from the University of Texas. Trio was at UT for the same four years as Luz and Jessie and majored in petroleum engineering, as did Aldo, who graduated a year ahead of them, and the two brothers are now managers in the engineering division of their father's oil-rig company. Linda, a year younger than Luz, graduated a year after the other four. She studied fashion design and today owns a studio in the Zona Rosa. During the three years all five of them were together at UT, they called themselves the Mighty Handful.

It was near the end of Jessie's junior year that she and Aldo had their "thing," as she calls it. They had agreed to be weekend sex buddies, but the arrangement had been in effect for only a month before he started pressing her for weeknight trysts, as well. She steadfastly refused, her weeknights strictly reserved for coursework, and his pouts, which at first amused her, soon began to grow tiresome. When she had to beg off one weekend because of the need to finish an important paper due on Monday, he angrily demanded to know if she was fucking somebody else. She wasn't, but didn't say so, telling him only that it was none of his business. But he persisted in his accusations and so she put an end to their thing then and there. For about three weeks afterward he made such a point of ignoring her whenever the Mighty Handful got together that Luz barred him from the apartment until, as she put it, "you pull your head out of your ass." Which he finally did just a few weeks before the end of the semester, telling Jessie he was sorry and admitting he'd been an asshole and asking her to forgive him and please come to his graduation ceremony. She did both. In the five years since, they have exchanged Christmas cards every season and a few e-mails of chitchat, but they hadn't seen each other again—not even on Jessie's previous visits to Rayo, when they each time got together with Luz and Trio—until the wedding rehearsal.

Francisco Belmonte sees Aldo and Jessie coming through the crowd and says, "Hay están," and Oscar Sosa says, Good, that's everybody. Make our good-bye.

A post-reception after party at the Sosa residence has been arranged for the bridal group, but first comes a formal farewell to the guests. Mr. Belmonte mounts a dais fronted by a microphone and thanks everyone for the great honor of their attendance on this happy affair. He wishes everyone good health and prosperity, reminds them that his house is their house, and invites them to stay and enjoy themselves for as long as they like. Some will take his invitation at face value and linger for a good while yet, but most will adhere to customary decorum and take their leave soon after their hosts.

Laughing and jabbering, the bridal party exits into the chill night and descends the verandah steps to the open doors of the waiting Town Cars, and the four parents are ushered to the one at the head of the line. Jessie notes how cleverly Aldo has positioned her and himself at the tail end of the group to ensure they will be riding in the same car, the last one. Their driver, a blond young man with a pleasant smile, stands between the open front and back doors.

Take the front seat, my captain, Aldo tells José Belmonte, his fifteen-year-old brother and a groomsman, and the boy happily complies. Aldo extends his arm toward the back door and says, Ladies. Jessie gets in and slides over to the window, expecting Susi—a bridesmaid and Luz's younger sister—to get in next, but Aldo cuts ahead of her and snugs up to Jessie, pressing his thigh to hers.

Susi says, Oh, thank you *very* much, Sir Galahad! and gets in.

The driver shuts both doors, goes around the car and slides in behind the wheel. The heater is on, the temperature cozy.

The small caravan gets rolling. The gate attendant waves as they exit to the street, both sides of which are lined for blocks with the attended cars of reception guests, and the Town Cars bear away into the deeper night.

3 — CHATO AND CHINO

Bound, blindfolded, gagged, alert to every ambient sound, the five agents of Angeles de Guarda lying in the back of the van feel the road passing fast beneath them.

The easy glide of the van suggests they're on a main highway. The radio is turned up loud, but the rocking rhythms of Chikita Violenta don't fully mute the sidelong rumblings of large trucks, the blares of car horns. At times they're jounced by a tap of the brakes and the driver curses somebody for an asshole who shouldn't be permitted to drive or a shithead who should be shot. In one instance, the other man laughs and says, Hey, Chino, pull up beside him and I'll hold the wheel while you shoot him.

After a time the van slows down and the men in back feel a mild lean and infer they're leaving the highway on a curving off-ramp. The road onto which they exit is also well paved. Soon afterward they feel a stronger pull as the van executes a tighter turn, and now the tires are reverberating over a rougher road face, perhaps of tar and gravel.

The radio begins to sputter with static. The tuner starts moving over a series of stations in a staccato of speech and music, and the driver, the man called Chino, says, What the fuck, Chato, I like that station. Put it back.

The Chato one says he's tired of that stupid rock noise and anyway can't stand the static. He settles on a corrido station.

Peon crap, the Chino one says. But the tuner stays where it is.

When the van slows almost to a stop and makes a careful turn and proceeds slowly over rugged rising ground, weaving widely left and right, the men in back cannot say whether they've been riding for forty minutes or for two hours. They proceed at this slower pace for a long while before the van stops and the motor shuts off.

The front doors open and close. The back door slides open and the one named Chino says, All right, boys, here we are.

The men in the van smell a horrific stench mingled with acrid smoke, and they know where they are—at one of the massive garbage pits all about the periphery of the city. Where a daily fleet of huge trucks brings its garbage for disposal, much of it by fire.

Peee-yoo, huh? Chino says. As you guys can tell, the house is right next to a dump.

The caustic stink loosens mucus from their noses and a couple of them begin snorting wetly, puffing hard through the little mouth hole in the gag.

Christ, man, Chino says. Let's get the gags off them before they choke to death.

As the tape comes off their mouths, each captive breathes in gasps, fighting for air and grimacing at the foulness of it.

Sorry about that, fellas, Chino says. But don't worry, you won't have to smell it for long. Tomorrow night, you're out of here. Right now we'll just line you up and take you over to the house and get those blindfolds and cuffs off you.

Bullshit! one of the men says in anger. I know what this is. He coughs and spits on the floor.

Chino disregards him. One of the others begins praying in low voice.

Chino helps the man nearest the door to get out and guides him away a short distance before saying, Right here, stay right here. He then retrieves the angry man and stands him at the side of the first man and goes back to the van for the next man.

You fuckers, the angry man says. You stinking shits!

What can we tell anybody? the first man in line says. We don't *know* anything.

We know what they look like, the angry man says. We know Huerta knows them. They can't trust us. Fuck them. Fuck their mothers.

The Chato one says, Man, I wouldn't want *you* for my lawyer.

Fuck what you want, the angry man says. Fuck your father. I hope your sister gets fucked to death by burros.

The Chato one laughs and says, *Burros!* Damn, man.

Chino sets the third man beside the angry one, then fetches the one who was praying and who now starts to cry.

Easy, man, Chino says, patting the man's shoulder gently as he stands him at the end of the line. I know the smell's bad. But it'll be all right soon, you'll see. You don't have to put up with it for long.

The angry man says, Stop sniveling, you cunt coward.

The smoky reek burns their throats. The blindfolded men cannot know they are within three feet of the edge of a bluff overlooking the vast excavation spread before them like a black smoke-hazed sea scattered with large and small islands of fire. A dozen feet below them is the apex of a large smoldering scree of noxious refuse reduced to bright orange embers. It is any man's guess how deep the pits are under the fires, under the accruals of ash and coal and dissolved organic matter of every sort. Popular belief holds that the pits have no bottom but in hell. Through the cold air, the men feel the wafts of heat.

The big man is the last to be brought out. His wounded arm is in grievous pain and bleeding through his makeshift bandage. Chino holds him by the elbow of his good arm and takes him over to the others. The man feels the strength in Chino's hands, but can tell, too, that he's shorter than average. He supposes that, as befits their nicknames, Chino truly looks Chinese and the one called Chato is in fact broad nosed. He is aware that he will never know. When he's positioned at the end of the line, he bumps against the crying man and says, Excuse me, and the man begins to sob more loudly.

You cocksuckers, the angry man says. I hope you die of AIDS. I hope your mothers drown in shit. I hope your sister chokes to death on a nigger dick.

The Chato one laughs. Jesus, man, you're a poet.

He and Chino confer in lowered voices.

The big man envisions one of them standing aside with a gun and ready to shoot anybody who might in desperate fear whirl and run, even blindfolded, preferring to be shot while trying to stay alive than just stand there and take it. He can picture the other one stepping up behind the first man in line and raising the muzzle to his head. He inhales deeply of the malodorous air, feeling his lungs swell wonderfully. His name is Salvador Martín Obrero and he now recalls a Sunday morning more than thirty years ago, his mother telling him as they leave for mass to comb his hair, for the love of God, it looks like a bird's nest.

He flinches at the blast of a gunshot and then come three more in quick succession . . . *bam* . . . *bam* . . . *bam* . . . approaching him and—

Chato and Chino watch the big man's body tumble down the slope to join the others in the fuming mound, vanishing into it in a geyser of scarlet sparks.

They return to the van and start back to the city.

4 — JESSIE

They no sooner head out for the Sosa estate than Aldo places a hand on Jessie's thigh.

"Stop," she says, pushing his hand away.

"Ho, ho, ze Americain girl, she wanz to play, how you say, har to get, eh?" he says in the terrible French accent of the Pepé Le Pew impersonations he used to do in college. He walks his fingers slowly down his leg to his knee and then hops them over on hers and begins walking them backward up her thigh.

"I said *quit*!" she hisses, and jabs a thumbnail into the back of his hand.

He pulls his hand away and tries to examine it in the bad light. "I think you drew blood, you she-devil." She sees his grin in the glow of a passing streetlamp.

"For Pete's sake, Aldo," Susi says. "She doesn't want to be pawed, so just stop pawing her, why don't you?" Susi is seventeen years old and in her final year of high school. In the front seat, young José Belmonte snickers.

Switching to Spanish, Aldo says, You kids mind your own business. This is a matter between grown-ups.

The only grown-up in this car besides JJ is the driver, Susi says, raising another chuckle from José and even from the driver.

They follow the other Town Cars to the brightly lighted thoroughfare of Paseo de la Reforma and meld into the northbound traffic, the four cars holding close to each other to prevent other vehicles from getting between them. Now they turn off onto the Periférico, the city's outer beltway, and bear south. Having been to the Sosa residence, Jessie knows it's on the south side of the posh Pedregales area.

They've been on the beltway less than a minute when the driver's cell phone chirps. He puts it to his ear and says, "Sí?" He listens, then says, "Ah, pues . . . sí, claro . . . muy bien," and puts the phone away. Staying behind the Town Car in front of them as it moves over to the exit lane, he says there's been an accident a few miles ahead on the beltway and traffic's been slowed almost to a standstill. We're getting off at the next ramp and taking side streets until we're past the point of the accident, the driver says. Then we'll get back on the belt. We're lucky we received word before we got stuck in that muddle.

Jessie inwardly groans at this additional irritation. The idea of extending the car ride with Aldo is irksome, never mind having to continue fending him off when they get to the Sosas'. She chides herself for not having faked an upset stomach or something at the reception and begged off from the after party.

The Town Cars exit onto an avenue of heavy traffic and stay on it for a few slow blocks before turning onto a less-congested street. Several blocks farther on, they turn into an industrial area of warehouses, most of them closed for the night. The fenced parking lots contain scatterings of semitrailers. Only one of the loading docks is lighted and at work and only one trailer is being loaded. Paper litter lines the bottoms of the fences.

The cars make another turn, and then another, and are now on a narrow lane, badly lighted and gouged with potholes, flanking a rail track that runs between rows of darkened warehouses with shuttered loading docks.

The driver says he's sorry for the rough ride and explains that the lead driver has chosen this detour because there aren't any stoplights on these backstreets and despite the inferior street surface they're faster than the main avenues. We'll be out of here soon and back on the beltway, he says.

A large vehicle with a red-and-blue flashing light behind its windshield appears from around a corner up ahead, its headlights dazzling. It stops at an angle across the lane, blocking the Town Cars' passage.

The cars halt.

Police, José says. What's going on?

Been a lot of warehouse break-ins lately, the driver says. Lots of thefts. They're probably checking anybody who comes along here at this hour.

The cars in front of them hinder Jessie's view. All she can see of the obstructing vehicle is the reflected radiance of its headlights on the warehouse walls, the rhythmic red-blue sweeps of its light.

Now their car is flooded with bright light from the rear and she squints out the back window at a similar vehicle with a flashing police light on the dashboard.

It stops a few feet behind them and its front doors open and two men come out, both wearing dark Windbreakers. They approach on either side of the Town Car. The one on the driver's side passes on by, but the one on the right stops at José's window and raps it with a knuckle, then holds up an open wallet to display a badge of some sort. His hair is bound in a ponytail that ends below his nape. The other man has gone around to the passenger window of the car ahead and is also displaying an open wallet.

The driver presses a switch to lower the right-side window a little and says, "A su servicio, oficial. Que pasa?"

"Policía," the ponytail man says, and puts the wallet back into his coat. "Abre las ventanas y las puertas, y corta los faroles y el motor."

The driver does as ordered, touching toggles to unlock the doors and lower all four windows into their door slots. He turns off the engine and the headlights. The two cars directly ahead of theirs also turn off all their lights, and the only illumination remaining is from the front Town Car and the two large vehicles, which Jessie now identifies as Suburbans.

The driver reaches under the seat, then opens his door and gets out with something in his hand. Jessie can't see what it is, but she notes that the interior light didn't come on when the door opened. The night chill floods the car.

Hey, man, Aldo says to the driver. What are you—

The driver raises the object in his hand and the sudden glare of a large flashlight forces them to turn their faces away, Aldo saying, What the hell!

You're under arrest, the ponytail man says. All of you! Hands on your head! Everybody! Keep them on your head or I'll shoot you.

Jessie recognizes the pistol in his hand as a compact Glock fitted with a suppressor, and while it's perfectly plausible that Mexico City cops would be working in plain clothes and unmarked cars, she wonders what need a cop would have of a silencer. No one in the car has ever faced a loaded gun before or been threatened with being shot, and all of them, even Jessie, for all her familiarity with firearms, are seized by a kind of fear entirely novel to them.

The ponytail man yanks open the door and tells José to get out and empty all his pockets, of pants and coat both, put everything on the driver's seat. Your watch, too, necklace, rings, *everything*, the man says. I'm searching you afterward, you little prick, and if I find anything on you, you're fucked. When your pockets are empty, take off your coat and put it on the seat too.

José complies as fast as he can, his motions jerky with fright.

Now the driver also brandishes a Glock with a silencer, and commands everyone in the backseat—each in turn and starting with Jessie, the nearest one to him—to do the same. Phones, wallets, jewelry, purses, on the driver's seat. Shawls and coats on the passenger side.

Jesus Christ, man, Aldo says to the driver. What are you—

"Cállate el hocico!" the blond man orders, and Aldo shuts up.

Robbers, Jessie thinks. They're just robbers.

She takes her phone from her purse and deposits both over the front seat, then her watch and shawl, then sits back. The necklace too, the blond says. She hadn't thought she'd get away with it but had to try. She takes off the fine gold necklace with the ivory brooch given to her by her great-great-grandaunt Catalina and drops it over the seat and sits back again with her hands on her head. She tells herself to stay calm, it's only a robbery, nobody's going to get hurt. Could be they're crooked cops, a common reality everywhere in the country, though no more so than robbers who pretend to be cops. Which she figures is what's going on here. They even got the drivers in on it. That, or somehow took the cars from them and put their own men in them. Whatever the deal, she thinks, they've hit a jackpot with this bunch of purses and wallets full of cash and credit cards. And the Town Cars. They'll take them too, she's sure of it. Bring a nice price on the black market. Her job as a crime reporter in Brownsville has taught her much about how these things work, and she's learned a few things from the experts in her own family. In a minute these guys will have everything and be gone, nobody hurt, only lighter of pocket and a little shaken, and everybody with a tale to tell. Much of her fear is giving way to a wary excitement. She's already thinking of the piece she'll write for her newspaper. Maybe a syndicated op-ed piece. Timely stuff, this. But damn it, she hates to lose that brooch.

A man with a large hooked nose has come from the forward cars with a plastic grocery bag and into it puts all their possessions from the front seat, then scoops up the shawls and coats and goes away with it all.

Yep, Jessie thinks. Robbery. Taking the coats and shawls in case there's anything of value pinned in them.

The front Town Car starts to move, easing its way past the Suburban ahead, then goes out of view around the corner, and Jessie congratulates herself for being right about the cars, too. The phrase "making out like bandits" comes to mind and she suppresses an inexplicable urge to laugh.

The ponytail man finishes frisking José then produces a small instrument shaped like a pack of cigarettes and only a little larger, and runs it over him, front and back, head to foot. A sweeper—Jessie knows one when she sees it. It can detect a GPS device too small to find in a pat down, one small enough to be hidden in a belt, a shoe. She's acquainted with various models of both devices—her family deals in them, legitimately and otherwise, among other electronic commodities. Pretty thorough, these boys, she thinks. Best to know if anybody in the party is showing up on a screen somewhere. Some richies carry a tracker on them every time they leave the house. Some have them implanted under the skin. She hopes nobody here has an implant. These guys seem the sort who will excise it on the spot.

The ponytail orders José to put his hands behind him, binds them with plastic flex-cuffs, and tells him to sit on the ground. José squats and then falls over trying to sit, and the man laughs and pulls him up and José sits with his legs crossed. The ponytail tells Susi to get out, and first cuffs and then searches her. She whimpers as his hands fondle her breasts and bottom, his fingers press between her legs. After sweeping and cuffing her, he helps her to sit down beside José, a tricky maneuver in the sheath dress, but she does it. Aldo is next to be cuffed and searched and made to sit on the ground, and then it's Jessie's turn. The ponytail subjects her to the same groping search he gave Susi and concludes it with a kiss to her nape that makes her cringe. He sniggers. She remembers Rayo kneeing the drunk dickhead in New Orleans, but she can't do that in this dress.

Besides, the guy in New Orleans didn't have a gun. As she's helped to sit down she almost loses a high-heeled shoe but manages to keep it on.

It's dark on this side of the Lincolns except for a portion of headlight glow from the vehicle behind their car. Jessie can vaguely discern that the other members of the party are also being bound and searched and made to sit in a bunch on this side of the cars. She's thinking that without a phone left among them they'll have to hoof it out to some busy street to find help. Some sight they're going to present—a bridal party on foot and with their hands bound behind them. Be great if somebody takes a picture of them before the cuffs come off. She can use it in her piece. She's fairly sure that if she kicks off her shoes she can make it to her feet even with her hands behind her and even though this dress will make a contest of it, but she's not so sure she could be of help to those who won't be able to get up, like the parents.

The process has been swift and without a word other than the robbers' orders. She hears low voices but can't make out what they're saying, and then the sounds of car doors closing. The cars start up and their lights come on. Like the first car, they carefully make their way around the large Suburban forward of them and their taillights disappear, one set after another.

She wonders where the hell the real cops are, the warehouse guards, *somebody*. How can these pricks be taking their own sweet time like this? Then thinks, Jesus, girl, what a dummy. There *aren't* any police or security patrols. Not here. Not tonight. These boys have taken care of that. Maybe even have some regular deal worked out for this area.

Everybody up, the blond man says.

She and Susi have to be helped. At least the bastards have put them all on their feet before leaving. The blond man moves and speaks with an easy confidence and it's Jessie's guess he's not a co-opted driver but one of the bandits, maybe even their chief.

Get the bride over here, the blond man says to the ponytail.

Luz! Jessie thinks.

The man goes to the other group and returns with Luz and stands her beside Jessie, who's so glad to see her she blurts, "Luzita, are you all—"

The ponytail man grabs Jessie by the nape, hard fingers digging into the sides of her neck. We told you keep your mouth shut, he says at her ear. His hand tightens and Jessie groans.

Let go of her and get the things, the blond man says.

The ponytail retains his grip for another two seconds, then releases her with a shove. Her eyes are flooded with reflexive tears. Mucus drains from her nose. She sucks air through her mouth and has a bleary view of the ponytail going over to the near Suburban.

Right again, she thinks. Blondie's the honcho. And that ponytail son of a bitch doesn't like it.

The blond comes over and holds a handkerchief to her nostrils and says, It's clean, blow. He gives her nose a few gentle squeezes as she does, then he readjusts the hankie and says, Again. And again she snorts into it. He turns her face toward the headlights and wipes her nose and says, Better?

She nods.

Can you breathe through your nose?

She sniffs and says, Yes. She thinks it a strange question.

Don't speak again unless you're told to or you'll get hurt, he tells her, and flings away the hankie. And don't speak English again if you want to keep your tongue. Understood? He says this in the same tone he might tell her the time of day.

She nods. Thinking, Holy shit.

Say it.

I understand.

He looks around at the others and says, That goes for all of you. You won't get another warning. Now form a line facing me. Guys on the ends, the women in between.

They do it, Jessie wondering, What's this?

The ponytail man returns from the Suburban with a bulbous plastic grocery bag attached to his belt, and the blond says, We're going to blindfold and gag you. Don't resist. Just do as you're told and you won't be harmed. I promise you.

The ponytail goes around behind them. He takes a black sleep mask from the bag and slips it over Aldo's head and over his eyes, then takes out a roll of duct tape and wraps a length of it over Aldo's mouth and around his head. Then sidesteps over behind Susi and begins doing the same to her.

Making sure we can't even go for help, Jessie thinks. That we won't be found before morning.

She flinches at the ponytail's touch from behind her. The sleeping mask comes down over her eyes, the tape seals her mouth, and the man moves on.

She stands bound, gagged, sightless, hearing only the rips of tape from the roll. Then hears what she's sure is a soft cry and her fear surges again.

Rape-robberies are not uncommon either.

Now someone takes her by the arm and says, "Por acá, güera." She recognizes the blond man's voice. She can't help resisting his light pull, and he softly repeats himself, saying, Come with me, blondie. No one's going to hurt you.

She'll fight, she tells herself. Kick the best she can. You can't give in without a fight. It's a rule.

He guides her a few halting yards and turns her around and the backs of her legs come in contact with a solid edge of some sort. She emits a muffled squeak as he hefts her by the waist and sets her on a hard surface, and then someone behind her—the ponytail?—slips his hands under her arms and drags her rearward and eases her down between two other persons lying there. She apprehends they're on the bare floor of the Suburban, whose backseats have been removed.

And now knows . . . this isn't a robbery.

It's a snatch.

5 — THE PARENTS AND EL GALÁN

The Town Car containing the parents of the bride and groom bears north on the beltway's river of traffic. Wearing large-lensed dark glasses, Espanto drives without haste, Huerta beside him, holding a pistol on his lap and half-turned to keep an eye on the two couples crammed into the backseat. The couples are neither gagged nor blindfolded—it wouldn't do for someone in another car to look over and see four persons in such straits—but their hands are cuffed behind them. No one speaks.

It had happened to the parents in such confusing swiftness . . . the Suburban wheeling from around the corner ahead, headlights glaring and police light flashing, blocking the lane . . . the ghostly figure of a spike-haired man in dark glasses at the front window, pointing a pistol at them and commanding them to silence . . . Huerta ordering Mr. Belmonte into the backseat, and the shocked realization that they had been stopped by either corrupt police or outright bandits and that Belmonte's security chief was in league with them . . . the divestment of their phones, wallets, purses . . . the spike-haired man asking if any of them had a GPS device on them and promising he would kill whoever lied, and their swearing in truth that they did not . . . Huerta handing a phone to Mr. Sosa with the instruction to call home and notify his staff that the after party group had decided to go to a nightclub rather than the Sosa residence and that he and Mrs. Sosa were returning to the Belmonte home for the rest of the night and would there spend the next day . . . their hands being cuffed . . . the spike-haired man getting behind the wheel and driving them away, Huerta beside him and assuring them they would not be harmed if they sat still and kept quiet.

So have they done.

The beltway now curves eastward and they stay on it for several miles before exiting onto a northbound highway. A mile farther on, they turn off into a shopping mall and drive around to a far corner of the rear lot where there are few vehicles and park in the darkness of overhanging trees. In the deep shadows, no face in the car is clearly visible.

The spike-haired man tells them that Huerta is going to put sleeping masks over their eyes but they need not be afraid. He holds a pistol on them as Huerta leans over the front seat and slips the elastic-banded masks on each of them in turn. Mrs. Sosa whines softly as the mask is placed on her. The spike-haired man tells her it's all right, there's nothing to fear, but she must keep silent, does she understand?

Yes, she says, yes, I'm sorry.

Huerta sits down again and takes out his Sig 9 pistol. Espanto removes the dark glasses and holsters his gun and exits the car. He walks out into the light of the lampposts and scans the sparsely occupied parking spaces of the nearby rows and spies the vehicle he's looking for, a silver Grand Cherokee, two men silhouetted in the front seat.

A man gets out of the Cherokee's front passenger side and comes to the Town Car. He is tall and lean, his movements fluid. His cream suit superbly tailored. A fedora shades his face above the trim mustache. In his professional circles he is known as El Galán.

"Todo bien?" he asks. Espanto says all is very well.

Espanto gets back behind the wheel and Huerta gets out of the car. Galán assumes the passenger seat and shuts the door and turns to face the masked captives. He tells them his name is Mr. X and that he is responsible for their circumstance. He regrets their discomfort but says there was no other way to do this. His voice has a pleasant timbre and his enunciation is precise.

Mr. Belmonte starts to say, "Por favor, señor, donde están—"

"Silencio," Galán says without raising his voice, and Belmonte falls silent.

Galán apologizes for his rudeness but says that in the interest of time he will do the talking and they must listen carefully.

To ensure that you understand, I will frequently ask you if you do, and you will respond by nodding or shaking your head. If you shake your head I will clarify my point and then ask again. Do not speak. If you speak, your spouse will suffer. Is everything understood so far?

They all nod.

Very good, he says. The state of things is this. The groom and the bride and the other eight members of your party are in our custody. Your three sons and two nephews, Mr. Belmonte. Your three daughters and your niece, Mr. Sosa. And of course the American girl. They are all safe and will be treated well during the short time they are with us. To regain them from our custody, you must pay a total of five million American dollars in cash. Am I clear, gentlemen?

The two men nod.

Excellent. Your people are being held in two separate groups in two different venues. I will not tell you which persons are in which group, only that there are five persons in each and there are Belmontes and Sosas in both groups. You will pay two and a half million dollars for each group, first one and then the other. The money will be in bills of one-hundred-dollar denomination. I'm fairly sure that you gentlemen do not personally handle cash of any great amount yourselves, so you may not know the physical size of this sum. It will fit handily in the gymnasium bags we are going to provide, two bags for each of you. With the money equally distributed in the bags, each bag will weigh roughly twenty-seven pounds. The bags have padded shoulder straps, but still, twenty-seven pounds on each shoulder can be a burden. However, you both look strong to me. Do you believe yourselves capable of such a burden?

Both men nod.

Good, Galán says. You have until four o'clock tomorrow afternoon to obtain the cash. Do not request more time. It will not be granted to you. Understood?

The men nod.

It should go without saying that it would be a regrettable mistake for you to contact the police, and if—

All four of them shake their heads vigorously.

No, certainly you will not. Still, it is possible that the police might in *some* way learn of the situation and insist on becoming involved. Should that happen, you must rebuff their assistance and immediately inform us. Besides, you cannot be sure that the police who come to you are not in partnership with us. It should come as no shock to you that we have such accomplices within all levels of law enforcement agencies. It is one more sad fact about this sinful world that so many public guardians are so venal. It is true even of private guardians whom one might hire at no small cost, eh, Mr. Belmonte?

Belmonte's mouth tightens at the allusion to Huerta and he nods.

Yes, well, Galán says. Are we quite clear about the police?

They all nod.

Good. I'm pleased with how well this is progressing. And believe me, gentlemen, although I know your primary consideration is the welfare of your children, I also know how much it distresses you to be robbed. Permit me to suggest you take a practical view toward it. I've had a look at your financial portfolios, and quite honestly, I was astounded. I can only imagine how difficult it must be for you to deal with such wealth. To a poor workingman like myself, five million dollars is a fantastic amount—my God, a *king's* ransom! To men of your means, on the other hand, well, pardon my presumption, but it's not a loss of great significance. That fact does not make you feel any better, I know, and in truth is beside the point, since nobody likes to be robbed. Even were I rich as you, I would be furious to be robbed of twenty cents. All the same, these things happen. In any case, both of you must surely agree that five million dollars is a bargain price for ten people. *Ten*. A half million each, six of them your children, three others also blood kin. I suggest you divide the cost between you. After all, half of the party are kin to you, Mr. Belmonte, and although only four of them are related to you, Mr. Sosa, the American girl is your daughter's guest, and that makes you responsible for her. We know she comes from a prosperous family in Texas and has wealthy relatives here in Mexico City, but to involve her people in this affair would only make matters more congested and complicated. That is why you, Mr. Sosa, will pay for the American. Whether you discuss reimbursement with her people afterward is your own affair. Am I clear, sir?

Mr. Sosa nods.

Is there any reason either of you might wish to do otherwise than equally share in the ransom?

The two men shake their heads.

Very well. Now then . . . both of you gentlemen have accounts with Banamex, Santander México, and Bancomer. Neither of you is to get your share of the money from any of those three banks. Mr. Belmonte, you also have accounts with HSBC México and with Banco Rosemonte.

You are to withdraw your share of the ransom from Banco Rosemonte. Understood?

Belmonte nods.

Good. As for you, Mr. Sosa, besides the banks in which both you and Mr. Belmonte have accounts, you also have accounts with Banco de Indio Tierra. That is the bank from which you will draw your share of the money. Clear?

Sosa nods.

Good. We have chosen these banks because they are somewhat smaller than the others and your relationships with their officers more intimate, and it should be simpler to gain their prompt cooperation than might be the case at the larger institutions. However, although both banks normally carry more than enough American cash to meet your need, their daily holdings of U.S. currency can vary greatly. It could be that one or even both of the banks may have to request a transfer of dollars from another branch, in which case the procedure may be a protracted one. Even so, you will have ample time to conduct the transactions. You will each drive yourself to your bank and you will each go alone. You will both be watched all the way to and from the bank. Mr. Sosa, you will park as near as possible to the rear doors in order to have easy exit from the bank to your car. Mr. Belmonte, your bank is without parking facility and you will have to walk two blocks from the nearest public lot. More than fifty pounds of money may come to seem quite heavy on the return to the car, but I believe we have established that you can handle it. Is everything still clear so far, gentlemen?

Both men nod.

Very well. The bankers will naturally be most apprehensive about a cash withdrawal of such size, and in American currency. Bankers are not entirely ignorant about these things, and in the absence of a plausible explanation for the withdrawal, they are apt to suspect extortion. It is imperative that you prevent them from acting on such suspicion. This is a crucial point. The best way to ensure that your bankers not contact the authorities is to tell them the truth. But you must impress upon them that your children's safety depends on their discreet cooperation. Is this understood?

The men nod. Unsure if they were included in the question, the women do too.

Excellent, says Galán. Except for the visits to the banks by you gentlemen, the four of you will remain at the Belmonte house until our business is completed. However, other relatives of wedding party members may become concerned about the lengthy absence of the party and the lack of communication from it. You must therefore provide them with an explanation that precludes their concern. I suggest you devise a good one before morning. If you find that you *must* tell a relative the truth, if only to keep him from worrying to the point of calling the police, it is your responsibility to ensure that this relative also keeps the secret. Understood?

Everyone nods.

Very good. Be aware that, thanks to the technological marvels of our age and Mr. Huerta's expertise with them—and his intimate access to your home, Mr. Belmonte—we have arranged to intercept any communications to or from the house. Landline phone, cell call, text, e-mail, everything, we will hear it or read it. Your communications with us, however, will be solely through a pair of telephones we are going to provide for you. One for each of you gentlemen. Both phones have been programmed so that we will know whenever they are used. We will know the numbers they call and the numbers they receive calls from. We will know if they are in any way connected to a recording device. We will know if either phone's cover is removed to expose its interior elements or if the instrument's security system should in any way be compromised. I stress, in *any* way. Am I clear to everyone?

All four of them nod.

The phones will not give you any indication of the numbers you are calling or, should we call you, of the number of the phone from which you receive a call. To call us on either phone, you need only to press zero. Understood?

The men nod.

Mr. Belmonte, you will call me at four o'clock tomorrow afternoon. At that time you will receive directions for conveying the payment for the first group. When you deliver that payment, you will be detained with that group until the remainder of our business is concluded. You, Mr. Sosa, will then receive instructions for delivering the second payment at the second location. When that payment is received, everyone in both groups will be liberated at the same time. Am I understood?

The men nod.

Very good. Now then, it pains me to say what I must say next, but it is important that all of you hear it from me and believe it absolutely. So listen well. . . . If you fail to get the cash by the appointed hour or fail to call me at the appointed hour . . . if we detect any attempt to infringe on the security of the phones we give you . . . if you or a relative or your banker or *anyone* contacts the police . . . if you in any way jeopardize this transaction at any point . . . if *any* of these things should happen . . . I promise you that every member of the party in our custody will be killed in a manner more horrible than you can imagine.

Mrs. Belmonte whimpers.

The remains of your loved ones will be disposed of where you will never find them, but photographs of those remains will be sent to you and will be distributed to newspapers and television stations around the country. Those pictures—forgive me, but I must be absolutely forthright—those pictures will be *unspeakable*. You will never be able to rid them from your memory. Or to forget that *you* were the cause of them.

Both women are weeping, struggling to contain themselves, but a moan escapes from Mrs Sosa.

Calm yourselves, ladies, Galán says. There is no need for such mortification. I'm sure nothing bad will happen to anyone. Your husbands will not permit it. They will do exactly as I have asked and all will be well. You will see. Your children will be back in your arms by suppertime tomorrow.

The four parents nod and nod.

Very well, Galán says. I believe that covers everything. Each of you gentlemen may now ask one question. Mr. Sosa?

Sosa is so surprised by the opportunity to pose a question that he has a mental blank and shakes his head.

Mr. Belmonte?

Do you promise not to hurt my children? I just want—

I have answered that question. They will not be harmed so long as you do as we instruct you. Now I bid all of you good evening and expect your call tomorrow at four. Be strong and be wise. My associate will drive you home.

The captives hear both of the front doors open and shut. A long minute passes and they hear a nearby vehicle start up and drive away. Now someone enters on the driver's side, and then the voice of the dark-glassed man tells them he's going to remove their masks and cuffs but they must then sit on their hands and remain silent if they don't wish to be hurt. He asks if they understand, and they all nod. One at a time, he has each of them lean forward and half turn and he slips off their masks and takes off the flex-cuffs.

Shed of their restraints, they sit back again, hands under butts, and stare at each other with a mixture of fear and relief. Huerta is no longer among them.

The dark-glassed man shoves the masks and cuffs into one of the plastic bags holding the other captives' possessions and replaces the bag under the seat.

All right, ladies and gentlemen, he says, starting up the Town Car, let's get you home.

6 — ESPANTO

The drive back to the Belmonte residence is fast and smooth, though to the four parents it seems interminable. Nodding his head in time to the radio rock music, Espanto might be alone in the car, so oblivious of the others does he seem, so disregardful of any possibility of being attacked from behind.

When they arrive at the street fronting the Belmonte residence, there are only a few vehicles still parked along the sides, their drivers lolling behind the wheel or smoking and chatting on the sidewalks. Espanto stops the car in the shadows alongside the driveway gate and permits the parents to free their hands from under their buttocks. They flap and massage them to restore circulation. He hands Mr. Sosa a shopping bag holding the parents' belongings and the two special phones Mr. X spoke of, then passes to Mr. Belmonte a larger bag containing the four gymnasium bags in which they will put the money. He tells Belmonte to inform the two Angeles men in the house that Huerta said for them to come out to the car for instructions.

There are still *two* of—? Belmonte stifles himself, unsure if the man's order to keep their mouths shut is still in effect.

Just tell them Huerta said to get out here. Don't say anything else to them. Understand?

Yes, yes. I will not say anything else.

Espanto watches them walk up the curving driveway, then removes the dark glasses and phones Rubio, in charge of the Alpha crew and its hold house in the distant southwest outskirts, who tells him in coded terms that his bunch is on the way to the house and all is well.

Excellent, Espanto says. If there's any problem with the invoice, let me know. Otherwise, I'll talk to you in the morning.

They click off, Espanto wishing he'd had the time to ask how the new man worked out, the ponytailed guy called Apache. Espanto had recruited him only three weeks ago to replace Chisto, who had been murdered in his sleep when a jealous girlfriend jabbed an ice pick through his eye. By then the plan was all set—the car assignments, the hold house crews, the street surveillance duties—and Galán ordered him to get a replacement fast. Espanto made inquiries around town, eliciting recommendations, and ended up with the Apache, whom Galán approved after an interview of less than two minutes. The other men seemed to have accepted him well enough, but there is something about him that makes Espanto uneasy. Then again, if the Apache had in any way proved troublesome tonight, Rubio would have said something about it, and he didn't.

He calls the Beta crew leader, Barbarosa, whose hold house is in the far northwest fringe of the city, and hears the same report—they're on their way—and Espanto tells him the same thing he told Rubio.

Now he phones Galán and reports that the cargo shipments are in fine condition and en route to the ports. I'm about to attend to the remaining security matter, Espanto says, and then I'll check to ensure the cargo's arrived.

Galán praises him for his good work. If there's any problem, call me, he says. If all is well, go home and get some rest. We'll talk again in the morning.

Until then, Espanto says.

The two Huerta men from the house appear at the mouth of the driveway. They see the Town Car and come toward it.

One of the men steps around to Espanto's window and says, Where's Huerta?

I don't know. He called and said pick up you two, then another guy, take you all to the Sosa place. Let's go.

What other guy? Who the fuck're *you*?

I'm the guy Huerta sent to get you. You coming or not? Makes no difference to me. He asks me, I'll tell him you said he could go fuck himself.

Hey, man, we been trying to get him on the phone for an hour but he doesn't answer. And Belmonte looking at us just now like we got two heads. What's going on?

Hell if I know, Espanto says. I just do what I'm told, same as you. Come on, let's go.

The men get in, one in the front, one in the back. They continue complaining about the way Huerta's always changing plans but never telling them about it until way later.

Tell me about it, Espanto says. Fucking bosses. All the same.

They arrive in a run-down neighborhood cast in misty vapor lighting and Espanto follows an isolate road to the gate of an auto junkyard.

Jesus Christ, the man in the backseat says. Who we getting *here*?

I don't know, some guy, Espanto says.

The watchman recognizes him and unlocks the gate to let him pass. He drives deep into the shadowy yard and parks in front of a garage building whose bay door is open wide and its interior brightly lighted. Not far from the garage door a large trash barrel is flaming high.

Before the two Angeles men can register what's happening, Espanto turns in his seat and raises the silencer-fitted Glock and shoots each of them in the head—the reports loud in the enclosed car, *THONK, THONK*—first the man beside him and then the one in back, spraying a raw paste of bloody brains on the door pillar and on a section of rear window cobwebbed by the bullet. In the enclosed confines of the car, the reports hurt Espanto's ears—only in the movies are silencer gunshots whisper quiet and without flash—and he curses himself for not having brought ear plugs and inserted them after coming through the gate.

He reaches under the seat and extracts the ragbags and plastic bags containing all other confiscated items, detaches the silencer from his pistol and puts it in the gun bag. He strips the two men of their possessions, adding their weapons to the gun bag, all else to one of the other bags, then gets out of the car and goes to the burning trash barrel and drops all the bags into it except the one with the guns. They will be added to the gang's weapons cache.

He enters the garage where the other three Town Cars are already receiving new vehicle identification numbers and new license plates and registrations before being shipped to buyers in different parts of the country. The other drivers aren't in sight and he assumes they've already gone to the hold houses.

The gray-haired owner of the yard comes out of the office and says, Finally, the last one. The utterance comes out in a muted parrotlike squawk, a consequence of his throat having been slashed in a long-ago attempt on his life, and the reason he has since been called El Loro.

Car's outside, Espanto tells him. Two dead in it. Needs a cleanup and new rear glass.

One of Loro's services for Galán is to dispose of corpses by putting them inside junked cars he then compacts in his crushing machine to the size of a suitcase.

I knew I wouldn't be lucky enough for the last one to come in as clean as the first three, Loro says in his parrot screech. He hands Espanto a key. White Sierra with extended cab, tinted glass, camper shell, he says. Around on the right side.

A *pickup*? Bullshit. I want an SUV.

Loro tells him the guys who dropped off the other Town Cars took the SUVs. The pickup's the only thing available.

Those pricks, Espanto says. I'm their *chief* and I don't get an SUV?

White Sierra with a camper shell, Loro squawks. Around on the right.

7 — GALÁN AND HUERTA

Galán and Huerta are in the backseat of the Cherokee, discussing their favorite dishes at La Nereida, a seafood restaurant where they plan to have supper, when Galán's phone vibrates in his coat.

"Dígame," he responds.

He listens, then says, Excellent. He commends the caller on his good work, gives him a few instructions, and says he will call him in the morning. Then slips the phone back into his coat.

"Tu segundo?" Huerta says. Is all well?

Yes, Galán says. A capable lieutenant, Espanto. And tomorrow, my old friend, *you* will be a wealthy man. And a disappeared one, no?

Yes I will, Huerta says, grinning back at him.

Huerta and Galán have known each other since their teens, when Galán's only name was Ramón Colmo and they belonged to a street gang called Malditos. They have fought against common enemies and both made their first kill at the age of sixteen. They have shared many drinks and stories, but they were both born to abject impoverishment—Huerta in a Puebla slum, Ramón Colmo in a shantytown in the hills west of the capital—and learned very early that friendship is above all else largely a matter of expedience. But both have also always been intelligent and ambitious, and Huerta was not yet twenty when he was befriended by an agent of a downtown security company who soon thereafter hired him as a street informant to keep him apprised of whatever talk he might hear about store break-ins and warehouse burglaries. Huerta grew fascinated with the security business and when he expressed interest in becoming an agent, the man became his mentor. Over the next two years Huerta learned the basic skills of the trade, how to dress for it, how to comport himself. In due course the agent recommended him to his company and he was hired and proved highly adept at the work. He was not without charm and verbal facility, and despite his youth was smoothly self-possessed. Clients liked him, and his amiable and confident bearing reaped the company many referrals. Yet certain aspects of his character would remain unchanged, and before long he was augmenting his income by abetting robbery gangs, instructing them in ways of bypassing basic electronic security systems. Over the next years he worked hard, saved some money, nurtured good relations with his employer's clients, and before he was thirty established his own company, Angeles de Guarda. He recruited a few capable pals from the old Malditos gang and trained them as agents, and he induced some of his former company's clients to switch their patronage to him.

During that same period, Ramón Colmo had risen too. He'd formed his own gang, Los Doce, so named because there were twelve of them, counting himself. He had made it a point to keep them at that number, and only recently, due to the death of a member named Chisto, had found it necessary to make its first replacement since the gang's inception. In its early years Los Doce concentrated on home burglaries and grew highly proficient at it—and for a share of the proceeds, Huerta was soon colluding with them, tipping them to affluent non-client residences and the means for penetrating their various high-grade defenses. Over time, the gang expanded into express kidnapping and robbery. Rotating teams of two or three in a car selected random victims as they exited upscale hotels, restaurants, theaters, office buildings. They snatched them into the car and stripped them of cash and credit cards, took them to every bank they had a card for and made them withdraw the daily maximum permitted at each automatic teller, then released them in some fringe part of town.

Ramón's aspirations, however, ran much higher, and last year Los Doce had begun kidnapping for ransom, with Huerta again colluding—his professional resources enabling him to identify prime targets for the sort of snatches Ramón had in mind. Swift grabs, swift payoffs, swift releases. Ramón did not want to hold a captive for more than one night, and liked it better yet if the entire process could be completed in the same day. The targets proposed by Huerta were well-to-do but not so wealthy they could afford full-time bodyguards, if any at all, so the snatches weren't very difficult, and although Ramón insisted on careful planning of each operation as the key to its speedy execution, Los Doce could usually pull two jobs a month and always at least one. The ransoms were not of such marvelous sums as one read or heard about in the news every so often, but they were ample, and even discounting Huerta's commissions, Galán and his men were earning far more than they had through burglary and express snatches combined.

Even as Los Doce developed into a smoothly functioning kidnapping crew, Ramón Colmo, too, underwent a remarkable transformation. He began dressing in increasingly dapper fashion, and for the past few months had been dressing chiefly in suits of white or pale yellow silk. In cool weather he wore a cashmere Chesterfield or a camel hair polo. He carried himself with poise and even seemed taller somehow—Huerta had checked carefully and knew it was not an effect of crafty footwear. He was now always freshly barbered, his nails manicured. But the greatest changes were in his manners and speech and pleasures. His demeanor had become almost courtly, his speech formal and precise, and Huerta could not recall the last time he had heard him use profanity. He had acquired an interest in classical music and could speak with authority on compositions emanating from a car radio or restaurant sound system. Huerta took great pride in having made himself a more stylish and better-spoken man, but Ramón had become a figure of elegance. Indeed, he wasn't even Ramón Colmo anymore. Some of his men had started referring to him as El Galán, and so was he now known to those of his profession, most of whom had never known him by any other name.

Still, there were stories suggesting that within El Galán's refinement, Ramón Colmo yet remained coiled and ready to strike. Just a few weeks ago a mutual acquaintance had told Huerta of an incident that occurred at a meeting he'd had with Galán in Chapultepec Park. They were sitting on a bench near a fountain, no one else about but a young couple on another bench, when suddenly the couple started arguing and the woman loudly called the man a prick and got up to leave. The man jumped up and grabbed her and began slapping her, cursing her for a lowdown bitch. Galán rushed up behind him and punched him hard in the kidney, then grabbed him by the hair with one hand and twisted an arm up behind his back with the other, forced him down on his knees in front of the ironwork bench, and twice rammed the man's face into the edge of the bench seat, audibly cracking bone and snapping teeth, pieces of which dribbled from his pulped bloody mouth. He let go of him and the man fell over, moaning, and Galán spat on him and called him a cowardly rat cunt and a few other epithets of the slums. But when he stepped back to adjust his cuffs and tie, the girl ran up to the man and knelt beside him, crying and crooning over him. Galán looked at her sadly, then looked at his friend and shrugged. They then went across the street to a cantina to finish their conversation, Galán showing no sign at all, the friend said, of just having destroyed a man's face.

Huerta had owned Angeles de Guarda for more than three years when, four months ago, Francisco Belmonte hired the firm at a princely fee to provide full-time guard service to his family and home. The comprehensive duties required Huerta's full contingent of seven agents working in shifts around the clock, and he had been obliged to remove his men from other bodyguard assignments. The rest of the company's clients subscribed only to electronic guard services that were easily monitored from the Angeles office by the firm's two women employees.

At the time that Huerta's company took over the security duties at the Belmonte estate, wedding plans were already under way for the upcoming marriage of Demetrio Belmonte and Luz Sosa. As chief of security, Huerta naturally became privy to every detail of those plans, and his position gave him access to a trove of personal information about both the Belmontes and the Sosas. Together with his extensive investigative resources, such access made it a simple matter to learn everything about both families' financial holdings. And the more Huerta learned, the more clearly he perceived the biggest opportunity of his life. And the more evident it became that he would need outside help to realize it.

So he had gone to Galán.

They have both decided they will order the broiled swordfish when they get to La Nereida. First, however, they are going to switch over to Galán's Mercedes coupe, which is parked at the home of one of his favorite lady friends, a wealthy widow of avid sexual appetite. Following a night of marvelous delights with her—which Galán has described to Huerta in almost poetic detail—he had slept late this morning while the widow departed for Paris to attend a week's showings of new fashion lines. Because Galán never uses his own car for business, the Cherokee had collected him for the meeting with the Belmonte and Sosa parents. Its driver, whom Galán addresses as Fuego, is a thin man with a pockmarked face. Huerta has never seen him before.

The widow's home is not far off the west side of the beltway in a residential community of spacious properties amid dense woods and small lakes. Galán's handheld remote control opens the barred driveway gate, which closes and relocks behind them after they enter. The widow employs one of the best security companies in the city, and there are sensitive alarms in every window and outer door of the house that on being silently triggered will bring armed agents to her door in minutes. But for reasons of personal privacy she has not permitted cameras to be posted on the property.

At this hour the servants have retired to their quarters. The house is dark but for the lights in the gated front courtyard and in the kitchen at the rear of the house, where the driveway ends at a large turning circle in front of a triple garage. The garage door is lighted by a low-watt overhead lamp.

As they get out of the Cherokee, Galán is laughing softly at Huerta's adamant refusal to tell him where he plans to go after he gets his share of the ransom tomorrow.

Galán points an electronic opener at the garage door but it stays closed. This worthless thing, he says. Doesn't function half the time.

He aims the opener again and presses its button, but still the door remains shut. Oh well, he says, and puts the remote in his pocket and heads for the corner of the garage, saying, There's a button on the wall over here.

Huerta hears the SUV's door open behind him—and even as he starts to ask himself why the driver's getting out, he knows.

He drops to a half crouch and starts to scurry around the vehicle, drawing his Sig 9 as gunshots *thonk thonk* behind him and a leg quits him and he hits the ground in front of the car and rolls onto his back and blasts two flaring shots up at Fuego's dark shape at the same time that Fuego fires twice more, both rounds punching through Huerta's chest and the second one stopping his heart.

Fuego kicks away the Sig, then bends down to probe Huerta's neck for a pulse. He straightens up with a grunt and puts his pistol back into its shoulder holster, then pulls open the other flap of his coat and probes his side. He winces and hisses.

Galán comes out from behind the corner of the garage, reholstering his Glock. He sees the dark stain on Fuego's side just above his belt. Bad? he says.

Nah. Went through. Stings like a bitch but not bad.

Galán gives him a clean handkerchief and Fuego wads it up and groans softly as he puts it over the entry wound and pulls his pants up higher to hold it in place, then puts his own handkerchief over the exit wound and tightens his belt over both makeshift bandages.

Galán picks up Huerta's Sig and thumbs the decocking lever and puts the pistol in his coat pocket. He stands in an attitude of alert listening.

Think anybody heard? Fuego says.

Galán shakes his head. The properties are large and well apart, he says. The hedges are high. Cold night, the windows shut.

If I'd killed him with the first two shots he wouldn't have got one off. Fucker heard the door and figured it.

Yes, Galán says. He always had good instincts for what was behind him. He wasn't as good at anticipating what might be ahead.

He gestures at Fuego's wound and says, Go to Mago and get that tended before you report to the Beta house. I'll put somebody else on the disposal.

Oh hell no, chief, it's not that bad. No lie. I'll get patched up after I take care of the disposal.

To prove his point, Fuego hurries to the Cherokee's hatchback and opens it and unzips and smooths out the body bag already unrolled on the floor behind the seat, then comes back to the body and squats down to grasp it under the arms and starts dragging it toward the rear of the vehicle. He is much smaller than Huerta and grimaces with the pain of his effort. Galán watches him a moment, then picks up Huerta's legs and helps carry him to the hatchback and lay him on the bag. Huffing for breath, Fuego tucks Huerta's arms and legs in the bag and zips it closed.

There, all set to go, he says. Whew. He readjusts his belt.

Galán is staring at the bagged body.

They would've tracked him down, chief, Fuego says softly, like you said. He would've made a deal. He had to go. Like you said.

Galán smiles. Fuego has always been a favorite of his. Quit flapping your mouth and get moving, he tells him. Then go directly to Mago.

Right, chief, don't you worry, Fuego says as he shuts the hatchback. I'll take care of this and then I'll see the doc and then I'll get out to the hold house. Fuego's grin is wrenched with pain.

He gets in the Cherokee and wheels it around the turning circle and drives away. In truth, he hates going to those garbage pits whose reeking firelight he is sure is full of evil spirits of no relation to the benevolent Santa Muerte. But he wants very much to rise in the world, and the best way to do that is to prove to Galán at every opportunity that he, Fuego, is a man who can be counted on to do a job. A man who can take it. Who is above the pain of wounds.

Galán watches him go, then studies the widow's house, seeking a sign of stir within, some new light, some silhouette at a window. The widow has a good intuition for hiring servants who know what not to see, not to hear. Besides, they know nothing more about him than she does, and she knows him as Mario Pérez, a sales representative for an international electronics company.

He turns on the garage remote control and presses a button and the door rolls upward with a low whir to reveal his Mercedes next to the widow's Eldorado.

He goes to El Nido, a small basement café in a downtrodden neighborhood of his days in the Malditos gang, for a bowl of what he regards as the best menudo in the city. He is revered by the local residents as one of their own, and although everyone knows his car and it needs no protection in the alley where he parks it, three large boys nearly get into a fight over which of them will stand guard over the Mercedes. He settles the dispute by appointing all three as its guardians and, despite their protestations, insists they accept payment for the duty.

After eating, he heads for his townhouse in a gated community at the south end of the Jardines del Pedregal. The deed is under the name of Alberto Molina, an uncle of his now dead for eleven years. The rain-black sky hides the westward hills and their scatterings of shantytowns, including Infiernito, where he was born and grew to an early manhood in the constant smoke and vile smell of a garbage pit. Where he learned to fear nothing—except, as he has never admitted to anyone, the dogs. The terrifying packs of feral beasts that roam the sprawling shanty settlements. Most of them starving, some rabid, all of them ever alert for a chance to attack the sick and helpless, to snatch away the small children of unvigilant mothers. He was nearly taken by them one night when he was very young. He woke to their low growls and then they had him, screaming in terror and pain as they dragged him from the hovel. His mother woke and began to flail at them with a tin pan and was also many times bitten. He well remembers the tumult of shadows and his great screaming pain and the dogs' fire-lit eyes and wild snarlings and slavering jaws, their piercing shrieks and yelpings at each swing of his mother's pan. He yet bears scars of that night on his arms and legs, on his scalp, hidden under his hair, remnants of his mother's crude stitchwork. But the only scars visible in public are on his jaw and neck, which his acquaintances believe were acquired in gang fights. He still at times has gasping dreams about those dogs.

At home he showers, wraps himself in a silk robe, then goes into the living room and puts a Dvorak CD in the player. As the "American" quartet issues from the speakers, he mixes a Jack and Coke and settles on the sofa to ponder the day's events.

He likes the feel of this operation, the speed at which it's moving. It is something he learned in the streets at an early age. Move in quick, do it quick, get out quick. Everything is proceeding exactly as it should.

When the quartet segues into the heartbreaking second movement he gives it his full attention, then nurses his drink to the end of the work, sipping the last drops from his glass with a small sigh of satisfaction. He would normally have a second one before bedtime, but it has been a tiring day and tomorrow will be a busy one, beginning with his morning meeting with El Ingeniero.

He stands up and catches sight of himself in a wall mirror, smiles, and raises his glass to his image.

Then goes to bed and is asleep at once.

Within an hour he is awakened by a call from El Mago, so named because of his wondrous surgical skills. However, as result of a scandal some years ago involving black market prescriptions and the overdose suicide of a college-student son of an important local politician, he lost his medical license, and his practice has since been restricted to select clients like Galán. He is calling from his home in a working-class neighborhood, from the well-equipped back room where he plies his trade. He reports that a man who said his name was Fuego had arrived at his front door not twenty minutes ago, saying he had been sent by Galán. He had a serious gunshot wound in his side requiring urgent attention, but as they were going down the hall to the treatment room the man collapsed. Mago did his best to save him but the blood loss had been too great and the man died.

Galán tells him he will send somebody there right away to take care of things, then calls a service he has used in the past. He explains the problem and the man he speaks with says it will be attended to at once.

He ponders how this occurrence might affect tomorrow's plan, settles the question in his mind, and uses the house line to call Espanto.

The phone rings only twice before Espanto responds, "Sí, jefe."

Galán apprises him of what happened regarding Huerta and Fuego, and tells him to notify the Beta crew that they will have to function with only three members.

Espanto says he will do so immediately.

Galan goes back to bed. This time it requires almost five minutes for him to fall asleep.

El Mago has bagged the body by the time three employees of the service engaged by Galán arrive in a van. One of the men drives off in the Cherokee, which he will deliver to Loro's garage. The other two men load the body into the van and bear it away for disposal in one of the fiery garbage pits that so often frightened Fuego with their aspects of hell.

8 — THE PARENTS

The three dozen guests yet in the Belmonte home are surprised by the return of the bridal couples' parents, embarrassed to be found still drinking and dancing and keeping the orchestra at work. The parents pass by without pausing, the men with shopping bags under their arms, Mr. Belmonte giving the guests a curt explanation that they're tired and have left the young people to their own fun at a nightclub.

Interpreting the parents' grim faces as displeasure with having discovered them still here, the guests hastily call good-nights after them, retrieve their coats, and phone for their cars as they head for the front door. The housemaids are glad to see them go.

Mrs. Belmonte has coffee brought to Mr. Belmonte's lower-floor office and then the foursome sit at the table in the middle of the room and talk and talk, going over everything Mr. X told them. They repeat his every word, making sure they all heard the same things and have the same understanding of them, each agreeing with one another that, Yes, yes, that's what I heard too, that's what he said, yes. In the course of these confirmations, there are bursts of outraged self-pity from the women. They dab at their eyes and ask how can such a thing happen to *them,* for the love of God? They're *rich!* What's the good of being rich if it doesn't keep you safer than those who are not? There are instances of one man or the other slamming a palm or a fist heel on the table and cursing, both of them at times seeming close to tears himself.

That Huerta bastard son of a whore! Belmonte says. I'll have his balls in a jar! He rarely uses profanity in the presence of women, but this time his wife does not reproach him.

Their angry indignation notwithstanding, they are agreed to do exactly as Mr. X has instructed. What other choice have they? The man was nothing if not precise in his instructions. They cannot even have their drivers convey them to the bank but must drive themselves there. Belmonte and Sosa debate whether to call their bankers at home right away to alert them to the large withdrawals they will be making. They decide not to, agreeing that they would only be raising troublesome questions and fears that could be difficult to deal with on the phone and at this hour. Besides, Mr. X said all communications to and from the house were being monitored, and while he did not say they could not call the banks, neither did he say they could. Best to wait until they talk to the bank officers in person. They curse the banks for their late hour of opening—that damned Indio Tierra and that Rosemonte bank still keeping the same business hours they did fifty years ago! The wait for them to open up will seem interminable, as will the wait afterward until four. Still, the sooner they have the money at hand, the better they will all feel until they can call Mr. X for their instructions.

There's nothing they can do for now but reiterate assurances to each other that everything will be all right, that the kidnappers don't want to hurt anyone, that they just want the money, that Mr. X bears no personal malice toward any of them and has no cause to harm their children as long as he gets the money and . . . dear *God,* it's just awful, it's despicable, it's beyond *vile,* what some people will do for money! But that's of no matter now. The only important thing is that the money will free their children from danger. There *is* that advantage to being rich.

They urge one another to get some sleep, there's no sense staying awake, it won't help anything. The husbands want the wives to go up to the bedrooms but the women refuse, saying they cannot sleep, and instead exhort their husbands to try to rest, they'll need it for tomorrow. When the men also refuse to go upstairs, the wives plead for one of them to lie down on the couch in the office and the other on the large couch in the adjoining den where Mr. Belmonte sometimes retires for a nap in the course of a long workday.

Where Rayo Luna Wolfe has been standing with an ear to the door, listening to it all.

9 — RAYO

Rayo and Gregorio had danced and danced, writhing against each other, unmindful of the grins they drew from others on the floor. They sometimes whirled off behind the stand of potted palms in the corner for a kiss and fondle before spinning back out on the floor again, enjoying the dancing foreplay and the excitement of where it was headed.

When Rayo nipped his earlobe during a slow dance and said, Enough of this dry hump, buddy, let's go somewhere and get naked, Gregorio laughed and said he knew just the place.

He'd many times before been a guest of the Belmontes and was well acquainted with the house. He led her around to a hallway off the other side of the dance floor and down to a room furnished with a small desk and bookcases, framed wall maps, and a long wide couch. They locked the door behind them and did not switch on the light, the room's darkness eased by the bright screen glow of a large digital clock on the wall. To one side was a door to an adjoining room Gregorio said was Belmonte's larger office, but they didn't have anything to worry about, as the Belmontes would be at the after party for hours.

They flung off their clothes and tumbled onto the sofa and Rayo laughed at his eagerness and petted him and told him to slow down. She was delighted by his adroitness when he put his tongue to her, and she helped out with a shift of hip and a light directorial hand on his head. After a time, she wriggled herself farther under him and drew him inside her, Gregorio in such a state of excitement she was afraid he would come too soon, but each time he approached orgasm he was able to restrain himself, and they were at it for a good while before he finally could not hold back, and she praised herself for her sound intuition that he would prove a good lover. She bet him a peso she could raise him to readiness again in five minutes, and four minutes later said somebody owed her a peso. After that, they were much more leisurely about it, sporting into the deepening night, panting and giggling, now one on top and now the other, now face-to-face and now he behind her, at one point falling off the sofa and putting a hand to each other's mouth to mute their laughter. She has always been quick to achieve release and able do so repeatedly, and she climaxed several times before he'd done so twice. He was making a heroic attempt at a third orgasm when he gave up and wheezed, Sweet Jesus, woman . . . I surrender.

She growled low and nudged him with her pelvis.

Then they heard the sound of someone entering the adjoining room, and various voices.

Oh Christ, what— Gregorio started to say before she put her hand over his mouth with a strength that should not have surprised him, given the torsions of her lovemaking.

She put her finger to her lips to keep him hushed, eased out of bed and wiped herself with his shirt, tossed him his clothes and picked up her own and went to listen at the door, stepping into her thong and slipping the minidress on and sliding her feet into her shoes. She recognized the voices of the Belmonte and Sosa parents, heard Mrs. Belmonte tell someone to please set the tray on the desk, heard the door shut. She wondered what they were doing back here and if the whole bridal party had come back. Whatever the case, it was time to depart, and she was just about to signal Gregorio to hurry up when she heard Mr. Belmonte say something about "rescate de los jovenes."

Rescue? Young people?

She kept her ear to the door and heard everything they talked about and understood the sort of "rescate" they were referring to was a ransom. Gregorio finished dressing and started toward her, but she motioned sharply for him to stay where he was. He grinned and kept coming and she turned and grabbed his arms, pressing her thumbs hard into the crooks of his elbows, and drove him back to the couch, her mouth at his ear and hissing through her teeth for him to sit the fuck down and keep quiet. She pushed him onto the couch and slipped quickly back to the door.

Now she's heard all of it, everything they have repeated to one another about the kidnapping—from the security chief's participation in it to their driver's spike haircut, from Mr. X's explanations and warnings and instructions for tomorrow to Mr. Sosa's agreement to pay the ransom for his daughter's American friend.

Of all she's heard, that's the most important item. The bastards took JJ.

Now the parents are telling each other there's nothing to be done until the banks open in the morning, and they begin a mild squabble about getting some rest, the women urging one of the men to make use of the couch in the neighboring room.

Rayo heads for the door without giving Gregorio a glance, but he swiftly follows. They hurry down the hallway to the guest-deserted ballroom and past the knowing looks of the tidying maids. She stops at the checkroom to get her shawl, and then they're outside and stepping lively down the driveway toward the gate, Gregorio practically giddy, gabbing without pause, saying it was damn sure a close one and what if they'd been caught going at it on the couch and he doubts he'd ever have been invited to the Belmontes' again and he's known some daring women but she's right up at the top.

She pays him no mind, her thoughts elsewhere.

The attendant grins at the sight of them and opens the gate and gives Rayo an appreciative ogle as she strides by with her shawl around her shoulders, high heels clicking. Their cars are parked blocks from each other and in opposite directions, and as she starts away from him Gregorio grabs her arm and says, Wait a minute, wait, give me your phone number.

She jerks free of his hand and points a warning finger in his face, then turns and stalks off.

He watches her go, admiring her flawless ass with a sickening certainty that he'll not have access to it again.

Bitch, he says.

But not loudly.

In her restored TR3 roadster, the canvas top up, she reviews the situation as she makes her way to the beltway and merges into it, then thumb scrolls her phone's directory of contacts and taps on her Uncle Rodrigo's name.

"Tío Rigo," she says. "Es Rayo Luna." Forgive my calling at this hour, sir, but it's truly important. Someone of ours is in serious trouble.

Tell me, he says.

After she relates to him everything she overheard between the Belmontes and Sosas, Rodrigo softly says, Oh Christ. Then says he will inform his father, Plutarco, and his Uncle Juan Jaguaro. The Texas family must be notified, but courtesy demands that the notification come from a patriarch of the Mexican side of the house.

Regardless of our own efforts, he tells Rayo, the Texans will send somebody down here immediately to look for their girl. It's how they are. Furthermore, they will want to speak with *you*, since you're the source of the information. It's convenient you're the one of us they know best.

But if they try to rescue JJ, Rayo says, won't that just put her in greater danger? Why not pay the ransom and get her back, *then* hunt down the fuckers who took her? Oh God . . . forgive my language, Uncle.

And your presumptuousness. We've spoken about that, miss.

I'm sorry, Uncle. I—

They won't trust the fuckers not to kill her even if they're paid, Rigo says. Neither would I. Now listen, I'm going to have Mateo himself handle this, and you'll work with him. He'll contact you shortly. Be ready.

Yes . . . yes sir, I will.

She hears his soft sigh before he says, I know you'll do well and exactly as you're told.

Yes sir. You can depend on me.

"And remember, chica," Rodrigo adds in English. "Like our gringo cousins like to say . . . watch your ass."

"Yes sir, I definitely will."

She'd been hoping Rodrigo might assign her to a part in this because of her close relations with their Texas kin—but to work with Mateo! He's Rodrigo's younger brother and the head of the family's enforcement squad. She almost bounces on the seat in her excitement.

Then she thinks of Jessie and rebukes herself for such selfishness.

10 — JESSIE

They haven't been on the road very long when she hears the chirp of a phone and then the blond man's voice saying, "Sí?" Then he says, No, no problems at all. The cargo's on the way to the warehouse right now. . .. I understand. Until tomorrow.

Let me guess, says the voice of the ponytail man. Espanto.

Who else? Mother hen, that guy.

Fucking toady, the ponytail says. Always sucking up to Galán.

He's not sucking up. He's the number two man doing his job.

Again the phone chirps. The blond mutters, Now what? And then says, Yeah, what is it? in an acerbic tone that makes Jessie think it very unlikely he's talking again to the one called Espanto.

There's a silence and then the blond says, Jesus Christ. Well, tell him to do it fast, God damn it. I want it ready when we get there. Yeah, yeah, yeah. Just tell him to do it fast.

Who was *that?* the ponytail says.

Cabrito. Water pipe busted on the lower floor. Flooded the place. He's got a guy working on it but it may not be fixed before we get there.

Fucking slums, man, the ponytail says. Pipes *always* busting, roofs *always* leaking. Walls and floors full of holes. Why the hell use those rattraps?

Because, the blond says, out there nobody ever sees anything, hears anything, knows anything. Galán tells Espanto to find houses out there and then checks them himself before giving the okay. You want to argue with Galán about his choice of hold houses?

The ponytail doesn't answer.

It's a slow drive at first, with numerous stops at traffic lights, with constant sounds of proximate vehicles. The bare metal floor jars them at every bump and pothole. It hadn't taken long for Jessie to accept the impossibility of working her hands free of the cuffs, but she's been slowly rubbing her left cheek on a rib of the metal floorboard and, bit by bit, she's managed to push that side of her sleep mask upward until its lower edge is on her upper eyelid and she can see.

The whole time she's been working the mask up, she's feared that one of the bastards is watching her, enjoying her effort, waiting to see if she'll succeed in uncovering the eye. Ready to bust out laughing and smack her for her trouble if she does. But she's done it . . . and still no laugh or punch.

She's on her side between two other captives, so all she can see in the intermittent light of passing lampposts is the dark form of someone lying in front of her. A man's back. Aldo, she's pretty sure. She very slowly squirms partway onto her back until she can discern the two men in the front seat. They stop for a red light at a loud, bright intersection and she cranes her head around and sees no one else in the back of the Suburban besides other captives, all lying motionless, hands bound behind them. The ones from her Town Car, she figures, plus Luz. The rest of the party must've been packed off in the other Suburban. They're being taken to hold houses, she's sure of it. She's had it explained to her by cops. Two houses, maybe three, it's how they sometimes work it with more than one captive. Parcel them out to different holding places, so that even if one place becomes known, a rescue won't be attempted for fear of getting the captives at the other places killed.

The sound of traffic becomes sporadic and gradually lessens to almost none. They enter a part of town with fewer stoplights. The road is bumpier. They go straight for a long way without streetlights or stops or turns until at last they make a turn to the right. It's straight ahead again for a distance and then she feels the light centrifugal pull of a long curve and then they're moving straight but more slowly and over a still rougher surface. There are streetlights again, but dimmer and fewer than before. They move slowly for block after block and then pass through a flashing green cast of light and she glimpses a raised sign reading "Chula's" and bordered with green lightbulbs.

They slow down even more, and the blond says, Gallo's here already. Always picks that Durango at Loro's.

Whose shitty truck?

Must be the guy's who's fixing the pipe.

They make a turn and come to a stop and the engine cuts off. Dogs close by break out in a rage of barking, joined by dogs at a greater distance.

They're parked in deep shadow but there is sufficient sidelight of some sort for Jessie to see the two men. The blond says he's going to check on things and gets out.

The barking intensifies and the blond yells, "Cállense, condenados!" but the dogs don't slacken a bit. Jesse guesses they're pent behind some barrier.

As the ponytail man twists in the driver's seat to look back at them, she turns her head slightly to conceal the skew of her mask. She hears the *snick* of a lighter, then smells cigarette smoke.

Long minutes pass in the steady yelpings of the dogs. Then the blond's voice is at the driver's window, saying that the plumber will be finished with the pipes in another fifteen or twenty minutes. The problem is that he can't restore running water to both the upstairs and downstairs of the house, not tonight. That job will take a couple of days. So Rubio chose to have water on the upper floor so it won't be necessary to take a captive downstairs every time one has to use the toilet.

These fucking rattraps, the ponytail says.

I'm gonna stay on the guy's ass to hurry it up, the blond says. Take this bunch over there so we can quickly move them all inside as soon as the place is ready.

The ponytail gets out and opens the right-side back door and says, All right, children, time to get out of the boat.

She hears Aldo being pulled out. He gives an angry grunt, and then a cry of pain through his gag.

Kick at *me,* cocksucker! the ponytail says. Aldo groans.

Come *on,* the ponytail says. Then he and Aldo are gone and there's only the barking of the dogs.

Jessie wonders if Luz and Susi and José are all right. If they have any notion of where they are. Even if she weren't gagged, she wouldn't dare speak. For all she knows, somebody's standing at the open door of the vehicle.

It seems not more than a minute before the ponytail's back. Susi whimpers under her gag, and the ponytail snickers and says for her to quit the act, he's not hurting her, she probably likes it. He tells her to wiggle forward, and Jessie feels Susi shifting about on the floor. Then she's gone with the ponytail.

Emotional stress can skew your sense of time, Jessie knows, and she concentrates hard, trying to be as accurate as she can in estimating how long the ponytail is gone. When you're in danger, keep your head and try to learn as much as you can as fast as you can about the state of things. The more you know, the better your chances of being able to do something about it. A rule she'd learned from Charlie.

The ponytail returns, and she guesses he was gone for two minutes, maybe a little longer. Now you, my love, he says. His hands slide up Jessie's legs and over her breasts to clasp her by the shoulders and pull her to a sitting position. He then holds her by the hips and tells her to work herself toward him on her ass. She keeps her face down and wriggles forward, feeling like a child, the hem of the dress bunching up at her knees. When her lower legs dangle from the vehicle, he puts his hands under her arms and pulls her out to her feet. Holding her by one arm, his other arm around her and his hand on her breast, he conducts her over uneven ground, bracing her each time a heel tilts under her. The night is chillier now. He's on her right and so she's able to peek up without his seeing the raised edge of her mask. It's a small yard containing a pair of wheelless cars propped up on concrete blocks, plus another junker, and he guides her around them. Directly ahead stands a house of unpainted concrete block, with a second story that covers only the right two-thirds or so of the building. At the far end of the house, the one-story part, there's a small front porch with a bare yellow bulb glowing above the door. The porch is fronted by a dirt driveway where a red Durango is parked, and a few yards past it is a stone wall of what is probably the neighbor's courtyard. Behind it are the yammering dogs. Only two, maybe three, Jessie guesses, but they sound fierce.

The ponytail steers her toward the other corner of the house, in the shadow of the trees, where she sees Aldo and Susi standing at the wall. He positions her next to Susi.

The blond man calls, "Todo bien?"

Jessie risks a peek at the porch and sees the blond at the open door in his shirtsleeves, his pistol holstered under an arm.

What's the holdup? the ponytail says.

Not much longer, the blond says, and goes back inside.

The ponytail flaps a hand in disgust toward the door and in mimicry of the blond man says, Not much longer, as he starts back to the Suburban.

Jessie tilts her head and surveys the narrow street fronting the house in the sickly glow of lampposts. There's no one in sight on the street or at a window. Some windows iron barred, some boarded up. Not a place for night strolls, she thinks, not when these guys come around. The street's littered with trash and lined with close-set little buildings of concrete block. Beat-up vehicles parked everywhere. The blond and ponytail were right, it's a slum—though this one's not nearly so bad as many she's seen. There are ramshackle quarters like this everywhere on the fringes of the capital, residential neighborhoods that sprang up next to an industrial plant or shipping depot that provided good jobs until the plant was shut down or the depot was excised from the transportation system, and then the neighborhood was left to wither into isolated slumhood. There is little police presence in these places, a patrol car is an uncommon sight. Hence all the dogs, the poor man's security service. Few crimes short of murder will bring the cops, though it can be hours after the fact before they arrive. A major blaze will draw the fire department, but hydrant hookups are a rarity, and often a fire must be fought with water-tank trucks until the flames are doused or the tanks run dry. People are born and die in neighborhoods like this with no record of either event. The Other Mexico City, she heard the slums called on a previous visit to Rayo, when she'd been escorted through several of them so she could take pictures and notes for a Texas magazine article about the different societies of the capital, from the wealthiest and artiest zones of the central city to the bleak outskirt localities like this one. Even bleaker than slums like this, however, are the shantytowns of the surrounding hills, where the dwellings consist mostly of discarded shipping crates and construction rubble, cardboard covered with shower curtains. Jessie has long been familiar with the shantytowns along the lower Tex-Mex border, but the squalor of those girding the outer reaches of Mexico City exceeds any she's seen elsewhere. Wretched, lawless settlements outside the regard of municipal authority, without electricity or running water, subject to chronic brutalities of every sort. The largest shantytowns border the enormous garbage dumps and fire pits where the city disposes its daily tons of rubbish. Yet even the meanest society desires identity, and every shantytown she's been to has had a name. She's passed through places called Absent Souls, the Devil's Patio, Little Hell, Tears of Mother, and a number of others dubbed in a similar vein. The air here smells mostly of exposed garbage, but it carries tinges of carrion and charcoal fires, open privies and putrid muck—olfactory indications that whatever slum she's in it isn't far from a shantytown that's a hell of a lot worse.

To her left, across a short span of gravelly, trash-strewn ground and just behind the trees, is a skewed picket fence silhouetted by a distant corner streetlamp and showing a small gap of missing pickets. Beyond the fence is a two-story building that may once have been a small hotel but now serves as a tenement. Few of its windows are lighted, and its forward ground is overgrown with high weeds. Past the tenement are other buildings, some dimly lighted, some totally dark. She's sure that the gap between the tenement and the next building is an alley.

That's the ticket, she thinks. Down that alley. With a two-minute head start you can be into it well before they even know you've gone. You cut through there to the next street and find your way to a phone somewhere, a taxi, hitch a ride, *something*.

What if the alley's a dead end? Go to the next street and make your turn there. You play it as it comes. What you goddamn well have to do is *try*. Might be the only chance you'll get.

She slips the pumps off her feet and kicks them behind her. Can't run in those. She'd grown up a barefoot tomboy and her feet were toughened all the more by years of ballet and modern dance. Her feet have known pain, and a few cuts won't be anything she can't endure. Better the cuts than a shoe heel giving way and twisting or breaking an ankle. The dress is no help, either, but there's nothing to be done about that for now.

The ponytail returns with Luz and positions her beside Jessie, saying, Stand here and don't move. Then goes off to get José, the last of them.

Jessie watches him until he goes out of sight behind the clunkers.

Then steps around Luz and bolts.

11 — JESSIE

She barely hears the sound of her feet on the gravel, but the neighboring dogs hear it and again burst into a frenzied barking—the ponytail yelling for them to shut the fuck up—as she runs for the fence, her dress restricting her to short quick strides. She runs through the fence gap and into the high weeds, keeping her head craned back in order to see under the sleep mask, fearful of tripping over something, of gashing a foot, expecting an outcry of pursuit any second. Stones bite into her feet.

She passes the dim entranceway of the tenement and reaches the alley and is elated to see that it joins a lighted street at the other end. She glances back toward the hold house and sees no one coming and dashes into the alley. It's darker in here and she fears even more for her feet, the threat of broken glass, upturned nails. Other dogs on other streets have joined in the general uproar.

She stops and squats and stretches her arms downward, sliding her bound hands under her butt, then drops to a sitting position and hunches forward, drawing her knees up to her breasts, and works her hands forward under her feet. She whips off the sleep mask and stands up, searches with her fingernails for the end of the tape gag, finds it, and peels it off, taking off some of her hair with it. She hears angry shouts through the clamor of the dogs—the ponytail has discovered she's gone. In the weak light of the alley mouth, she spots a large chunk of brick and crouches and sets it just above the hem of her dress, holds it in place with one foot, and yanks hard on the skirt to make a tear in the hem. With both hands she then rips the tear open all the way up her thigh.

Now she can run.

She races to the end of the alley and hears the ponytail yelling that he's spotted her—"Ya la veo! Ahí va!"—from behind her as she rounds the corner onto a street.

She fights down her fear, ordering herself to breathe in a rhythm, *breathe*. She can outrun these bastards if she doesn't panic.

The street she's on is as ghostly as that of the hold house, as bare of traffic and people, streetlights as hazy, buildings as dark. She goes past a house from which a voice calls something she doesn't catch and then goes silent.

Back in the alley, the ponytail is shouting, "*Por acá!*" She's over here!

Before he comes into view, she dodges into the next alley. She sprints to its other end and out to another street, catches sight of someone vanishing into the shadows and hears a door slam. She's sure she's being watched from the lightless windows. The neighborhood is a tumult of enraged dogs alarming everyone into staying in hiding.

Holding to a mental map of the location of the hold house relative to her position, she moves away from it, turning left and right into alleys and streets, once stepping on something soft and slimy and almost losing her footing, twice reversing her course on entering an alley and seeing only the darkness of a dead end ahead.

She knows that if she keeps bearing away from the house she's bound to arrive at a street with traffic and people. Even if there's not a cop around, there's sure to be a café or store, someplace she can duck into and get free of the cuffs and borrow a phone and—

Damn it!

She's come deep into an alley before realizing it's another cul-de-sac. Behind the alley fences, dogs are insane with fury.

She whirls around to backtrack, and, in the dim light from the street, sees piles of old fruit crates and cardboard boxes, one of them heaped with empty food cans with the opened lids still attached. She plucks a large can from a box and sits down and sets it between her feet and saws through the plastic cuffs with the edge of the lid.

A vehicle's coming, engine rumbling low. She scoots over to the shadowed wall and hunkers next to a stack of empty crates.

An SUV comes in view, moving slowly. The Durango. No one in it but the driver. It stops. A driver-side spotlight comes ablaze and plays into the alley. She makes herself as small as she can, thinking the game's up, they've got her.

The spotlight beam moves over the opposite walls and fences, inciting dogs to higher pitch, then flicks over to her side of the alley and flashes along the wall above her head. Through the din of the dogs, she hears the driver's voice—speaking on a phone?—and the Durango speeds away.

She gets up and goes to the corner and peers around it to see the Durango make a turn at the end of the street. Holding to the shadows, she jogs along the broken sidewalk, stripping the severed cuffs off her wrists. She pauses at the corner, looks both ways, sees no one, and runs across the street to the shadows of the next block.

As she nears the entrance of the next alley, hoping it won't be another blind, she hears footfalls behind her and turns to see the ponytail man not ten yards from her and coming fast.

She runs into the alley, the ponytail yelling for her to stop. "*Párate*, pinche concha!"

It's an open alley but a long one. She's gasping as much in fear as for breath. She stumbles and regains her balance, hears the man's running feet, his cursings louder. Some of the alley fences are of concrete, some of wood, all about seven to eight feet high, and it sounds like there are raging dogs behind every one of them. The only chance she sees is to start hopping fences and damn the dog bites.

The alley lamppost shows no glass shards on top of a stone fence on her left, and she veers to it and jumps and catches hold of its top with both hands. She pulls herself up chin-high to the rim of the wall and works her right foot up to the top of it, but before she can bring up her other leg, the ponytail catches it by the ankle and yanks her down.

She drops onto him and he topples backward and hits the ground with her on his chest, the air bursting from his lungs. She rolls onto her hands and knees and starts to get up but he again snatches her ankle with both hands, holding her down as he fights for breath. She kicks and kicks at his face with the heel of her free foot, kicking his mouth, his eyes, and one of his hands slips off her foot. She keeps kicking and her ankle comes free. She scuttles rearward on hands and heels and butt as he fast-crawls after her, snarling like one more dog trying to get at her, grabbing at her feet. She kicks him in the face again, then rolls over and starts to get up but he dives and tackles her around the thighs and brings her back down. Dogs for blocks around going mad.

She's on her side, writhing and twisting like a lunatic amid the dogs' crazed howlings, trying to detach from him, her hands in frantic search of the ground for anything that might serve as a weapon. He's cursing in gasps, punching her ass and hips, struggling to keep his grip on a fistful of dress at her waist as he tries to get to his knees.

Her hand closes on a large chunk of concrete block and she twists around to face him as he starts to rise to his knees and she swings the concrete chunk with her arm extended and hits him hard on the ear. He grunts and his hand lets go of her dress and he falls over sideways.

She kicks free of him and scrambles to her feet. He's breathing but not moving, and she has an impulse to hit him again, harder, to break his goddamn skull. But she doesn't. She drops the concrete chunk and again jumps and grabs the top of the wall, and it's a greater effort this time to lug herself up.

The wall is flat-topped and almost a foot wide, and on its other side a pair of large dogs are leaping and leaping, jaws snapping at her overhanging face as she labors to get her legs up on the wall top, then does. She sits with her knees drawn up, catching her breath. Then notices the man and woman watching her from the open back door of the house. It's too dark to see their faces, but as she stares at them they go back inside and shut the door.

The ponytail groans and stirs.

Go! she thinks.

She stands up and quicksteps with sure balance to the end of the wall, where it abuts the top of the neighbors' wooden fence, behind which a small dog is apoplectic at her looming presence. She follows the stone wall to the left until she's about three feet from a neighboring house with a flat roof not two feet higher than her head. It's a tricky jump that requires her to catch hold of the narrow eave without banging her knees on the side of the house—and she does it, grabbing the eave and lighting on the wall with the balls of her feet, then hefts herself up onto the roof.

From up here, the furious racket of the dogs sounds even louder. She sees a wide orange glow in the looming foothills and reckons it for one of the fire pits that consume the city's garbage. Its position gives her a clear fix on which way to go—in the other direction.

She proceeds from rooftop to rooftop, the houses so close to each other it's less a jump than a running skip between most of them. The people inside surely hear the thumping of her footfalls, but no one comes out to see who's tramping on their house. Some of the roofs are of corrugated tin, some of gravel over wood, some no more than tar-papered planks that yield somewhat under her weight as she crosses them. Some are festooned with clotheslines and she has to bat her way through hung laundry.

She's moving over ground of slight upward incline, and now she reaches its summit, atop a roof from which she spies brightly lighted streets straight ahead and about twelve blocks distant—red-yellow-green blinking of traffic lights, the play of neon. *That's* where she has to get. Maybe half a mile, she figures, maybe a little farther. The moon has vanished in the growing mass of clouds, and a wind has come up. She shivers in her thin dress.

She crosses another few roofs before finding herself on one that's too far from the neighboring houses for her to make the jump. A tall tree stands close and she descends it to the ground.

She has no idea how far she's come from the hold house, but there's less barking now. She thinks she's reached the perimeter of the slum because the streets are a little better paved here, most of the residences fronted with small yards and shrubbery.

She's advanced another two blocks, staying in the deeper shadows along the side of the street, when she hears something behind her. The tread of running feet? She darts over to a row of bushes and crouches behind them and holds still, listening hard. Now hears nothing except the most relentless dogs.

But maybe whomever she heard has also stopped and is listening as hard for her to make the next move. It occurs to her the ponytail was probably armed and she feels stupid not to have thought of it and taken his weapon when she had the chance. Damn it, girl, *think*.

She silently counts to sixty, alert for any suspicious sound, but at the end of the count she hears nothing but the dogs and the rustlings of the trees in the rising wind. She resumes moving slowly down the street.

Before she's gone another block she hears a vehicle approaching from the rear and hurries back to the bushes.

A compact car drives past, trailing rock music behind it.

Get a grip, she thinks. You've lost them. You have. Just keep moving to where the lights are.

Another vehicle is coming. She stays hidden and watches an ancient Volkswagen van pass by, a hand-painted logo of a crossed rake and shovel on its side. Two men in the front seat, two or three others in the back. Itinerant workers bound for yard jobs in some better section of town. As the van's single taillight fades down the street, she regrets not having tried to get a ride with them. A lot less risky than being out here on foot.

She moves on, alarmed by every rustle of leaves in every surge of wind, growing more conscious of how cold she is. A sweep of headlight beams comes around the corner behind her, and she again takes cover behind some shrubs.

It's an old pickup truck with slatted wooden sides on the bed. It clatters toward her in the weak glow of a streetlight. Another crew heading for a day's work in the greater city. She looks all about, sees no one else. Do it, she thinks.

She runs to the edge of the street, into the margin of the headlights, and waves her arms over her head. The truck slows with a squeal of brakes and stops a few feet from her. There's no one in it but the driver.

She runs up to the open passenger window and says, "Por favor, señor, necesito—"

The door flies outward and knocks her sprawling.

Stunned, she's trying to get up when she's grabbed by the hair and pulled to her feet. She sees it's the blond man and tries to knee him in the crotch but he pivots to take the blow on the hip and counters with a punch to her midsection that doubles her over, stopping her breath and practically paralyzing her. Her knees give way but he grips her under the arms and drags her around to the other side of the truck and braces her up against it, holding her turned away from him.

Her stomach feels crushed and she can't breathe. She thinks she's going to die. Then her lungs abruptly inflate and she's breathing again, though every inhalation is a wrench of pain under her ribs.

You going to throw up?

She shakes her head. Then bends forward and vomits, her knees buckling at the pain, but he holds her in place.

After several excruciating heaves, she can bring up nothing more. She hacks dry a few times and stops.

Done? he says.

She nods.

Sure?

She considers, and nods again. She now feels even colder than earlier and hugs herself.

A vehicle appears a few blocks away. He helps her to get in the truck and tells her to sit on her hands, then reaches past her and turns off the ignition and removes the key.

If you move from there or show a hand without my permission, I'll break your arms. You understand?

She nods.

Say it.

I . . . understand. She's still dazed. What she wants more than anything is for the pain to subside.

He shuts her door and waits beside the window for the vehicle to go by, an old sedan with a whining engine, then takes out his phone and makes a connection.

I got her, he says. Get back to the house.

He listens, then looks at Jessie. Really? he says. Well . . . it's another thing she'll pay for.

He puts away the phone and goes to the rear of the truck. She hears him rummaging in its bed. After a minute he reappears at the door and opens it and tells her to get out and stand facing him. She steps down, her balance largely recovered though her knees are still tenuous.

He holds her by an arm and says, All right?

She nods, fixing her gaze on the holstered pistol under his coat.

Don't even think of it, girl, he says. You'll get hurt worse.

He's got a wide roll of black electrical tape and he binds her wrists together in front of her with snug around-and-over loops of tape, and then winds a few loops over her upper arms and around her waist, securing her arms to her sides. He tears the roll free and lobs it into the truck bed.

He helps her back onto the cab seat and closes her door and goes around and gets in and cranks up the engine. Then makes a U-turn and heads slowly down the street.

Who taught you to fight?

She stays silent.

When I ask you something, answer me.

Nobody, she says, staring ahead.

Liar. I was just told you beat the shit out of the Apache. That's very funny, although you shouldn't have done it.

Apache, she thinks. Of course.

12 — JESSIE

He parks the truck in front of the house and leaves the motor running and comes around to her side and helps her out. The dogs next door have resumed their commotion.

The pain in her chest and stomach is such that she's hardly aware of the soreness of her feet. The Durango is parked behind the Suburban along the front of the yard.

As the blond assists her to the house, two men come out the front door and one of them starts toward them, carrying a large tool chest. She doesn't see the Apache. The man with the toolbox passes by without word or glance. She hears a truck door open and shut behind them and the old pickup rattles away.

The other man is still on the porch, sipping from a bottle of beer. The hook-nosed man who collected their phones and valuables. He grins at her and says, Hey, wildcat, glad to have you back.

She looks away.

You can take the cuffs off the women now, the blond tells him. But first shut those dogs up.

The hooknose nods and heads for the wall.

Jessie stumbles on the porch's bottom step, but the blond steadies her, then helps her up the other steps and through the door. The living room is dimly lighted by a crookneck lamp at one end of a worn sofa, and, at the other end, by a shrine of glimmering candles around a three-foot statuette of a black-robed Santa Muerte, a sequined mantilla atop her grinning skull, a scythe in one hand. The Mother of Death, worshipped by outcasts of every sort, and the patron saint of Mexican gangsters. There's a redolence of fried chiles and other spices, of maize tortillas, pintos, cooked tomatoes. On the table of the adjoining dining room is a black-and-white television no one is watching, its volume barely audible. Jack Nicholson and Marlon Brando are in Old West costumes and conversing in dubbed Spanish. Adjacent to the dining room is a kitchen at whose door stands a dark bony woman holding a wooden stirring spoon.

Jessie hears a *thonk* and pained yelping, then three more *thonks* in succession and the dogs are silent.

The blond man steers Jessie toward a hallway entrance, then draws her aside to let a girl pass by, a large pail of water in each hand. At first glance, Jessie thinks the girl is winking at her, then realizes she has a squint eye.

Come on, the blond says, and leads her into the dim hallway. At its far end is a staircase, the dark form of a man sitting on its bottom step. She supposes the others are being held upstairs and she's being taken to join them. But midway down the hall the blond opens a door on the right and says, In here.

The shadowy figure at the staircase stands up and the blond says, Wait there. Then he guides Jessie into the room.

It's a small, spare bedroom lit by a bedside lamp. Her first notion is that they're all being put into separate rooms. From the outside, the house hadn't seemed that big, but she supposes it might be, if all the rooms are this small. Then she thinks of a likelier reason he's brought her to a room with a bed.

She starts at the touch of the blond's hands on her back. He carefully removes the tape binding her arms to her sides and sticks the tape to the rail headboard.

She feels a tentative relief. He wouldn't have to untape her arms to rape her. She offers her hands to him so he can free them too, but he doesn't.

Do you need to use the bathroom?

What? she says. No.

You're sure?

No. I mean, no, I don't have to. Why do—?

Lie down, he says.

Her alarm renews. She tries to read his eyes in the low light.

Don't make me repeat myself.

She sits on the edge of the bed and says, What are you going to do to me?

Nothing. Lie down.

She does. He pulls her bound hands over her head and uses the removed tape to secure them to a headboard rail.

Why do this? she says. I can't run away again, not from in here. Leave my hands taped if you want, but . . . please, you don't have to tie me to the bed.

It's as if he doesn't hear her. He tests the firmness of her bonds and is satisfied. Then goes out into the hall, leaving the door open.

She tries to free her hands from the headboard rail, twisting this way and that, trying to push herself backward and effect some slack in her arms, but her contortions serve only to tighten the tape around her wrists. Her frustration churns in her chest, burns her eyes.

The blond returns and sees the disheveled bedcover and shakes his head. A man comes in behind him and closes the door.

The ponytailed man called Apache.

Her skin tightens. One side of his face is darkly swollen, its eye half-closed, its ear a raw mass. His lips look like small blue jellyfish, his nose bloated. There's no white at all in his eyes.

The blond takes out a switchblade and opens it and cuts her dress straps and puts away the knife. Without uncovering her breasts he slides his hand under her and unhooks her strapless bra and pulls it off her and drapes it over the headboard.

She feels tears forming and angrily blinks them back. *Don't*, she commands herself. Don't you dare fucking cry. Don't say anything. They'll hear it in your voice, how much they scare you. Don't give them the satisfaction, do not.

Catalina, she thinks. *Catalina.*

You harmed this man, the blond says to her, and he believes you owe him compensation. Unfortunately for you, you also caused *me* distraction and extra work. Had you been successful in your escape, I may have been severely punished for it, and I certainly would have seemed a fool. Like I can't hold on to a prisoner—a woman prisoner, worse yet. What you've done must be punished. Don't make a fuss about it. All you'll do is frighten the other women. Nothing's going to happen to them because neither of them tried to run away or kicked anybody in the face. The truth is, you're getting off very easy. Your only punishment is to be fucked by somebody you don't have any choice about. So what? We all have to do things with people we have no choice about. Think of it as just another dick.

She's stupefied with disbelief. Charged with dread.

Just don't hurt her, he tells the Apache.

She did this, man, the Apache says, indicating his face. She *owes* me.

That's why you can have her and that's plenty enough payback. Just don't hurt her.

The Apache's damaged mouth warps in a grotesque sneer.

Understand? the blond says. He unholsters the Glock.

Or what, you'll *shoot* me? Bullshit.

You hurt her, I'll bust you on the head so hard you'll never remember your name.

The Apache attempts another distorted sneer and returns his attention to her.

Understand? the blond says.

Yeah, yeah, Apache mutters, his eyes on her.

Say it.

I got it, man.

The blond goes to a ladder-back chair in the corner and sits down and crosses his legs and holds the pistol on his lap.

What're you doing? the Apache says.

Get to it or get out, the blond says.

Fuck you, the Apache snorts. Think I won't if you watch? Watch all you want. Jack off. What do I care?

She watches in terrified outrage as he takes off his pants and undershorts at the same time. He's already hard.

She wants to plead that he please please please not do this, but she remembers the look in her Aunt Catalina's eyes and the sound of her voice when she'd recounted some of the things *she* had survived. It was Catalina who had told her never to beg for mercy, never. Eat shit if you must, she had said—that proud woman who rarely spoke a coarse word—but there's no greater shame than to beg for mercy. You can always wash shit from your mouth, she had said, but begging for mercy will leave a vile shame on your tongue you can never get rid of.

She bites her lip and glares at the Apache as he looms over her, his grin distorted. He tugs the dress down her body and over her feet and drops it on the floor. He pinches her nipple and she twists and kicks at him, striking him on the thigh and just missing his erection.

He snarls, *Cunt!* and punches her leg and she cries out.

Don't hit her! the blond says, springing from the chair. Then points a finger at Jessie. *You!* Any more of that shit and I'll *let* him hurt you.

He returns to the chair.

The Apache gets on the bed and rips away her panty and flings it aside, then pushes her legs apart and positions himself and spits into his hand. She wants to laugh at him, insult him, tell him how much fun it was to kick his ugly face and how she'd fight him again if he were man enough to unbind her, but speech fails her as he tries to insert himself and curses her tightness. She wants to vomit, to loose her bowels, *anything* to repel him with disgust, but all her effort is concentrated in clenching herself against him—a resistance suddenly breached, her teeth baring in a yowl of raging shame at his invasion, at his grunting and grunting with the guttural pleasure of impaling an enemy, his rank odor shrouding her, his exhalations hot on her face.

And despite her resolution not to cry, not to show any sign of defeat, she cannot keep the tears from coursing.

Blurring his bloody grin.

II

RUDY

13

The plane is a five-passenger business jet belonging to the Three Uncles, but it isn't ready. Something about a faulty instrument light. It's not till a couple of hours later that Charlie shakes me out of my doze in an office chair and we board the plane and take off. It's a little four-seater but we're the only passengers.

The rain has stopped but the cloud cover's still thick. As we turn southward, the lights of Brownsville and Matamoros are patchwork glimmerings. Then we're over Mexico and there's only darkness down below.

Uncle Harry Mack has seen to the clearances for us to land at an auxiliary strip at Benito Juárez International in Mexico City, where we'll be met by our cousin Rodrigo Wolfe. We've got passports and a bag of clothes. Everything else we need, the Mexican Wolfes will provide.

I can't remember the last time Charlie left home to attend to a problem personally. That's what Frank and I are for. From the time we graduated from college almost twelve years ago, we've worked as field agents for Wolfe Associates, which makes us state-licensed investigators, a handy sanction. According to the firm's job description, a field agent traces witnesses, serves subpoenas, runs background checks and so forth, and sometimes we actually do such things, though the firm contracts with a private company to do most of that. For us Wolfes, "field agent" is mostly an occupation of record we enter on our tax forms. In truth we work for Charlie Fortune, mainly as gunrunners and sometimes as "fixers" for both him and Wolfe Associates. Whenever the firm is faced with a serious difficulty that can't be resolved in a courtroom, or whenever someone fails to hold up his end of a deal with Charlie or in any way threatens a family project, we're called on to resolve the matter. To fix it, if you will. Sometimes someone who wrongs us will haul ass and go into hiding, and so we first have to find him. We always do. At present, there are two other fixers in addition to me and Frank—a cousin named Roy Wolfe, and as of six months ago when he graduated from LSU, Eddie Gato. Roy likes to work alone, while Frank and I usually work as partners, but because Eddie's new to the trade, Charlie has had him working with me since last summer.

Frank was irked at being left out of this one, but Charlie needs him to run things in his absence. Eddie Gato wanted to come too, naturally, but was already assigned to go to New Orleans tomorrow night to lend a hand to the Youngblood family. They're our relatives through marriage, and our most important arms supplier east of Texas. They're having a problem with a smuggling outfit that's been trying to poach some of our southeastern sources and is suspected of hijacking shipments meant for us. It's not so much that the Youngbloods need the help, but Charlie's been wanting Eddie to get acquainted with them and saw this as a good opportunity to send him on his first solo job.

Immediately following the call from Harry Mack, Charlie filled us in on the situation with cousin Jessie. We knew she'd gone to Mexico City a few days ago to be a bridesmaid at the wedding of a couple she's known since her college days, and she was expected to return to Brownsville the day after tomorrow. But according to Harry Mack—who received the information from Juan Jaguaro, the head of the Mexican Wolfes—she'd been kidnapped tonight, she and nine other members of the wedding party, including the bride and groom. Kidnapped late last night, to be more accurate, since it's now Monday morning. The ransom's five million, U.S., and the bridal couple's parents have agreed to pay. The transfer's set to begin at four o'clock this afternoon. The parents do not intend to tell anyone about the snatch and are unaware the Mexican Wolfes have learned of it. That's all Harry Mack knew. We'll get the details in Mexico City.

Evidently, the parents believe they have no choice but to trust the kidnappers. That's their prerogative. We choose not to. We're tolerant and liberty loving, as I've said, but we're not free with our trust except with each other, and even then we can sometimes be chary. It could be that the snatchers truly intend to release the captives on receipt of the money. It works out like that more often than it doesn't. But we know of too many kidnappings in which the ransom was paid in full and in exactly the manner dictated and without any violation of the agreement with the kidnappers, and the captives were killed anyway. Mainly for the age-old reason that the dead don't tell tales. Even if the perpetrators don't plan on doing away with the captives when they get paid off, they might get riled or panicked about something for whatever reason and decide to kill one for effect. To make a point of their seriousness. In such a case, the likely victim would be the captive who's most expendable. The only one of the bunch not related to either bride or groom. Meaning Jessie.

It's a possibility we can't risk.

Find her before the money changes hands—and move fast to get her out. That's our plan in a nutshell.

By tonight we'll know how it went.

As we make our descent, the cloud-blurred lights of Mexico City materialize. It's almost dawn but the overcast is well entrenched and the pilot says the prediction is for rain all day. I managed a catnap but I can tell that Charlie didn't even try to sleep.

I've been to a number of places in northern Mexico, but this is my first time in the capital. Some might find that odd, considering the large family we have here, but that's how it is. The Three Uncles have all come here at one time or another, but I don't think any of them have been here in ages. Other than Charlie Fortune, who comes down once or twice a year to see the Jaguaros about things that neither he nor they will discuss in any way but face-to-face, Jessie's the only Texas Wolfe who's been in Mexico City in recent years, so far as I know. The Mexican Wolfes are the same way about Texas. The only one of them who's visited us in years is our cousin Rayo Luna. We're all under the same roof and in business together, but the two sides of the family generally tend to keep to their own side of the house.

The Beechcraft lands smoothly and taxis to a small building where a mustached man in a dark suit stands waiting by a door. We debark into a light wind threaded with the scent of rain. The man comes over and welcomes us, saying, "Bienvenidos a México, primos!" He introduces himself to me as my cousin Rodrigo Álvaro Wolfe but says to call him Rigo. We shake hands and embrace each other tight in a backslapping abrazo, then he and Charlie do the same. Charlie has met with him a number of times before and thinks highly of him. They're about the same age, and as operations chief of the Jaguaros, Rodrigo is Charlie's Mexican Wolfe counterpart. He has a degree in economics from UCLA and is as fluent in English as any of us. Like Charlie, he reports only to the heads of his family—his father, Plutarco, and his uncle, Juan Jaguaro, who is Plutarco's big brother and the top man.

"Let's get the customs bullshit over with," Rigo says. "Then we'll talk in the car."

Over the generations, the Mexican side of the family has prospered even more than ours. They own two investment firms and are part owners of two banks. They own data processing companies. They have controlling interest in a shipping line. They're established in Mexico City society and are prominent philanthropists who have endowed a number of education foundations and research institutes. And under the guise of Los Jaguaros, they've long been buying arms from us and selling them all over Mexico. Like us, they don't deal in guns only for the money or because they believe strongly in the right of self-defense and in ownership of the means to exercise it. They do it because, like us, they believe in greater allegiance to our own rules than those of governments owned by powerful interests who play the public for fools. It's a matter of self-respect as much as anything else.

Although the Jaguaros have received very little attention in contrast to the major crime cartels, they haven't wholly escaped public notice. As periodically described by the news media, they're the most covert criminal organization in the country, and some reports call them a cartel of their own. No one can say when their name first became known. Their home territory is rumored to be the capital itself but no one has ever proved it. The number of members in the organization is anyone's guess, and so far as journalistic investigators have been able to determine, not a single member of the Jaguaros is known by name to any government agency. The only thing the federal authorities know about them is that they traffic solely in the sale of firearms, but on a scale that makes them the largest arms dealer in Mexico.

Some news outlets, however—their editors in the pay of shadowy intermediaries of the Jaguaros—have expressed chronic doubts that a Jaguaro organization even exists. They've repeatedly conjectured that the Jaguaros are nothing more than the fabrication of federal officials, one more ploy to distract the public from the government's failure to stem the arms flow into Mexico or curb the spreading violence of the real cartels, and maybe even—as some of the bolder tabloids have insinuated—to cover up their collusion with those cartels. Some apprehended members of various crime gangs have told police that the Jaguaros certainly do exist and that their organizations have many times bought guns from them. The same skeptical media sources have dismissed these claims as a clever tactic to keep secret the cartels' true suppliers.

The truth is that not even the other cartels know who the Jaguaros are. They know the Jaguaros work out of the capital, yes, and they know how to make contact with them to arrange an arms purchase, certainly. But to this day, none of the outfits has any inkling that the Jaguaros are connected to the estimable Wolfe family of Mexico City.

14

A white Tahoe picks us up in front of the terminal. The smell of the coming rain has grown stronger. In better weather the sun would be up now, but the cloud cover is so thick I don't even know in which direction the sun might be. Rigo takes the shotgun seat and Charlie and I sit in back. Despite the overcast, the driver wears dark wraparounds. Wood-faced dude. He nods when Rigo introduces him as Chuy.

Even at this early hour the traffic into the city is already something to reckon with, but Chuy navigates it with ease. According to Charlie, you haven't really risked your ass until you've tried driving in Mexico City.

Sitting half-turned toward us, Rigo asks how much we know about the snatch.

"Only what Harry Mack got from Juan Jaguaro," Charlie says, and gives him the spare rundown.

Rigo then gives us the full account, which he says originated with his cousin—and ours—Rayo Luna, though he doesn't say how she came by the information. The key points are that the kidnapped party's being held in two groups at different sites, each group to be ransomed in turn, then all the captives released at the same time, and that the guy who claims to be running the show calls himself Mr. X.

"Number of perps unknown," Rigo says. "But no question it's an inside job involving the Huerta guy, the security chief working for Belmonte. What we don't know is if Huerta's the only security guy involved or if some of his men are in it too. It's a small company, seven agents, all of them on duty at the reception, but we haven't found any of them. Could be the whole outfit's in on it. He's got two secretaries, both single, both live alone. We've braced them, told them we were federal cops, grilled them good. Neither one seems to know anything. Got them under house arrest, man posted with them so they can't contact anybody. We tossed the office but found nothing."

"What do you have on the Mr. X dude?" Charlie says.

"Nothing but what the parents said. Came across as a cool customer. Smooth talker, they said, educated."

"Cartel?" Charlie says.

"Don't think so," Rigo says. "They'd be breaking an agreement the big guys have about Mexico City. The cartel honchos have to live somewhere, too, after all. A lot of them have homes here, their families. The understanding is it's okay to talk business here but not *do* business here, and for damn sure not make war here. Some of their cowboys might get in a dustup now and then but it doesn't happen often, and it's always some personal deal, not war. The big guys don't want undue attention here. They don't want to alarm the good citizens or the tourists or hurt the city's business. The government will deny it till doomsday, but word has it that as long as the resident big boys don't make trouble in the capital, the feds will leave them alone in the capital."

"So you figure small-time locals for the grab," Charlie says.

"Who else?" Rigo says. "God knows how many kidnap gangs there are in Mexico City. Hell, man, snatcher gangs have made the bodyguard business a boom industry in this town. The thing is, most of their grabs are middle-classers who can't afford a ransom like—"

"Smalltimers fuck up," Charlie interrupts. "They're reckless. The people they grab tend to get hurt, even killed, sometimes by accident, sometimes not. That's what *I* know about small-time snatcher gangs. It's riskier to Jess if it *is* a small-time bunch."

"Normally I'd agree with you, cuz. But these Mr. X guys, they grab *ten* richies at once, *and*, according to the parents, without hurting anybody. Pretty smooth, no? The parents treated politely, taken to meet Mr. X so he can explain the deal in person instead of by phone or a letter. He has them driven home. Cool. Reassuring. They're smart, these guys, they're not greedy. They could tag these people for more than five mil but they don't. They figure the families can pony up the five faster than, say, even ten. *And* they figure that two and a half mil from two banks is easier and faster than five mil from one. I think speed's their thing. The faster it moves, the less chance of cops coming into it, of anything going wrong. My money's on a small and highly competent bunch that's looking to move up in status and knows there's no percentage in harming the hostages. They get the money, they'll let them go."

"Unless they don't," Charlie says. "Look, man, ease up on the fucking comfort campaign. I don't need it."

Rigo gives him a narrow stare. "Fuck your comfort, Charlie. You wanna believe they're gonna do her, whoever they are, go ahead and believe it. *I* don't. Odds are they're not gonna hurt any of them. All I'm saying. Those are the *odds*."

For a minute nobody says anything. Charlie stares out the window. Rigo makes a show of checking his watch, the overcast sky.

"Sorry, man," Charlie says without looking at him.

"Skip it, cuz," says Rigo.

We're in the central city now, in a six-lane river of nearly bumper-to-bumper traffic ranging from scads of limousines and luxury sedans to hordes of junkers trailing clouds of smoke. The Mexico City soundtrack, some call the steady blaring of car horns.

Rigo tells us his people have the groom's parents' house under surveillance from a house two blocks away. A three-story house whose top floor affords an excellent telescopic view of the Belmonte place. An associate of the Mexican Wolfes, a realtor dealing in exclusive homes, knows the owner of the house, who is vacationing in Hawaii. As a favor to the Wolfes, who told him they're doing it as a favor to a filmmaker friend of the family, the realtor was able to rent the property for two days and nights so the director could shoot a few scenes set on a sumptuous estate. A Jaguaro team went there with movie equipment and told the household staff they could take the next two days off and paid them all a sum equal to a week's wages.

We're headed for the offices of Jiménez y Asociados, a legal firm dealing mainly in customs and international trade contracts. It's only a few blocks from the Zócalo—the city's immense central plaza containing the major federal offices, the National Palace, and the Metropolitan Cathedral. Jiménez has got the top six floors of a twelve-story building whose owner of record is Grupo Azteca Mundial, SA, a Latin American conglomerate whose financial ties would be very difficult for anyone outside the firm to unravel. In fact, the conglomerate is headed by Plutarco Wolfe, Rigo's daddy, and the building belongs to the Wolfe family.

"The top floor is our operations center," Rigo says. "It's got a suite, if you'd like to clean up, have a bite."

"Rayo be there?" I ask.

"For sure. I figured you'd want to talk to her, since she's the one came up with the info. I've put her on this thing. Her first biggie."

"She's a *Jaguaro*?" I say.

He nods with a look of mock rue. "Insisted on a tryout. Wouldn't take no for an answer. Thing is, and just between us, she might actually work out."

I grin back at him, not really that surprised by any of it.

Rigo clears his throat. "Look, guys, I know how you—"

Chuy hits the brakes and we all sling forward and hear the screech of tires behind us. A green-and-white microbus that cut in front of us from the lane to our right now cuts into the faster-moving lane on the left, squeezing in ahead of a braking taxi whose driver leans hard on his klaxon as if its squall means anything in the incessant cacophony. Then the traffic in that lane slows and we come abreast of the microbus. It looks like an oversized bread box, and I'd noticed a number of them since leaving the airport, all of them as packed with riders. Look like they can seat maybe two dozen and carry that many more standees holding to overhead rails. The driver of this one wears a red bandanna headband and looks to be in his twenties. He's obviously irked at his mistake in moving into a slowing lane and he's flicking glances at ours, looking for a break to slip back into it.

Chuy lays on his horn to attract the driver's notice and says, "Chinga tu madre," enunciating slowly so the guy can read his lips.

The driver's eyes cut away from Chuy and go wide as he points ahead of us and mouths, Watch out!

Chuy taps his brakes as he whips his attention forward—and the microbus zips into the sudden gap in front of us.

The driver sticks his arm out and gives us the finger. Then he swerves ahead of a full-sized bus in the lane on the right, and the micro's gone.

Motherfucker, Chuy says under his breath, the deep darkness of his ears evincing his embarrassment at having been faked out.

Rigo tells us there are thousands of such micros plying the streets of Mexico City, the cheapest form of public transportation in the capital. A lot of people still call them peseros because for many years their fare was one peso. Only after they've earned a daily quota determined by the company do the drivers start to earn their own pay. It's a cutthroat competition, Rigo tells us, and hardly any wonder the drivers take such chances.

Charlie's staring out at the passing traffic, not really listening.

"Hey, cousin," Rigo says, and Charlie turns to him.

"They didn't just take your niece," Rigo says. "They didn't just take a *Texas* Wolfe. They took somebody from the *house*, man. Jessica's our blood, too, and we want to find her as much as you do, as fast as you do. I want to find her yesterday. But I don't know if it can happen before payoff time. All I can say is we'll probably hear something soon. We've got our spiders on this. Gave them the word without giving them specifics. They know how to do it, ask around without tipping anybody off. We don't want the perps getting wind of somebody maybe being on to them. We want them believing they're the smartest guys on the planet and this is the coolest snatch that ever was and nobody knows about it but them and the snatchees and the two sets of parents. The longer they believe that, the lower their guard and the better our chances of getting a fix on them."

Charlie nods. Then goes back to staring out the window.

I understand why Rigo's so confident about getting a quick lead of some kind. Charlie's told me all about the "spiders" Rigo mentioned. They're the Jaguaros' information collectors. Every day, they range through an enormous web of sources that extends into every corner of the Federal District, sources from every social level—street rats, corporate staffers, shoeshine boys, political aides, cops, whores, bartenders, newspeople, you name it. The federals are wrong about the Jaguaros dealing only in guns. They also sell information. Almost exclusively to the cartels, who are always ready to pay for any report or rumor concerning anything that may affect them by way of the federal authorities and their American advisers, who are in this country in greater numbers than either the American or Mexican public knows. All the crime outfits have their own information sources, naturally, but, according to Charlie, they all know that none of them can match the network of Jaguaro connections in the capital.

The way Charlie explained it to me, the spiders are unknown to each other and don't even know who they're really working for. They relay their information to their district managers, who note its source and origin and get it keyed into computers, after which the data's encrypted and sent to one of the many depots, as the Jaguaros call them—computer dealerships and tech support shops they own all over the city under the names of dummy corporations. The depots recode the information and then transmit it to a so-called warehouse through a routing system so labyrinthine that not even the depot techies know where it ends up. According to Rigo, those warehouses are some of the research institutes the Mexican Wolfes have endowed, a research institute being a perfect cover for filtering, cataloging, and storing coded information in readiness for Jaguaro computers seeking specific kinds of data.

That information network is why we came with the hope of finding Jessie fast. If there's anything to be picked up out there that'll lead us to her, the Jaguaros will find it.

15

The first fat raindrops are spattering the windshield and there's a low roll of faraway thunder as we wheel into the building's garage and park in Rigo's reserved spot near the elevators. He uses an electronic key to activate an office elevator that takes us to the top floor.

In a spacious foyer appointed in colonial Spanish decor, a sleek young woman at the reception desk, her hair woven in a black braid extending to the small of her back, greets Rigo with warm informality. He introduces her as Ángela and she smiles and welcomes us to Jiménez y Asociados.

We go down a long hallway flanked by spacious offices and enter a storeroom whose walls are lined with ceiling-high shelves loaded with office supplies, then pass through another door and into a huge room spanning the width of the building but for one side that's lined with private offices and the suite Rigo had mentioned.

The remainder of the room is full of cubicles containing computer terminals. The screens flicker. Printers hum. Young men in shirtsleeves are moving from cubicle to cubicle, reading screens and talking with the casually dressed technicians at the terminals.

Rigo tells us the techs have put in a coded request to the storage institute's computers for all spider information gathered in the Federal District in the past three months that contains any reference, large or small, to kidnapping, as well as all information ranging from rumors to public records pertaining to Jaime Huerta or the Angeles de Guarda security company. The information has been coming in bits and pieces for the past three hours.

The techs scan it, Rigo says—speaking in Spanish for the first time since greeting us at the airport—and channel everything of related interest over to *those* computers.

He points to a table on the far side of the room where several men and one woman are seated at a long desk in front of a row of computers and focused on the monitors.

The woman looks up, and I see she's Rayo Luna.

She grins at me in recognition, then says something to a young guy standing nearby who takes her place at the terminal and she rushes over to us. She hugs me and kisses me on the cheek and then does the same to Charlie, saying how happy she is to see us.

Then her face gets serious, like she just remembered why we're here. We're going to find her, she says. "Ya lo veras."

Charlie makes no response. I smile and resist the urge to run my hand through her pixie haircut. We've known her since her first visit to Brownsville back when she and Jessie were around sixteen and Jessie was still living with Harry Mack and Mrs. Smith. Like Jessie, she's a beaut—more of one, in my book, but then I've always preferred morenas, with their black hair and brown skin. She's also something of a free spirit and nobody's fool, I know that much, even though Jessie's always tended to monopolize her on her visits and the rest of us never have much chance to spend time with her. In one of the few private exchanges I've had with her, I remarked—God knows why—that it was interesting we were both orphans as a result of our parents having vanished in the Gulf. She'd given me a strange look and said yeah, that was real interesting, all right. Can be hard to read her sometimes. Not a man of us isn't impressed by the fact she's a stunt woman. I've seen her run partway up the trunk of a palm tree and flip backward off it and land on her feet as lightly as a bird. She was wearing a flared skirt when she did it, and the peek of her undies made the exhibition all the more memorable. Frank once observed that she's right out of Shakespeare. "Though she be but little, she is fierce." She's not really all that little, maybe five seven or eight, around Jessie's size, but she's definitely fierce. Jessie's told us about guys who were fools enough to cross her boundaries and suffered for it. The outfit she's wearing—a black T-shirt and a pair of faded jeans—holds to her so nicely it's an effort not to gawk. Plus she's got this full-lipped mouth you can't help but imagine yourself kissing . . . and yeah, yeah, yeah, she's my cousin and so what? That's never been an impediment to amorous liaisons in our family. The Mexican Wolfe patriarch, Juan Jaguaro himself, married his first cousin back when. Didn't raise more than one or two family eyebrows.

We're joined by a guy whose smile is a little awkward. Not in a way that suggests shyness but as if smiling is something he doesn't do very much. He and Charlie clutch in an abrazo and say it's good to see each other. Rigo introduces him to me as his younger brother, Mateo Genaro Wolfe. He's clean-shaven like I am, and built about the same. Quick-eyed. We embrace and smack each other on the back.

Though we haven't met before, I know a lot about him by way of Charlie. He's only a few years younger than Charlie and is in charge of a crew of guys called Los Chamacos—the Kids—who are the equivalent of us fixers, only there's more of them than us, Charlie told me. When the Jaguaros come up against a problem they can't settle in standard business fashion, they turn it over to Mateo and his Chamacos to right the matter. The word on him is that he's very damn good at his work—and capable of a fury belying his reserved manner. The family tales about him are legion, but the one that's always stuck with me is the one Charlie told about Mateo's first assignment as a Chamaco, when he was hardly more than an actual kid. He was sent to collect the outstanding difference, plus interest penalty, on an underpayment for an arms shipment. The debtor was the chief of a Toluca street gang and not much older than Mateo. When Mateo tracked him down at a plush house just outside of Toluca and told him to pay up, the kid told him to fuck himself and had four of his guys jump him. They gave him a pretty good going-over, breaking his nose and blacking his eyes, then stripped him of his gun and wallet and took him out in a car and dumped him on a four-lane highway full of midday traffic. The way Mateo told it to Charlie, he went bouncing over the pavement for what seemed like forever with tires screeching and cars swerving and whipping by him, and he was sure he was going to get splattered. When he stopped rolling he was just a few feet from the shoulder and still in one piece and he crawled to it as fast as he could as an 18-wheeler sped by within a foot of him, its blow-by knocking him rolling. It was God's almighty wonder he wasn't killed or didn't break anything more than the pinky of his left hand. His clothes were torn, his elbows and knees gashed, his head knotty with bloody bruises, and he was going to be sore from head to foot for a month. But he was intact and could walk. The only vehicle that pulled over to see about him was a large truck full of field workers. They gave him a ride into town and he practically had to force them to accept the money he pressed on them. He called the capital from a pay phone and waited on a park bench until a quartet of Jaguaros came for him and took him to a clinic where he was sewn up and bandaged and given injections. That evening, he and the four Jaguaros overpowered the outside guards at the gang chief's house and slipped inside and took care of another three guys without much fuss or noise. They searched the house as quiet as cats until they found the young boss in a bedroom, asleep with a girl on either side of him, everybody bare-assed. The kid woke to Mateo's pistol muzzle on his mouth. Surprise of the fucker's life, Mateo told Charlie. The kid was made to produce every last peso and dollar in the house, which amounted to twice as much as his debt to the Jaguaros. Mateo even got his gun and wallet back. He thanked the kid very much for his cooperation and then took him, still naked, down to his car and out on the same highway and had him kicked out of the speeding vehicle. There wasn't as much traffic at that late hour as earlier in the day, but the kid wasn't nearly as lucky as Mateo had been. In the brief moment before they lost sight of him, he was repeatedly struck and dragged and dispossessed of body parts. "You could say in complete truth," Mateo had told Charlie in English, "that he paid more than an arm and a leg for his mistake."

We spend the next half hour with Rigo and Mateo and Rayo in a private side room, where we're shown a folder of photographs of the Belmonte and Sosa family members. Portrait photos, school pictures, newspaper and magazine shots taken at one or another soiree or sporting event or civic function.

Partly in English, partly in Spanish, sometimes in both languages within the same sentence, Rayo tells us everything she's already told the Jaguaros several times. She says she was fooling around with a guy in a room in the Belmonte house when the bridal parents unexpectedly entered an adjacent office and she overheard them talking about the kidnapping. "Fooling around" is her phrase, spoken without hint of embarrassment. Which is another thing I've always liked about her—she's as forthright as they come. She's absolutely sure of what the parents said because they kept repeating things to each other, comparing their memories of what Mr. X had said to them.

"When I checked my landline messages this morning," she says, "there was one from Sosa. Me díjo que JJ had gone with the rest of the wedding party a un rancho en Cuernavaca for another day of good time. Pero she lost su teléfono and so asked him to please give me a call and let me know she wouldn't be home till tonight. He was covering for her absence."

Rigo's going to post men at the banks where Belmonte and Sosa will get the money. Lookouts for anybody shadowing either man. Mateo nods at Rayo and says, The kid and I will watch Sosa's bank. It's closest to the Belmonte house. Anybody looks right, we tail *him*. If he keeps on looking right, we grab him, see what he has to say. Same for the lookouts at Belmonte's bank.

That'll be me and Rudy, Charlie says.

Rigo nods like he was expecting that. If you wish, he says. Mateo will assign another man to you, too, just in case.

Duarte, Mateo says. Good one.

Charlie shrugs.

Rigo tells us that so far all the kidnapping items his communication techs have received have been in reference to snatches no more recent than two weeks ago, and the file searches on Huerta and his security company have uncovered nothing more than repetitious data attesting that Angeles de Guarda is a fully registered business with impeccable financial records and client evaluations that universally laud the company's good service. Except for the bureaucratic data relating to his proprietorship of the company, there's nothing on Huerta himself but a single police record of arrest for fighting in the streets when he was sixteen.

Something will come up, Rayo says. It's hard to keep a secret in a small town, and you know what they say about Mexico City. It's a small town of twenty million people.

Rigo goes off to the suite, and Mateo and Rayo take us into a room furnished with only a couple of long bare tables in its center and rows of lockers along the walls. Mateo opens one of the lockers and extracts a pair of cell phones and hands one to Charlie and one to me. Their directories contain no names and only three numbers—the first is Rigo's, the second his, the third Rayo's. All the phones are equipped with trackers. He withdraws a wallet from the locker, takes a gander in it, and hands it to me, then gets out another and gives it to Charlie. The wallets contain two kinds of identification with our picture and physical description—a Federal District driver's license and an ID card for employees of Montoya Investigaciones SA, a private Mexico City investigation company. Montoya Investigaciones is a real company, Mateo tells us, owned by the Jaguaros through a combination of fronts. Its owner of record is a retired and highly venerated naval captain named Alejandro Montoya whose nephew is a ranking attorney in the mayor's office. The company's office is on a lower floor of the building we're in.

If you should have to deal with the police, Mateo says, show them the card. The federals don't care for private investigators, but they know Captain Montoya and give his people some latitude.

There's a knock at the open door and one of the computer guys beckons Rayo. She excuses herself and goes off with him.

Mateo takes a pair of pistols from the locker and places them on the table and beside each one sets two 13-round double-stacked magazines and a shoulder holster. Beretta .380 Cheetahs. He asks if they'll do or if we prefer something else.

Truth to tell, I prefer revolvers, big ones like my Redhawk. Revolvers don't jam. Plus I hold with the view that if you need more than six shots to hit something, you really shouldn't risk getting in a gunfight in the first place. But Charlie likes pistols and regards the Beretta highly. They'll do fine, he says.

We join Rigo in the suite, where a table in the outer room is set with platters of sandwiches and bowls of fried chicken and baskets of pastries. There's a large urn of coffee, and the refrigerator holds juices and soda pop and beer. Mateo fills a plate with pieces of chicken and cracks open a beer and sits at the table to eat. Rigo's slumped on the sofa, watching a weather channel with the sound off. He says he likes the maps, the colors of the temperature bands. It's very soothing, he says, the weather channel.

A radar map shows a pulsing bright green swath, wide and ragged, extending from South Texas down through central Mexico and all the way to a strip of coast that includes Acapulco. The forecast is for the rain to continue into the night.

Charlie says he's going to take a fast shower, but as he starts for the bedroom, Rayo comes in with a printout paper in her hand and says, We got something on Huerta.

Everybody looks at her.

Nothing big, but it's something, she says, suddenly looking a little nervous with so many expectant eyes on her. She tells us that just two weeks ago Huerta was seen coming out of the Alameda park in the company of two unidentified men, one of whom had a spike haircut. Huerta departed on foot, and the two men were picked up at the curb by a silver Grand Cherokee driven by a man of distinctly Asian extraction. The spider reported it because he knew Huerta owns a security company and such people are often of interest. The third man was said to be as tall as Huerta and wore a wide-brimmed hat and expensive white suit.

We stare at her.

And? Mateo says. The spider get a name? A plate number?

Well . . . no, she says. But the man with the spike hair . . . he has to be the one the parents mentioned, no?

It could well be, Mateo says. So now we know for certain that the parents can identify a spike haircut when they see one. And that one of the kidnappers dresses well. Was there anything *else* in the report?

No, sir, Rayo says. I just thought . . . no sir.

Thank you, Rayo, Rigo says. Attach it to the file, please.

It's *something*, isn't it? she says, a little flushed.

"It's *nothing*," Charlie says in English, getting up and going off to shower.

I don't care for their tone. She was just trying to help.

When she leaves the room, I follow her out and say, "Oye."

She looks back and stops, her eyes bright with anger and injured dignity.

"Listen," I say. "It *is* something. It shows that the parents' accounts are pretty accurate and reliable, which is a good thing to know."

She nods and gives me a small smile. "Yeah, well . . . thanks."

I watch her walk off. God, that rump.

When Charlie's done with the bathroom, I take a turn in the shower and get into a pair of jeans, a sweater, the Beretta shoulder holster, a waterproof Windbreaker. Charlie's dressed the same way. The spare magazines go in an outer zip-up pocket, the wallet with Mexican ID in an inner one.

In the dining room we help ourselves to sandwiches and coffee, then sit on the couch with Rigo and Mateo, who are talking about a pal of theirs who's about to get married for the third time. The guy never learns, Mateo says.

He's hardly the only one, Rigo says. Men tend to remember the best things about the women they've loved and to forget the worst, which is why so many men make the same mistakes with women again and again. Women tend to forget the best things about the men they've loved and to remember the worst, which is why so many women are so bitter about men.

I can see Charlie's not listening. He just stares at the pulsing green colors of the TV weather maps and checks his watch every two minutes.

16

Hardly anybody really knows Charlie Fortune. It's not that he's aloof or closed-mouthed. He enjoys kidding around and batting the breeze as much as the next guy, and he's always liked swapping jokes with me and Frank. It's just that he's never been one for *sharing his feelings*, as they say. The truth is Frank and I probably know him better than anyone else does, even his daddy, if only because nobody else has spent as much time with him as we have. We've worked for him for around a dozen years now and have lived practically next door to him for the last sixteen, ever since he took us in when our parents died.

At least, everybody assumed they died. All anyone's ever known for sure is that on a fine spring day of ideal weather and mild seas, they went out for a weekend sail one Friday morning in their sloop, the *Annie Max*, and never came back. When nobody had heard from them by Monday morning, the Coast Guard was notified and air units made a wide search for the next three days without spotting any sign of them. No flotsam, not a life jacket, nothing. After another two weeks, the family accepted their death as a fact. There was a memorial service for them and plaques were set in the family graveyard.

Frank and I were our parents' only children, seventeen and sixteen years old at the time, but both of us heading into our senior year of high school by dint of our parents' finagling my enrollment in first grade when I was only five so that Frank and I could be in the same grade all the way through school. They had willed us the house and we wanted to continue living in it, just us two, but some of our relatives were very much opposed. They said it would be unseemly and irresponsible of the family to permit any of its children to live without adult supervision while they were still in school. Frank and I said we weren't children and could take care of ourselves quite well, thank you very much. So they took the matter to the Three Uncles. Whenever there's a family conflict that the principals can't settle on their own, the Uncles are asked to decide it. In this instance they ruled that we had to live under direct adult supervision until we graduated. Either an adult relative moved in with us or we moved in with an adult relative. We didn't like the choice worth a damn, but in our family the rules are the rules, and one of the most basic is that a decision of the Uncles is final. Most of our relatives were willing to take us in, but the only one willing to move in with us was our spinster aunt, Laurel Lee. She's a nice person in many ways and a real whiz with digital gadgetry, but she's got some rigorous views about the proper governance of the legally underage, and the idea of being under her authority was as appealing as a yearlong stretch in reform school. Still, it was a better option than moving in with another household. We intended to inform her of our decision right after the memorial ceremony, but as soon as the service ended, Charlie Fortune came up to us to express his condolences and ask how we were doing.

We didn't know him very well then. He'd gone off to Texas A&M when Frank and I were in elementary school, but even as little kids, we knew about his athletic achievements in high school. He had set a state broad jump record that stood for five years and he twice made all-state in football as a running back and three times in baseball as a catcher. He went to A&M because he wanted to stay in-state and preferred College Station to the other university towns. He majored in history, took full-time coursework even in the summer sessions, and got his degree in three years. He has many times said he would've gone on to law school except he didn't meet the entrance requirements because he'd been born of married parents. You wouldn't think that old joke would continue to get as many laughs as it does in a family with a half-dozen lawyers in it, including Harry Mack. As soon as he graduated, Charlie came home and went to work for our daddy, Henry James Wolfe, whom everybody called HJ, and who by that time had been chief of the family shade trade for about ten years, since shortly after I was born. Daddy had promised him a position as soon as he met the rule that requires any family member who wants to work in the shade trade to get a degree first, which is why Charlie had matriculated year-round at A&M, to get it over with as soon as he could. Frank and I would do the same thing at UT Austin. Charlie quickly became Daddy's number two operative, behind Uncle Harry Morgan Wolfe, but even then Frank and I still didn't see much of him. Unlike Daddy, who commuted daily from Brownsville to the Landing, Charlie lived out there from the day he entered the shade trade and but infrequently came into town. The only times we saw him were at family gatherings on holidays or birthdays, and our exchanges with him were pretty much limited to "hey" when we arrived and "so long" when we left.

Frank and I were in junior high when he got married. Her name was Hallie Rheinhardt and she was nineteen years old and the marriage lasted exactly eight days. Frank and I never did meet her. Nobody did except some of the folks who lived or worked at the Landing back then, including Daddy. All he ever told us about it was that Charlie met her in Galveston and married her two days later, then brought her home to the Landing, where they mostly kept to themselves for a week before she lit out while Charlie was making a gun run to Laredo. When he got back and found out she'd left, he went looking for her and was gone for almost three weeks before he came back and told everybody the marriage was over and done and he did not ever want to hear a word about her. Daddy said everybody was wise enough to take his warning to heart, and nobody ever mentioned Hallie Rheinhardt within earshot of Charlie again. So far as I know, that's still true. It's a whole story of its own, Charlie's marriage.

For a while after it happened, though, he kept to the Landing and refrained from attending family events. Daddy figured he was feeling humiliated and probably thought everyone saw him as a fool, though in truth nobody did. Charlie Fortune was not the first man to fall in love with the wrong woman, Daddy said, and he would get over it by and by. In the meantime, Charlie made him an offer on the Doghouse Cantina and Daddy took it. He had inherited the place and never cared for the onus of operating it, but Charlie loved the joint. He enjoyed the badinage of bartending, and its management was no burden to him. Daddy believed that operating the Doghouse and socializing with the patrons did a lot to help Charlie get over the embarrassment of his marriage, and he pretty soon resumed attending family get-togethers.

It was at the family Christmas party at Uncle Peck's house just a few months before our parents disappeared that Frank and I had our first real conversation with Charlie. It came about when Daddy mentioned to him in our presence that Frank was now the best high school pitcher in the county and I was the best third baseman and so on and so forth. His bragging on us made us uncomfortable in light of Charlie having been one of the best-ever players in South Texas, but the baseball talk got the conversational ball rolling between us. He was only twenty-six then, yet there was an air about him that made us address him as "sir" until he said to quit it and just call him Charlie. We jawed about baseball with him for about an hour before he said he had to leave and had enjoyed the talk and hoped we could do it again sometime. But we didn't see him again until the memorial service, when he came up and asked how we were doing. By then the Three Uncles had appointed him to take Daddy's place as chief of the shade trade.

It so happened he hadn't heard about our residence problem and the Three Uncles' edict about it, and Frank told him the whole thing.

"Jesus," Charlie said. "You guys are gonna live with *Aunt Laurel?*"

All we could say was it beat the alternative.

He looked at us in a way he never had before. Like he'd just been asked a question about us and was trying to come up with a good answer. Then he asked if we'd like to live out at Wolfe Landing in one of the rental trailers, a double-wide in good shape that happened to be available. We wouldn't have to pay rent, not even if we sold our parents' house—which we would end up doing—but we'd have regular chores to do in lieu of rent. Our homework would always come first, but then would come the chores. He said it would be a long drive to school in Brownsville, but he'd provide the vehicle, and because we were under eighteen, he'd see to it we were given "hardship" driver licenses so we could drive without a licensed adult in the car.

We couldn't believe it. A house and a car and the licenses to drive it on our own. We also couldn't believe the Uncles would allow it, since they'd said we had to live under the same roof with an adult.

Charlie said to leave it to him, he'd talk to the Uncles that night.

We didn't think they would okay it, but they did. They said his offer to be our guardian and supervise us until we were of legal age met the terms of their ruling, and, notwithstanding the protests of some in the family, the matter was closed.

So Frank and I moved to Wolfe Landing.

Like all Texas Wolfes, we've known about the shade trade from the time we were kids, and we'd been taught never to speak of it to anyone outside the family. Until we moved to the Landing, however, we'd been there only once, back when we were still in grammar school. We nagged Daddy into taking us out there one Saturday but he wouldn't let us go exploring, so there was nothing for us to do but fish off the dock, and we got so bored we never asked to go out there again. That suited Daddy just fine and very much pleased Momma, who never liked the Landing or its "denizens," as she called its residents.

When we went to live there, though, we not only were older but had a whole summer to get acquainted with the place, and we came to love it. We loved its distance from the rest of the world. We loved its shadowy green daylight and the awesome blackness of its dank nights, the raw smells of the passing river and the surrounding resacas. The sudden frantic splashings in the dark. The ghostly calls of owls. The hissing of wind in the palms and the mossy hardwoods. We loved its wildness.

Our daily chore was to maintain the Landing's dock, to keep it swept and mopped, ensure that the cleats and mooring lines and tire bumpers were in good shape and replace whatever wasn't, and to help out Len Richardson at his Gringo's Bait & Tackle store in any way he might need. Richardson had come to the Landing only a few years ago, supposedly from Florida. He knew a thousand good jokes, but he never said much about himself. Probably for good reason, since rumor had it he was on the run from more than one felony warrant. He was hardly the only resident of the Landing with such a rumor about him.

Twice a week we also had the duty of burning the Landing's garbage in a pit—all except the large meat scraps and bones from the Doghouse kitchen. Those we took to the Resaca Mala and dumped into the water just before dark. The first time we were told to do it, we asked how come. It was a much longer haul from the Doghouse to the resaca than to the burn pit, and we'd have to transport the garbage bags in a pickup. Charlie said he did a lot of fishing there and liked to fatten up the fish, the turtles too, which made fine soups and stew. So off we went in the truck into a risen gray dusk. We were dumping the second garbage sack when the alligators came tearing out of the shadowy reeds of the opposing bank. We hollered and nearly pissed ourselves and put some fast yardage between us and the water's edge before we stopped to watch them chomping up the scraps. Then we busted out laughing at both our fright and the thrill of the feeding frenzy. It was a hell of a spectacle. We then dumped the rest of the scraps, working our way along the bank, the snapping, growling armada of gators churning along behind us.

When we told him about the scare we got, Charlie laughed and said he knew there was something he'd forgotten to tell us. He said Resaca Mala has always been full of gators. "Those fellas long been useful," he said, "for disposing of, ah . . ."

"Mortal testimony?" I said.

"Why yes, Rudy Max," he said. "That is precisely their inherent and perennially valuable function." He can talk like that when he wants to.

He was obviously pleased we weren't shocked by the revelation about the gators, and from then on he took as much delight in telling us smuggling stories as we took in hearing them. By the time we had to go back to school we knew the shade trade was for us, and one evening when we were having supper with him, we told him so.

"Oh hell, gents," he said. "I've known that since the first time you fed the gators."

Thus began a routine that held throughout our last year of high school and during which time Charlie became more of a big brother to us than an older cousin. We drove the thirty-five-mile round trip to school every weekday and then usually went there again on weekend nights to take our dates to the movies or a dance, and then afterward, if they were the adventurous sort, out to a secluded stretch of riverside for a little moonlight dallying. We were diligent about our schoolwork and made good grades, and we conscientiously tended to our chores.

And best of all, we began to learn the shade trade.

Daddy had taught Frank and me to shoot when we were just boys, and we kept in practice and were both good shots. But under the tutelage of Charlie Fortune and Niño Ramirez, who back then ran the gun shop, we really came to learn about guns, about the workings of every type of small arm that came through the Republic Arms. On road and topography maps, Charlie showed us the overland passages to key delivery points in the geographic triangle formed by Brownsville, Laredo, and Monterey. He taught us astral navigation and how to read nautical charts. He showed us the locations of the hidden cuts into the Mexican stretch of the Laguna Madre and showed us the channels and transfer points inside the lagoon. In the spring, he brought Uncle Harry Morgan Wolfe into our training. Captain Harry, as everyone calls him, manages Wolfe Marine & Salvage, as well as the family's shrimp boat and charter boat businesses, and some of his smuggling adventures in younger days are legendary. He's about fifteen years Charlie's senior, on which basis he could have succeeded our daddy as chief of the shade trade, but he didn't want the job and preferred the Uncles give it to Charlie. He was satisfied with prepping the boats to make the runs, and from time to time making a delivery himself, just to keep his hand in. He and Charlie familiarized us with the smuggling vessels—the shrimp boats for offshore deliveries, a charter boat with a modified hull for deliveries in the lagoon shallows—and taught us to pilot them by day or night, on open sea and in coastal channels.

Although Charlie strictly adhered to the family rule that doesn't permit a Wolfe to take part in any shade trade operation until after he's out of college, I believe that by the end of the ten months Frank and I lived at the Landing before graduating from high school we were already better prepared for the trade than anybody our age had been since our ancestors back in the day. That's how well Charlie trained us. And he did more than that. He *taught* us. He taught us the rules of the family, and he taught us a lot of truths as he saw them. The most important of them—Frank and I have always agreed on this—is that the only things you can ever truly own cannot be bought with money.

All of that is why I believe Frank and I know Charlie Fortune as well as he can be known. I don't think anyone else, not even his own daddy, can make that claim.

Except maybe Jessie Juliet.

Besides being her uncle, Charlie is Jessie's guardian. Not in a legal way—there's no court document involved—but in the more binding sense that he had promised her daddy, his brother, Axel, that he would always watch out for her. When Axel was sent to prison for thirty years for the armed robbery of a Dallas jewelry store, he was just twenty-two years old and Jessie was two. It was a stiff sentence for a first-time conviction, but there had been shooting as the robbers made their getaway, and some people were wounded, including Axel, who took a bullet in the leg and was captured. He hadn't fired a shot, but he refused to rat on his accomplices, both of whom got away with a load of jewels, so the court came down hard on him. Not even the Uncles' most talented criminal law associates could get him a lesser sentence. He'd been inside the walls a year when his wife took off for parts unknown, deserting baby Jessie. Axel's and Charlie's sister, Andie, their only other sibling, had two young children of her own and wanted to take Jessie into her family, but Axel wouldn't have it. He'd never approved of Andie's poor choice of husband, and he asked Charlie's promise to always take care of Jessie and not ever let Andie get custody of her. Charlie made the promise, but he was in his senior year at A&M at the time and couldn't do much about tending to Jessie himself. So he went to their daddy for help, and even though Harry Mack looked on Axel as a severe disappointment, he agreed to take Jessie into his home under the care of Mrs. Smith, who had been his household employee for more than twenty years. She had only recently been widowed when he hired her to attend to his three young children after his wife died giving birth to Charlie, and even after Charlie left for college she stayed on as Harry Mack's cook and housekeeper. Everyone liked her, but she wasn't one for revealing much about herself, and though her first name was said to be Rachel, nobody, not even Harry Mack, so far as I know, ever referred to her or addressed her as other than Mrs. Smith. She was a handsome woman and a model of probity through all the years she worked for him, but there were whispers that she had long been more to him than his housekeeper and children's nanny. Maybe she was, and if so, good for them. Frank and I had known Mrs. Smith since we were little kids and thought she was wonderful, and not just because she made the best pecan pies in Cameron County.

When Charlie graduated from A&M and came to work in the shade trade, he and Harry Mack both felt it would be best if Jessie remained under Mrs. Smith's care. But he kept his promise to Axel to watch out for her. During the thirteen years she lived under his daddy's roof, Charlie made it a point to go into town twice a week and take her out for a movie and a pizza, ask her about school and so forth, just generally chat. So far as I know, neither of them ever shared with anyone else the things they talked about, including her feelings about her daddy. Charlie did tell me and Frank that she only once asked to go visit him, back when she was about ten, but as they were about to enter the prison she suddenly busted out crying and ran back to the car. Charlie couldn't persuade her to go inside. He went ahead and saw Axel, who said he understood. She never again asked to go see her father, and has repeatedly turned down Charlie's invitation each time he goes. To this day she's never been to visit him.

She was in her senior year of high school when Mrs. Smith died of a heart attack. Harry Mack was doing a lot of casework all around the state in those years and was often gone for days at a time and sometimes a week or more, and neither he nor Charlie wanted Jessie to be home alone. All our relatives offered to take her in, and Harry Mack wanted to hire another housekeeper, but Charlie said she was his responsibility, and although he'd been okay with Mrs. Smith watching over her, nobody else would do. So he rented a house in Brownsville for the two of them to live in until she graduated. As soon as Jessie would leave for school in the mornings, Charlie would go to the Landing, and he'd return home in time for them to have supper together. At that time, Frank and I had been in the shade trade about three years, and on most weekends we'd join the two of them for a patio barbecue and a rented movie. We saw a lot of Jess and Charlie over the course of those months until she finished high school, and if I hadn't seen it for myself I wouldn't have believed Charlie could look on anybody with such tender affection as he did her. It was the same for Jessie. You could see it in her eyes even as she'd mock-sass him or make him the butt of some joke he'd end up laughing at along with me and Frank.

However, people being how they are, a nasty rumor about Charlie and Jess began to circulate not long after they started living together. Frank or I or anyone else of the family would have loved to be the ones to deal with whoever started it, but we all knew Charlie would want to attend to it himself. He made inquiries and learned the rumor had originated with a former football teammate who'd long been resentful of Charlie's having stolen a girlfriend from him. The fella now owned his own construction company, and that's where Charlie ran him down one morning. Frank and I tagged along to make sure nobody else stepped in. The guy had been a defensive end and was every bit Charlie's size, but Charlie pounded his ass from one end of the parking lot to the other. The fight being in public view, somebody called the police and they showed up pretty quick, which was a good thing or Charlie might've hurt the guy even worse. As it was, he was all busted up—broken jaw, one eye shut, a broken foot where Charlie stomped his arch, a few other ailments. Nonetheless, he was able to convey to the cops that he'd been the one to start the fight and didn't want to press charges, which all in all was a right thing to do. Not too long afterward, Jessie got a note from the fella, expressing his regret for having said the awful lies he did and asking her to forgive him. She asked Charlie if she should, and he said it was up to her. And she did.

At the conclusion of her high school graduation ceremony, Jessie came running up to the family bunch of us in attendance and waved her diploma in Charlie's face, saying, "My emancipation paper, Mr. Charles Fortune Wolfe! I'm free of you *at last!*" Then she flung herself on him and whooped like a kid as he whirled her around.

Yeah. If anybody else knows Charlie as well as Frank and I do, it can only be Jessie.

III

17 — JESSIE

She awakens in fright and confusion, staring at a puzzling gray blankness. She's lying on her side. A knot of pain pulses in the center of her chest. She's wrapped in a blanket, her head half-shawled with it, her face only partially exposed to the grayness before her. Despite the blanket she's cold.

She makes no move, no sound. Takes shallow, silent breaths through her open mouth. Listens hard. All as Charlie had taught her, though she had not believed she would ever have need of such instruction. She senses a proximity of others but hears no voices. The only sound is a low, drumming monotone, not unfamiliar, yet it takes her a minute to recognize it as rain on the roof. And now she remembers she's on a cot in a dimly lighted room and understands that she's staring at a bare wall not a foot from her face.

Then she remembers everything. . . . Running through the streets and alleys. The fight with Apache. Crossing from roof to roof. The sight of the bright lights of better streets—how *close* those streets had seemed! The old pickup truck and the blond man and the astonishing pain of his punch. The little room and being bound to the bed. Being made naked. The Apache . . . the miserable failure of her vow not to cry.

She thinks of Catalina, who has never wept in self-pity. Tears are a natural part of life, Aunt Cat has told her, and at times unavoidable, as with great grief or great pain. Tears of self-pity, however, are inexcusable and always to be withheld. The thought that Catalina would be ashamed of her for weeping prompts an urge to cry again, but she locks her jaws against it and derides herself for even having to fight the impulse. I'm sorry I cried in weakness, Señora, she thinks. Forgive me. No more. I swear. . . .

When the Apache had finished with her, he'd picked up her torn underwear and wiped his cock with it and hung it on her big toe and laughed when she kicked it away and called him a cowardly shit. As he put on his pants he remarked to the blond man that he ought to take a turn while the opportunity was there. The blond made no response but just sat staring at the floor, still holding the pistol. She had never before wanted to cause anyone pain, but she nearly quivered in her desire to inflict screaming agony on the blond man and the Apache. Her capacity for vengeance was a frightening realization.

Without looking at him, the blond told the Apache to take over for Gallo as outside lookout. You're on till dawn, he said.

Gallo, Jessie had thought. The hook-nosed guy. Rooster-looking.

Why do *I* get the graveyard shift? the Apache said.

Just do it, the blond man said.

The Apache stared at him, then showed Jessie his mutilated smile and blew her a kiss. Then he went out and slammed the door.

The blond then covered her with the sheet and went out too.

Bound to the seamy bed in the cold little room that still held the smell of the Apache, she had never felt so helpless in her life. So alone. There's a future beyond this room, she told herself, but had been hard-pressed to imagine it. Nor could she have said how much time passed before the blond man returned, seeming angry, though not with her, carrying a plastic bottle of water and a full paper grocery bag. He set the water on the bed and then emptied the bag's contents beside it—a change of clothes, plus a small towel and a washcloth—then freed her from her bonds.

She sat up and held the sheet to her breasts with her forearms so that she could massage her sore wrists and half-numb hands. He went back to the chair and sat down and partially averted his eyes while she turned her back to him and wet the washcloth and cleaned herself, then dried off with the towel and got dressed. The cotton panties were large but the elastic waistband sufficed to keep them up. She forwent the strapless bra—the act of putting it back on seemed somehow too intimate to perform in front of the blond—and pulled on a big yellow T-shirt. The khaki trousers were loose at the waist but snug on her hips, and she had to roll up the legs a little. She guessed they belonged to a teenage boy. The warmth of the large gray sweatshirt was unexpected—she hadn't been conscious of how cold she was. After washing and patting dry the abrasions on her feet she pulled on a pair of thick wool socks and marveled at their comfort. Her soles hurt but she could walk without limping.

He took her up the stairway to a narrow unadorned hallway with only one window—at the far end of the hall—and one door, midway down and on the left. The blond man opened it and stepped aside to let her enter before him into a large stark room that, together with the hallway, constituted the entire upper story.

Directly across the room and between its only two windows, their drapes closed, sat two men who looked up at her from the magazines in their laps, the hook-nosed Gallo and a slight man who looked too young for his wispy-white, billy-goat beard—aptly named Cabrito, she would soon learn. They were in shirtsleeves and sat on chairs to either side of a small table and low-watt floor lamp, the room's sole lighting, the Cabrito one apparently unarmed, Gallo with a shoulder-holstered Glock.

Good to see you again, wildcat, the Gallo one said to her. Dressed a little less formal than last time, I see.

She wondered if he knew what happened downstairs. If all the bastards knew. Her eyes burned and she thought, So what if they do? Damn them all.

Sitting coatless on a cot positioned lengthwise along the right-side wall, young José Belmonte, his hands still cuffed behind him, was staring at her with an expression of confused awe, but he lowered his face when she looked at him. Jessie wondered if *he* knew. On an adjoining cot, Aldo lay on his side and facing her, also coatless and still cuffed, but his eyes were closed and the cheekbone under one of them was darkly swollen. His respiration raspy.

Susi and Luz sat on cots along the front wall, unbound and barefoot and still in their ceremonial dresses, but their shawls had been returned to them and they held them around their arms and shoulders. Their faces were unreadable. Jessie found it hard to envision the image she presented to them.

She was relieved to see the Apache was not there. She'd feared he might be, despite the blond having ordered him to replace Gallo on outside watch. It angered her to be so afraid of him.

The blond ushered her to a cot next to Luz's in the far corner of the front wall. As soon as she sat down she was dizzy and felt herself sway, but the blond caught her by the shoulders and eased her onto her back.

Better? he said.

She nodded. But the discolored ceiling began to waver and she closed her eyes to it.

She heard him tell the others they were now permitted to talk among themselves and that they would soon be fed. He was still speaking as his voice faded, and then she was aware of nothing more. . . .

Staring at the shadowy gray wall before her, she hurts everywhere. Chest and stomach, joints, muscles. Her *ass*? Then remembers the Apache punching it in the fight. Her fingers ache, her palms are sore, but she can work her hands, her feet, she's not incapacitated. She recalls now that she partially awoke sometime earlier, feeling the blanket placed over her and tucked gently about her, then half woke once again after that, when somebody—Luz?—put a hand on her shoulder and asked if she was hungry. Did she want some soup? She had wanted to say yes, but must have fallen back to sleep before she could speak.

She's thinking clearly now, trying to assess the thing. Wherever they are, they by now are surely known to be missing. Maybe already known to have been snatched. Maybe already under ransom demand. And from whom demand ransom but the parents? Who have certainly been warned not to tell anyone. But there's still Rayo. When she gets home and sees you're not there, she *might* think you decided to go off with Aldo for some fun of your own, but chances are—

She gasps and flinches at the touch of a hand on her shoulder.

It's all right, sweetie, it's me, Luz says.

Jessie rolls onto her back and Luz sits down beside her on the edge of the cot, silhouetted against the low light of the floor lamp on the other side of the room. Someone else is standing close behind her. Susi.

Sorry I scared you, Luz says, speaking softly. You made sounds. . . . We thought you might . . . oh God, JJ, are you *hurt*?

Jessie shakes her head. "I'm all right," she says. "I just—"

"Nada de'se pinche inglés!" the Gallo one commands from his chair by the lamp.

We can talk, Luz tells her, but like the man says, no English.

Susi sits on the cot and takes one of Jessie's hands in both her own. In the soft sidelight of the lamp, her eyes shine with tears. Jessie pats the girl's hands and says, I'm all right, really.

Keeping her voice low, Luz says, My God, Jess, the Apache's face. We saw it. They said *you* did it. That true?

Jessie smiles.

Good Lord, girl! He could've *killed* you. They might've . . .

I'm all right. Little sore is all.

Luz and Susi scan her clothes. At least they gave you something warm to wear, Susi says. Your dress, it must've . . . you must've . . .

It got all torn up, Jessie says. You should've see me going over those fences.

They don't know what the Apache did to me, Jessie thinks. They may suspect but they don't *know*. She's not about to tell them.

You hungry? Luz says. We saved you some soup in case you'd want it. It's gone cold, but still. . . .

The mention of food makes Jessie aware of her hunger. Yes, please, she says.

They help her to sit up and put her stocking feet on the floor. Luz asks Gallo if she may go to the table for Jessie's food. He nods, and she heads for the left-side wall where a high narrow table holds a plastic cooler and other items.

José is now lying on his side with his back to the room, his bound hands in view. Aldo appears not to have moved since she last looked at him, and his breathing is still labored.

I just want this to be over, Susi says. She seems on the verge of crying again. Jessie pats her hand and says, I know, sweetie. It will be. Soon.

She attempts a mental picture of the configuration of the house, the way the upper floor is situated over the lower, but has no idea what it's like in the rear of the building.

There's the sound of a toilet flushing, and only now does she notice the small door at the far left corner of the room, adjacent to the windowed wall. The Cabrito one emerges, leaving the door open. He sees her and says, Ah, the sleeping lovely has awakened. I thought I would have to do it with a kiss.

He plops into his chair and loudly informs Gallo that he feels ten pounds lighter. Gallo picks up the deck of cards on the small table between them and starts shuffling it as Cabrito's bathroom stink begins to infuse the room. Jesus Christ, man, Gallo says. You been eating roadkill again?

Cabrito laughs.

Luz returns with a small plastic bowl of soup and plastic spoon in one hand and an opened can of cola in the other. She hands the soup to Jessie, then sits on the other side of her and sets the cola under the cot, saying, This is here if you're thirsty. She wrinkles her nose at the malodor from the bathroom. *My God*, she says, and looks over at Cabrito.

He grins and winks at her, and she turns away. He gives his attention back to the card game.

What time is it? Jessie asks.

Luz shrugs and says that Susi asked Gallo a while ago and he said it was no concern of hers. About an hour ago the Cabrito guy pulled the drape open a little to take a look out, but all she could see was that it's all gray and rainy. She guesses it's around midday.

The soup is covered with a thin layer of congealed grease, but in Jessie's hunger the strips of chicken are delicious, the rice and bits of tomato. She has to restrain herself to keep from gobbling.

Aldo coughs without waking, moans lowly, then goes quiet again.

Jessie nods at him and says, What happened to him?

The Apache. He got—

No, wait, Jessie says, tell me *everything*.

Luz takes a look at Gallo and Cabrito, then tells Jessie that when she ran away, Rubio—the blond man—had the rest of them brought up to this room and sent the other men after her. He removed everybody's mask and gag but left their cuffs on. He said they had been kidnapped for ransom and were being held in two groups that would be ransomed by turns, but they would all be freed by early evening at the latest. He assigned everybody to a cot and ordered them to stay on it unless they were given permission to get up. He had the shawls brought up for the women, but not the men's coats.

Luz hesitates, saying, Then, ah . . .

What? Jessie says. Tell me.

Well, Luz says, Aldo said he had to pee really bad, but Rubio wouldn't uncuff him and asked if anybody wanted to help him out, and . . . well Christ, *somebody* had to do it, and José sure wasn't going to, and Susi's just a kid, so I said yeah, I would. So he uncuffed me and I took Aldo in there and unzipped him and, you know, *held him* while he peed. Rubio then let me use the toilet in private, then Susi too, then cuffed us again. Christ, JJ, if Trio finds out I held Aldo's thing, he's not going to like it one damn bit.

Jessie grins in spite of herself. I don't know, she says. Given the circumstances, he'll probably understand. So go on.

It seemed like a long time later, Luz tells her, when Cabrito came in and said something to Rubio, who then went away and left Cabrito in charge. They were all still cuffed. She couldn't say how much time went by before the Apache came in with his face all beat-up and went in the bathroom to wash. When he came out he glared at Aldo and asked him what he was looking at. Aldo said he wasn't looking at anything, which enraged the Apache for some reason and he went over and punched him so hard that Aldo fell back and hit his head on the wall and Luz was sure he'd cracked his skull. The Apache left and hadn't returned since. Aldo was unconscious and Cabrito couldn't wake him, so he tugged him around and stretched him out on the cot, but then he started choking, and Cabrito rolled him on his side so he could breathe better. Some time later Gallo came in and told Cabrito they'd caught the gringa and that Rubio said it was okay to take the cuffs off the women but not the guys. Cabrito asked him what happened to the Apache's face and Gallo said the gringa was what happened to it, and they had a big laugh about it. Then Gallo saw Aldo's condition and Cabrito told him what the Apache had done. Gallo pulled up Aldo's eyelids to examine his eyes and said it was probably a concussion and he'd be all right, but Rubio and Espanto wouldn't like it.

Who's Espanto? Jessie asks.

Luz shrugs and says, The head chief, maybe? She tells Jessie that Rubio then came up to the room to fill a water bottle and when he saw Aldo out cold and with that big swollen cheek he looked angry. Gallo told him it was the Apache's doing, not theirs, and was probably just a mild concussion. Rubio didn't say anything, just filled the bottle and left.

The next time he came up, Luz says, he had you with him.

José stirs on his cot, keeping his back to the room.

He hasn't said a word from the time we were taken, Luz says. Hasn't eaten, hasn't had to pee. Nobody's hit him, though, thank God.

Cabrito starts arguing about a play Gallo has made in their card game and Gallo laughs and says it was perfectly legitimate and if he doesn't think so he should learn the rules.

Jessie puts the bowl aside and says, Excuse me, addressing Gallo, and asks him if she may use the toilet. Gallo flicks a hand for her to go ahead.

She goes in the bathroom and shuts the door, which has no lock. It's a small room with a remnant odor of Cabrito's visit, and it's colder in here than in the larger room. There's a small sink under a frame absent its mirror. A toilet, a couple of rolls of paper towels. And a high window framing a dark gray sky. The window's at least a foot and a half wide, by her estimate, and maybe a little higher. The sill a half foot above her head, the top of the frame two feet from the ceiling. A swing-in sash with four square panes, two of them missing their glass, hence the greater coldness of the room.

She can fit through there! A man couldn't, or even most women, but *she* can. She knows she can! Take some doing, because she'd have to go out feetfirst and how on earth can she do that? *Somehow,* that's how. Just a matter of body torsions and contractions, some arm strength. . . .

Easy, girl, she thinks. Might be sealed shut.

On tiptoes, she reaches up to the sash lock and it turns easily in her fingers and she opens the window to the right like the back cover of a book. She'll need a ledge or something on the outside wall below the window to set her feet on, so she can then maybe sidle her way over to the end of the house and. . . . Quit dreaming, for Christ's sake, she thinks, and take a look.

She pulls herself up on the sill like she's doing a chin-up, assisted by the rough texture of the concrete block wall that gives good purchase to her socked toes. The effort infuriates every sore muscle in her body, but she's able to work her elbows up over the sill and poke her head out. The rain dampens her hair and face as she looks out on a long muddy alleyway of gated concrete walls and lined with trash and garbage containers of all sizes. It's intersected by several cross alleys and extends on her right to a dead end where an old car is propped on concrete blocks. To the left, the alley runs to a distant street, and close by, a boy and girl, both around six or seven, are sopping wet and playing in the mud. Sure to catch hell from Momma.

Beneath the window, the wall's a sheer drop of some twenty feet and offers no footholds at all. High enough to break an ankle or leg and maybe her butt bone. But just off to the right along the base of the wall is one of those big heavy-duty plastic trash bins around four feet high with a flip-top lid and a push handle and pair of little wheels. Crammed to overflowing with crumpled rain-sopped cardboard boxes, it's a beat-up thing standing somewhat tilted on a badly canted wheel, its lid hanging on one hinge. All of that cardboard could cushion her fall sufficiently. Maybe.

And so what? The thing's too far off to the side.

The two kids have come over and are looking up at her, wiping rain from their eyes. They return her smile. She gestures for them to reposition the trash container under the window. The boy seems not to comprehend, but when the girl goes to the container and tries to move it he catches on. He goes over and takes hold of the handle with both hands and tilts the container back on its misaligned wheels and the girl helps him to steer it. Jessie cuts a look at the bathroom door, fearful that Cabrito or Gallo might at any minute come in to see what's taking her so long. She directs the kids with her hand until the container's directly beneath the window, then grins and gives them the OK sign, and the kids grin back and ape her gesture.

She waves good-bye to them, then lowers herself to the floor and reaches up and closes the sash. She massages her throbbing arms, thinking that the thing to do is wait a little bit, then ask to use the toilet again. Less suspicious. A gringa with intestinal strife. She'll have more time that way than if she tries it now.

She's excited and afraid. What if it's just a layer of flattened cardboard boxes over a lot of broken bottles or sharp tin cans or God knows what? Even if there's only cardboard, it might be so saturated she'll plunge through it like tissue and break her legs. Think you hurt now, girl. Broken leg or two, *that* would be some pain.

She flushes the toilet, dries her face and mops her hair with paper towels, and exits the bathroom, affecting a look of some relief.

Cabrito grins at her and says, Everything come out all right?

She looks away and he laughs.

Aldo's breathing sounds somewhat better, though still raspy. José is now on his back, asleep or appearing to be.

She assures Luz and Susi that she feels much better and just needs a bit more rest. Then lies back and closes her eyes and wonders if she's going to try it.

And asks herself, What would Catalina do?

18 — GALÁN AND MELITÓN

White of hair and beard, his girth thick with folds, Melitón Santana—El Ingeniero to his associates—sits on a cushioned bench along the wall of a large steamy cubicle in a public bathhouse and watches a naked young couple engaging in sex a few feet from him. On the tiled floor, the man and woman have been lingually ministering to each other by turns and at times simultaneously, and now both of them kneel on small plastic cushions, the woman on all fours, and the man mounts her from behind in what is commonly called the dog fashion. The man only infrequently looks at Melitón, and when he does his gaze remains distant, but the woman at times meets Melitón's eyes and smiles. They are all three pouring sweat. Melitón has never exchanged a word with them, nor has the couple ever spoken to each other in his presence. Three months ago he happened on them in this cubicle by accident and they tacitly permitted him to observe them. Since then, they have met here for the same activity every Monday morning at quarter to eight, the couple always here first, awaiting his arrival before they commence.

Melitón has loosened the towel from around his waist and is fondling his semihard cock as he observes their exhibition. For almost a year now, a partial erection is the best he is able to muster. At first a sporadic condition, it had after a time become chronic, and so he went to see a doctor. The prescribed medication enabled full tumescence, but the erection would persist beyond his need of it, and the necessity of awaiting its abatement was an annoyance and sometimes made him late for appointments. Furthermore, his nagging perception of the effect as a synthetic rather than a natural achievement soon diminished his pleasure in it. So he quit the pills, even though the only way he can now attain even semihardness and, with effort, a meager ejaculation, is by means of his own manipulations in response to visual stimulus. This couple is the most effective arousal he's yet found, not only because of their performance, but because their enjoyment of his presence makes him more participant than mere voyeur. Some weeks ago, however, he was diagnosed with prostate cancer of advanced stage, and extensive medical consultations have persuaded him that—in his case, and notwithstanding his age—surgical excision, rather than chemotherapy or radiation, offers the best long-range survival odds. Unfortunately, it will entail the certain side effect of impotence and, quite probably, incontinence as well. Melitón had surprised himself by his choice of the surgery. He hadn't known how badly he wants to continue living for as long as he can, at whatever cost, even that of a lifeless dick and daily diapers. The operation will take place in three days.

He is fully familiar with the couple's rhythms, and as they begin the culminating phase of their lovemaking, he alters his own touch and tempo, and like a well-rehearsed team they all climax at the same time. The couple then lies spooned on the floor with their eyes closed, the man snuggled to the woman from behind, while Melitón gets up and goes to the locker room, showers, and gets dressed. It is customary that he leave the locker room before they enter it, but this being the last time for him, he has an impulse to return to the cubicle door and say good-bye and express his great appreciation for the enjoyment they've given him in his final days of frail virility. But no. They have granted that enjoyment under an unspoken but understood code, and even now it would be wrong to violate it. Besides, they might view his gratitude as pathetically sentimental.

The clerk at the lobby desk sees Melitón coming out of the locker room and makes a brief phone call, and a minute later a black Chrysler sedan pulls up at the curb. The driver, burly and well dressed, gets out and comes around to open the rear passenger door as the clerk escorts Melitón to the car, holding an umbrella over him against the light rain.

As they move out into traffic, the driver says, "La Golondrina, jefe?"

Yes, Gómez, Melitón says. After we pick up Miss Salas.

Miss Salas is one of a large number of lovely and highly discreet women he retains as occasional escorts.

Very well, chief, Gómez says. An exquisite young lady, if I may say so.

Gómez knows that his boss tends to melancholia after a bathhouse visit, and he always tries to distract him from the mood with small talk and jokes.

She is, isn't she? Melitón says.

A mountain rose, chief, to brighten this miserable weather. They say it'll be like this all day.

Well, Melitón says, what cannot be remedied must be endured.

Gómez chuckles at the old saying. You're right about that, chief, he says. It's a sad truth. Say, have you heard the one about the German blonde and the piñata?

Galán maneuvers the Mercedes through the gray morning drizzle, the wipers clearing the windshield in soft sweeps. The radio report is of terrorist bombings in public places of the Middle East, women and children among the murdered.

Cowardly raghead cocksuckers, Galán thinks. Men make war on men, not on women, not on children. He'd heard somewhere that a dog or a woman is the most insulting thing you can call a raghead, so *daughter of a bitch* was just about right for these marketplace bombers.

A Beethoven cello sonata begins to play. Galán raises the volume and says aloud, Cleanse me, maestro. Work your magic.

In the verdant upscale neighborhood of Colonia Roma, he finds a parking space two blocks from La Golondrina, then walks there under his umbrella, muttering curses at the water beading on his oxblood Florsheims. It is a fashionable district of colonial-era architecture, many of its old mansions converted into offices, art emporiums, trendy shops, upscale apartment houses. With its faux nineteenth-century decor, La Golondrina fits in well. Melitón spotted the café in passing a few years ago and has ever since been a daily patron. He has said it reminds him somewhat of a café in his boyhood neighborhood before it was lost to the bulldozers. The Golondrina staff believes Melitón to be a retired executive of a heavy machinery manufacturing firm, and his favorite table—in the far front corner and next to a sidewalk window—is on daily morning reserve for him.

Galán pauses under the front door awning to shake the raindrops from his umbrella and furl it, then enters. As always, Melitón is already there, and as usual accompanied by a striking young woman, a dalliance from the night before. He has told Galán that he enjoys an early morning coffee with the ladies before sending them on their way, but Galán suspects he also enjoys exhibiting them to him and everyone else in the place. To show the onlooking world that the grizzled lion can still gratify the sleek lionesses.

Melitón smiles at his approach and stands to embrace him, then steps back to admire Galán's fine suit. What an elegant picture you are, he says. The very embodiment of your epithet.

I can only dream of ever achieving such elegance as your own, Mr. Engineer, Galán says. By way of Melitón's recommendation, Galán now gets his suits from the same local branch of a distinguished London clothier.

Melitón laughs and says to the young woman, This gentleman is a supreme diplomat as well as a model of fashion.

She's a beauty with lustrous brown hair and bright black eyes, skin the color of creamed coffee. Melitón introduces her as Miss Elena Salas Delarosa. She offers her hand and smiles warmly when Galán kisses the back of it and says, "Encantado, señorita."

Melitón takes a phone from his coat, keys it, and says into it, We're ready. He asks Galán to please be seated and says he will be right back, then escorts the woman across the room. Galán's eyes are not the only ones that trail after her in admiration. Through the room's front window he sees the black Chrysler arrive at the curb, and then Gómez comes around to open the back door and shield the woman with an umbrella as she gets in. She blows a kiss at Melitón. He raises a hand in farewell.

On his return to the table, Melitón smiles impishly and says, Let me tell you, son, *that* one was nearly the death of me last night. These young ones today! They don't understand that I'm *old!* I need a little rest between sessions in the course of an evening.

Galán says, Listen to you. Millions of men half your age would kill to have your woman troubles.

Melitón grins and shrugs with his palms upturned.

Without consulting the menu, they give the waiter their orders and he thanks them and retreats.

"Pues?" Melitón says.

As expected, Galán says. The security force has been withdrawn from the project.

Though their table is well removed from the nearest other diners, they have lowered their voices to near whispers.

Melitón nods. As expected, yes. All else is good?

Yes. My assistant had already checked with the crew chiefs before I called him this morning. No problems. Well, except for a bad smell of some sort at the Beta site. You would think they could put up with it till this afternoon but the crew chief claims it's quite severe. My assistant will have the owner of the place look into it, see if he can ease the condition.

It must be a very bad smell, Melitón says, to stand out among slum stinks. You know what the most common air freshener is in the slums? A dead rat hung from the ceiling.

Galán smiles at the old joke.

So, Melitón says. Now you wait until the principals have processed the funds and call you this afternoon.

Correct. My agents will observe the process to make certain the funds are conveyed to the repository until the hour of transfer.

I'm sure it will seem a long time until then.

Waiting can slow the clock, says Galán.

And yet the operation from start to finish will have taken less than twenty-four hours. Absolute lightning, my friend. Most impressive.

Thank you, Mr. Engineer.

There are others who will be no less impressed.

I hope so.

Be assured of it, Melitón says.

Their breakfasts arrive, and they apply themselves to the dishes with gusto.

They had first met on a Sunday night last spring. Galán had just come out of a downtown restaurant when he saw a woman in a little white dress displaying much of her exquisite legs getting out of the backseat of a black Chrysler at the curb, assisted by a corpulent but finely attired man who looked more than twice her age. It was early evening and the sidewalk traffic was fairly light, and Galán paused to light a cigar and admire her. The man spoke to the driver and shut the door and the Chrysler drove away. Just then, a pair of young men with buzz cuts and dressed in denim, their sleeveless shirts exposing sinewy arms, came strutting by on either side of the woman, and when she turned to keep an eye on the nearer one, the other stepped over to her and grabbed her ass with both hands, saying, "Ay, que bonitas nalgas!" The woman yelped and whirled around, backing away from him, and then the other one slipped his hands under her arms from behind and squeezed her breasts, saying, And these too! The woman cursed and broke free, slapping at him, but the kid just laughed and easily dodged her hand. The fat man yelled "Bastards!" and tried to grab the tit squeezer by the shirt, but the kid batted the man's arms aside and punched him hard in the face, knocking him to one knee. He was about to hit the old man again when Galán flicked away the cigar and grabbed him by the shirt collar with both hands and slung him around headfirst into the stone wall. The kid's head struck with an ugly sound and he dropped into a motionless heap. The other thug then brandished a knife and started toward Galán in a crouch. But the old man grabbed him from behind, locking a forearm around his throat and clamping his other hand on the wrist of his knife hand, and Galán stepped up and kicked the kid in the balls. The kid made a croaking sound and sagged in the old man's hold. The man let him drop and Galán kicked the thug in the mouth and then stomped on his head twice, the second time grinding his heel into an ear.

A small crowd had bunched to either side of them on the sidewalk, some faces shocked, some grinning.

Come, the fat man said to Galán, extracting a phone from his coat and pulling the girl along by a hand, the crowd parting with alacrity to let them pass.

I'm going around the north corner and heading east, the old man said into the phone. There's three of us. Make it fast.

The old man could move with haste, but the girl wailed that she was about to lose a shoe, and they paused to let her remove both of them and carry one in each hand. They were almost to the end of the block when the black Chrysler swooped up beside them with a small toot of the horn and stopped in the street. They all hustled into the backseat and Galán shut the door and the car gunned away, the old man saying, "A los taxis." As he'd entered the car, Galán had seen the driver slip a pistol into a holster under his coat.

The Chrysler made a series of sharp left and right turns for a few blocks and then doubled back before pulling into the parking lot of a taxi company. The car stood with its engine idling while the fat man, who had introduced himself as Melitón and the girl as Silvia—Galán saying he was Ramón—gave her money for a cab and, in addition, a few bills of large denomination. He apologized to her for their missed dinner and promised they would go to an even better restaurant the next time and said he would call her tomorrow. Then he caught the look that passed between her and Galán, and he said, I'll also give Ramón your number so he can call you if he pleases. His tone was good-natured sincerity. I mean, what the hell, he said. We've been in battle together, we three. We're comrades. Comrades share, do they not?

They all laughed and the girl kissed Galán on the cheek, then very gently put her lips to Melitón's swollen eye that was already discoloring, then got out of the Chrysler and into a cab. The following week Galán would bed her for the first time. They would thereafter get together once a week for almost two months before exiting each other's life as easily as they had entered it.

Shortly after dropping off the girl, the two men were seated in a softly lighted Argentine restaurant, perusing the menu. On arriving, they had tidied themselves in the men's room, and Melitón grinned at his bruised face in the mirror and said, Look at me! Mr. Street Fighter! Galán laughed and told him he had very well held his own.

As they decided on filets and a bottle of Barolo, Melitón saw Galán tapping his fingers in time to the low-volume music from the ceiling speakers and said, You like the sixth Brandenburg, eh?

Galán felt himself flush and said he'd recently heard that music somewhere and had liked it very much, but he had no idea what it was called except classical. He said he wished he knew more about such music.

If you wish to know more, learn more, Melitón said. He took a small notebook from his coat and wrote something in it and tore out the page and handed it to Galán. Meet me there for breakfast tomorrow, he said. I'll have some books for you. Some recordings for you to try. If you don't like them, donate them to the nearest library.

Galán saw that the café address was in Colonia Roma. He pocketed the paper and thanked him and said he'd be there.

They conversed with ease, and over the next hour they progressed from cordial guardedness to tentative candor to complete frankness. Galán had never before conversed so openly with anyone. By the time their table had been cleared away but for the glasses of amber brandy glowing in the candlelight, Galán had learned that Melitón was raised in a working-class home and had been in his share of boyhood fights. But he had been lucky to go to an adequate public school and eventually earned degrees in economics and in art history from the National Autonomous University. He had worked as a government accountant for several years before finding his true calling as a broker of sorts for Mexico City street gangs, which has been his main trade ever since. He is known to them as El Ingeniero for his ability to engineer almost any enterprise proposed to him that he finds promising. In exchange for a share of the gains, he provides whatever capital is necessary, plus, if also necessary, the venues for caching or brokering goods or for hiding out for a while. At times he even suggests improvements on the proposals themselves. The ventures he engineers range from burglaries, robberies, and drug transactions to larger and longer-term objectives such as brothels, gambling halls, and opium dens. Melitón's shares from all such projects amount to a steady and considerable income. In truth, he told Galán, he is not the one staking them, but only a front man for the Gulf cartel, which gets fifty percent of everything he earns from the gangs. In this way does the Gulf organization receive a steady revenue from Mexico City without attracting attention to itself in the capital. Melitón is fairly sure that other major organizations operate similarly through their own Mexico City middlemen. If any of the gangs who do business with those middlemen suspect their connection to the cartels, they also know the wisdom of keeping such suspicions to themselves. The cartels prefer not to wage war in the capital, Melitón said, with either each other or the police.

For his part, Melitón had come to know of Ramón Colmo's origin in an abysmal shantytown—his father unknown to him, his two sisters dead in their infancy, his mother uncertain of the date of his birth but for the year, and herself dead before he was thirteen. Ramón had since chosen the midyear, the first of July, as his birth date. He told Melitón of his days with Los Malditos, of the small but efficient organization of his own making called Los Doce and its successful kidnapping trade, of his efforts to improve his manner and dress and speech. And of his great ambition—which he had never before revealed to anyone—to have Los Doce accepted as an associate gang in a major organization. As a cartel undergang, they would not have to look for jobs, but rather the jobs would be assigned to them. Bigger, more lucrative jobs, whether burglaries or kidnappings or whatever else. They would no doubt have to turn over to the cartel a large share of their reap, but Galán believed that as his gang proved itself equal to any task assigned them, they would gain in reputation and rise in the cartel's esteem. As he saw it, he would either work his way up to an underboss position or, better yet, other small outfits of the organization would be assigned to Los Doce, enlarging it into a major undergang of the cartel with its own regional jurisdiction.

I can see it quite clearly, Melitón said with a smile. But with more than twelve members, you would have to change the name.

Indeed. Maybe to . . . Los Cincuenta? Galán smiled. Dare I think that big?

In a gang worthy of your leadership, at *least* fifty men, Melitón said. A hundred would be more like it.

Galán said he liked the sound of it—Los Ciento. It is a large ambition, he said. I know that.

Melitón said it was, yes, but what was life without a large ambition? In the meantime, and even though Los Doce was doing quite well on its own, he wanted Galán to know that if he should ever find himself in need of capital for some particular endeavor, it would be his great pleasure to provide it.

The next morning they met at La Golondrina as agreed and Melitón presented him with the books and CDs he'd promised, and Galán's instruction in classical music began in earnest. Melitón also gave him a book about world history. You want knowledge, Melitón said, and tapped the book. It begins here.

They continued to meet at La Golondrina on every Monday thereafter. Under the guidance of Melitón, Galán further improved his general education, his elocution and manners, and at every meeting he learned more about the workings of the crime cartels. Before long, he too was dressing almost exclusively in white suits of superior tailoring. Moreover, it pleased him to know that even at his age Melitón was still enjoying himself in bed with such lovelies as were always with him on Monday mornings. Melitón in turn always took great enjoyment in Galán's tales of past street battles and of his own latest sexual adventures.

And then a little more than two months ago Jaime Huerta had come to Galán with an audacious proposition to kidnap an entire wedding party of ten members, all of whom belonged to wealthy families. Over a succession of meetings between just the two of them—sometimes in Chapultepec Park, sometimes at La Nereida, sometimes near the Palace of Fine Arts in the Alameda municipal park—they discussed the project at length. They carefully formed a plan, reviewed it, refined it, came to accord on its logistics. They haggled about the ransom amount and finally agreed to a demand of five million American dollars. After further wrangling, they agreed as well that Huerta's share would be two million, the enormous cut premised on Huerta's argument that the project was after all his idea and, most important, could not be carried out without his inside information and access. Without Huerta present, Galán then gathered Los Doce at their usual meeting place, El Nido, the basement restaurant in his old neighborhood, and told them of the plan he and Huerta had devised. The men were excited by it but displeased with Huerta's share of the ransom. Then grinned in unanimous approval of Galán's suggested reapportionment of the shares. They were all in favor, as well, of his proposal for allying Los Doce with the Gulf cartel.

He met with Huerta a few times more after that, the last time just two weeks ago, when he took Espanto with him so Huerta could meet the man he would be working so closely with in making the snatch.

Galán had by then told Melitón of the project, and had asked him to convey an offer to the Gulf organization. He wanted him to tell them that, on completion of the job, Los Doce was willing to pay the cartel one million Yankee dollars for admittance into its ranks as an undergang.

A sort of membership fee, Galán said. Also, our successful exploit to acquire that money should testify to our proficiency. All I want is for them to admit us to the organization and give us a chance to prove ourselves worthy of remaining a part of it.

Jesus, kid, Melitón said. A million. You want in *that* bad?

Galán stared at him. If you race cars for a living, he said, you want to compete at Le Mans, no? If you play soccer, you want to play for the World Cup, is that not so? For what *we* do . . . he turned up his palms. What but membership in a top company?

I understand, Melitón said. But, well, how do your boys feel about giving up a million? It leaves your bunch with two million yes, but divided among—

Actually, it leaves us with four million, Galán said.

Melitón tilted his head and studied him narrowly. I see. The security chief is in for a surprise.

He's the only one of us they can identify, Galán said. If they track him down, he'll betray us. Look what he's doing to his own men.

Yes, I understand. Still, the captives will know you, too.

They'll know our faces, our nicknames. No matter. I've already frightened them with the possibility that any police officials they deal with might be friends of ours. But why would they go to the police? To try to get their money back? For *justice*? At the risk of angering us? Of having us revisit them? And even if they go to the police, so what? There are hundreds of known kidnappers at large. Untold hundreds of killers. The police have more important business than searching for unknown kidnappers who release their captives unharmed.

Unless some of them are not released unharmed, and especially if they are rich, Melitón said. Unexpected turns can occur. Exigencies arise. Dire surprises.

Yes, the unexpected is always possible, Galán said. You try always to plan so that the possibility is minimal.

Naturally. But *if* an exigency should arise?

Then you do whatever must be done.

Melitón smiled. *That*, he said, raising a finger for emphasis, is the creed of the top ones. It is the creed that carries them to the top and keeps them there. He leaned closer and said, Tell me, do you know of the Zetas?

Of course he did. They were the enforcement arm of the Gulf organization, most of them deserters from the Mexican Special Forces. They were widely regarded as the most fearsome enforcers in the country.

They are everything you have heard and more, said Melitón. Not so long ago they persuaded their Gulf employers to let them operate their own drug trade, and now it is said that their aspirations have grown even larger. The Gulf bosses have become very nervous about them, and they have reason to be. The Zetas are on a rapid ascension. Indeed, if I were a small gang seeking to join with a major organization, I might pass up a larger one that's afraid of its own enforcers and turn instead to the feared enforcers. It is only a matter of time before the Zetas establish their independence from the Gulf clan, and I have it on good authority that they have already begun to recruit their own network of undergangs. I think they would be highly receptive to a million-dollar membership fee from a gang they might otherwise reject as, ah . . . insufficiently seasoned, let us say.

And who better to carry my offer to them, Galán said, than someone of their acquaintance who is himself ready to transfer his full allegiance to them? Who may even be awarded a cut of the membership fee.

Melitón smiled back and said, What is friendship but a bond of mutual advantage? The important question is whether you and your boys would rather serve a large but nervous organization or join with a small self-confident one that will do whatever it must to achieve its high ambitions.

I take your point, Mr. Engineer.

Melitón smiled. Well then, you and your men have a decision to make.

I'll call you tonight, Galán said.

That evening he gathered Los Doce at El Nido and explained their choices and stated his preference. Every man of them opted for that choice too. He then called Melitón and said, You may take our offer to the Zetas, Mr. Engineer.

The next time they met at La Golondrina, Melitón introduced him to another fetching companion and then excused himself and escorted her out to the Chrysler. Then he returned to the table, resumed his seat, leaned toward Galán and said, It's a deal.

The light rain persists. As the waiter clears away their dishes, Galán excuses himself and tells Melitón he will be right back. He goes outside and stands under the Golondrina's entranceway awning and takes out an old clamshell phone, then waits for an arriving couple to walk by him and enter before he makes his call.

Señor Belmonte sounds alarmed when he answers on the special phone Espanto gave him, *Yes?* Hello?

This is X, Galán says. Is everything well?

As if baffled by the question, Belmonte hesitates, then stammers and says, Yes, yes. I will be . . . *we,* we will be leaving for the bank soon. They don't open until—

Be calm, Mr. Belmonte, Galán says, watching the traffic hissing past in the rain, the world proceeding about its business. I know the bank hours. You and Mr. Sosa must be calm when you deal with the bankers. I am calling only to reassure all of you that your children are well and safe. Also to ask if you have spoken to anyone else of the situation.

No, no, certainly not. We won't in any—

Not even other relatives of the party members?

Oh! . . . Yes, I see what . . . *Yes*, we told them the wedding party decided to spend today at my ranch in Cuernavaca . . . riding horses, canoes on the river, a barbecue. There are only four in the party who are not our children, and so—

I know, Galán says. Your nephews Carlos and Colón, Mr. Sosa's niece Francesca, and the American girl. And I know Mr. Sosa spoke to his cousin and you spoke to yours. I know Sosa received no answer at the apartment of the American girl's cousin, but he left the same message on her phone. As I have told you, Mr. Belmonte, we are aware of all communications transmitted from or to your home. I wanted to remind you of that—and to say you did well in ensuring the relatives will not become alarmed. Continue to do as well for the remainder of this day.

Yes, yes, we will. Whatever you—

Do not for a minute forget that your children's welfare depends completely on the four of you.

Yes, sir, yes . . . we understand, believe me. I—

Very good. I await your call at four.

Yes. At four. Exactly.

Until that time, Mr. Belmonte. Stay calm and be strong.

Galán ends the call. He goes into the men's room off the foyer, finds it unoccupied, breaks the little phone apart in a sink, and deposits the pieces in a trash receptacle. Then washes his hands and returns to the table.

Melitón smiles. Your face suggests that all is well.

My face cannot lie, Mr. Engineer, Galán says, and they laugh.

Lingering over coffee in the pleasant warmth of the café, they are content in each other's company. They talk of music, of a new exhibit at the Palacio de Bellas Artes featuring the fascinating collection of a young photographer from Morelia.

Galán will soon repair to El Nido, where he will pass the day contemplating the future of Los Doce, reading, taking phone reports from Espanto. Waiting for Belmonte's call.

19 — THE BETA HOUSE

The stink in the Beta hold house is unyielding. The place is far from the Alpha house but in a similar neighborhood of rutted streets littered with trash and rattletrap motor vehicles. But this house is smaller—a one-story, four-room structure of cracked block and weathered wood.

The Beta chief is Barbarosa, so known for his short red beard. His two-man crew consists of Cisco and Flaco. The three male hostages have been put in one of the small bedrooms under Cisco's watch, the two women in the other, with Flaco guarding them. The sole furnishings in each bedroom are inflated camping mattresses on the floor for the captives, a chair for a guard, a little table with a lamp. The crew has brought bottled water and sandwiches, but the awful smell has stoppered all appetites.

They have determined that the stink comes from the basement. It seeps up through cracks in the wooden floor and from under the basement door at the bottom of an enclosed stairwell off the kitchen. But they can't investigate the source because the heavy door is secured by a padlock the size of a brick, its shackle protected by shoulder shrouds, and the reinforced steel hasp has no exposed pins or screws. The door's hinges are also on the inward side. The men had taken turns trying to cut into the lock with a hacksaw but gave up after half an hour, having made but a minor scratch in the metal and blunted the saw's teeth.

Cisco had suggested they shoot the lock off. Barbarosa asked if he'd ever tried shooting off a padlock, or even seen anybody try it outside of the movies. Cisco admitted that he had not, but it seemed a damn good way to him and he'd like to see the lock stand up to a nine-millimeter bullet. Barbarosa said he once witnessed someone try to shoot a padlock off a clothes trunk with a .45-caliber pistol. There were four guys there, and in less time than it takes to blink, the bullet ricocheted around the room and hit one of them in the arm and crippled it. That was in a *room*, Barbarosa said. In a stone stairwell like this, the ricochet will be like a machine gun burst. You want to try it, that's fine, but wait till I go upstairs. Cisco declined to try but wanted to know if the bullet opened the lock. Barbarosa said it did not, but it bent the cylinder, and when the key was found five minutes later it no longer fit the keyhole. The owner of the trunk then tried using an axe on the lock but the blade glanced off it and chopped into his boot and maimed his big toe. The guy howled and swore like the devil while they bandaged him, then said fuck it and had another guy hack the trunk apart to get the clothes out.

That worked, Barbarosa said. I don't believe that option would succeed with this door, but if you want to try chopping through it, I have no objection.

Cisco declined that opportunity as well.

Thinking that electric fans might effect some relief, Barbarosa had sent Flaco to a twenty-four-hour store in the city to purchase a half dozen, but they only generated a foul cold wind through the house and caused a short in one of the outlets. The house lights have since flickered every so often as if preparing to quit altogether.

When Espanto called late last night to tell him of Fuego's death from wounds received in a gunfight with Huerta and that the Beta crew would have to operate with just three men, Barbarosa—who'd been close friends with Fuego and was angered by the news—had complained vehemently about the stink and the locked basement and the erratic electrical system. Espanto had expressed surprise. He said the house hadn't smelled too bad when he'd looked it over last month, no worse than most slum houses, anyway. He admitted, however, not having bothered to check out the basement, since the Beta crew wouldn't be making use of it. He said he would get in touch with the owner of the place and have him go there and see what he could do about the stink, but he doubted there was anything to be done about the flickering lights.

The remainder of the night at the Beta house had been an ordeal. They had partly opened all the windows in an attempt to ease the stink and had only made the place colder and danker. The two women captives—Linda Sosa, and her cousin Francesca—sniveled even in half sleep, hugging each other for warmth. In the other room, the complaints of the bridegroom, Demetrio, and his cousins Carlos and Colón, two of his groomsmen, grew so tiresome that Barbarosa threatened to gag them again if they didn't shut their snouts.

Early this morning Espanto had called again, to check on things and report that he was having trouble locating the house's owner, a man named Spoto—a slumlord from whom he has rented hold houses before and who knows Espanto only by a false name. Espanto said he would keep trying to get hold of him. He didn't call Barbarosa again until late morning. He had located Spoto but the man didn't have a key to the lock. Before Spoto rented the house to Espanto he had been letting his nephew use it, and the boy had confided that he and some pals were printing counterfeit government documents in the basement and swore to him they were being very careful to keep the activity secret. When Espanto rented the house, Spoto told his nephew he would have to stay away from there for a while, but he hadn't known the boy would padlock the basement. Because the nephew had complained about rats, it was Spoto's guess that he had set a bunch of traps before locking up and that a bunch of dead rats was the cause of the stink. He didn't know where the nephew might be but said he would try to find him and have him go over there and open the lock. Espanto told him to forget it. It would be quicker to send a locksmith.

I've called a guy who's a maestro with locks, Espanto told Barbarosa. Right now he's on a job that's almost done, and then he'll go straight to you. It's amazing the things I do for you pansies just so you don't have to put up with a little stink for a few more hours.

Hey man, Barbarosa said, if you think it's such a little stink, *you* come out here and wait till the payoff and *I'll* sit in a nice warm café drinking coffee and making phone calls.

Maybe next time, Espanto said, and they both laughed, but in different tones.

Now it's past midday and still no locksmith. Everyone's tired from lack of sleep, still damp and shivering from the cold rain blowing through the windows all night. As Barbarosa is debating whether to call Espanto and give him hell, his phone buzzes.

It's Espanto, informing him that the locksmith had been on his way to the Beta place when his fan belt broke. He was now waiting for roadside assistance and figured it wouldn't take long to get rolling again. He was only a few miles away from the hold house.

Jesus fucking Christ, Barbarosa says.

Hey man, the guy can't help it the belt broke. He'll be on his way again in a few minutes.

Yeah, right, Barbarosa says.

I'm telling you, the guy'll *be* there, Espanto says. You might still get a few hours free of the stink. *If* you find what it is, and *if* it's something you can do anything about. I mean, if it turns out it's a body, there won't be much you can do about getting rid of it. Even if you could, you know how *that* stink sticks around. Same for dead rats if there's a bunch of them.

Barbarosa hears the note of amusement in Espanto's voice. Fucker thinks this is funny. It occurs to him that Espanto's playing a joke, that he hasn't called a locksmith, that he probably hasn't talked to anybody about the stink. As the only one in the gang from a working-class family, Barbarosa is occasionally the object of mockery from the other members of Los Doce, all of whom come from the slums or the shanties and through a perverse turn of prejudice tend to view him as their social lesser. Barbarosa is so enraged he doesn't trust himself to speak.

Hey, man, still there? Espanto says.

Yeah, Barbarosa manages.

I was afraid maybe you'd passed out. Bad stinks have been known to do that to people with a sensitive nose. Anyway, buddy, the guy will be there soon.

Barbarosa grunts and cuts off the call, wishing the phone had a receiver he could slam.

20 — ESPANTO

Ensconced in a rear booth of the Casa Toltec restaurant a few blocks west of Chapultepec Park, Espanto smiles as he puts up his phone. Jesus Christ, so much carping about a little stink. Barbarosa's a good man, reliable, you damn well want him with you in a fight, and he's rarely one to complain. When he does, though, it can be about the most trivial thing. He deserved to be kidded about it. A bad smell! Like he'd grown up in some flower garden. It could be, Espanto has to admit, that by now some bad smell may have cropped up, but a stink is only a stink. It won't kill them to put up with it for such a short time.

The staff of Casa Toltec know Espanto only by an alias and are fond of him for his free hand in tipping. He has on occasion spent the better part of a day here with no company but his phone and laptop, and he will do so again today. The staff will take care to see that he is undisturbed and to keep other patrons seated at a distance from him.

He is monitoring all communications to or from the Belmonte house and overseeing the operations of the hold houses and the two street guys, Chino and Chato, and he will relay information to Galán as necessary. He had managed to get four hours of sleep before coming here just after the place opened its door and he'd had a breakfast of coffee and a sweet roll. The restaurant is almost equidistant from the hold houses, both of them just outside the city perimeter and more than twenty miles from each other on a north-south line.

He beckons the waitress, Betina, who takes his lunch order of three chicken tacos, nothing on the side, and another cup of coffee.

Eating so little today, handsome, she says.

Watching my weight, he says, patting his lean midsection.

You? she says. *I'm* the one who needs to trim this fat ass.

He reaches out and pats her bottom fondly and tells her it's just right. She beams and says she'll be right back with his tacos and retreats to the kitchen, its entrance flanked by the waitress station—a short counter and some stools, the counter holding a television tuned to an old Pedro Infante movie, its volume turned low.

On the table before him stands an open laptop computer. Any e-mail sent from or received at the Belmonte home will appear on the screen as it is transmitted or received. In his coat pocket is an audio receiver with an ear bud connection. Any phone call made from or to the Belmonte place will vibrate the receiver and automatically trigger the receiver's recording function, as it did thrice in succession this morning. Espanto each time listened to the call and then relayed the recording of it to Galán. Who then made a call to Belmonte.

The whole thing is going so smoothly he has to check an impulse to whistle.

21 — JESSIE

Pain is only pain, Aunt Catalina once told her. If it hasn't killed you, it hasn't beaten you.

Lying on her back with her eyes closed in pretense of sleep, hearing Cabrito and Gallo at their card game, her body aching, Jessie's thinking of her great-great-grandaunt, one of the oldest living persons in the world—and, who knows, by now maybe the oldest. Not long ago she had asked Aunt Cat how she felt about that distinction, and she had said, A little lonely. Jessie has written a book about her, though she doesn't feel she's actually written it so much as simply transcribed it. Except for a few of Jessie's expository passages, the book is in Catalina's own words. She had agreed to be interviewed and narrate her life story into a tape recorder on the condition that the book would not be published—nor any of its details revealed—until after her death, and Jessie had so promised. That condition, some in the family have joked, might ensure the book never sees print, since Aunt Cat is now 113 years old and in better health than some of her kin less than half her age. The family is well acquainted with the larger incidents of Catalina's life—her killing of her husband perhaps the most sensational—but only Jessie knows the full story of that event and of many others besides. She is privy to details of Catalina's life unknown to anyone else, and admires her great-great-grandaunt above everyone else she's ever known.

So . . . what would Catalina do?

She ponders the situation from every angle. Could be there's really no reason to fret. The exchange will go smoothly and that's that. All she has to do is keep calm for the next few hours, wait it out. They get their money, they turn them all loose, end of story.

But what if the exchange doesn't go smoothly? What if something goes wrong? There's always that possibility. If that should happen, what will this bunch do?

For that matter, what will they do even if nothing goes wrong?

She's heard the stories. What if they decide on no witnesses?

Maybe they've already decided.

Maybe is way too risky. She can't assume they're going to set her free. Can't just *hope* they will.

Catalina wouldn't.

She'd use the window.

22 — BELMONTE AND SOSA

Following the surprise call from Mr. X, the parents tell each other how good it was to hear from him that their children are well and safe. How good to have had the opportunity to tell him there are no problems with the other relatives of the wedding party, and how good that he had known it for the truth.

After sharing these comforting words, they revert to sitting in silence, all of them haggard for lack of sleep but none of them sleepy. The house servants have been given the day off—in honor of the previous day's celebration, they were told—and the four parents have been sitting without breakfast or any desire for it. Watching the antique clock on the mantel. Listening to its ticks.

At 9:30 Belmonte and Sosa take leave of their wives, saying they will return as soon as they can. Under their umbrellas, they go out to the garage, each man carrying a pair of folded gym bags and each with his special phone, just in case. The wind has relented but the rain continues to fall through the cold grayness.

So uncommon, this rain, Sosa remarks. It falls lightly, then hard, then lightly, but does not stop. The wind, as well. It comes, it goes.

Yes, Belmonte says. He suggests that Sosa take the yellow Cadillac, which stands nearest the garage door, and Sosa says that will be fine. Belmonte retrieves its keys from the garage office, as well as those to the black BMW that's next in the line of cars.

They drive out along the curving driveway and past the front courtyard and around to the front gate, where the attendant has seen them coming and is already opening the barrier.

23 — THE GATE ATTENDANT

The gate attendant, Arturo, smiles and raises a hand as they exit onto the street. Then he takes out his phone and a small piece of paper with a number on it and calls the number.

A man answers, Tell me.

Mr. Belmonte just now left, Arturo says.

What kind of car? the man asks.

BMW. A black BMW 335 Coupe.

Anyone else leave?

Yes. Mr. Sosa. In a Cadillac. Yellow CTS.

Was anyone else in either car?

No. No, sir.

The connection goes dead. Arturo pockets his phone and tells himself he has done nothing wrong. Only told a stranger that the patrón has left the premises and the make of the car he is driving. Mr. Sosa too. If any of that was supposed to be a secret, no one ever told him so.

A few nights ago in a cantina called Angelito's, the stranger—a stocky man with a broad flat nose—had squeezed through the crowd to stand at the bar next to Arturo's stool and asked him the score of the soccer match on the back bar TV whose audio was inaudible in the boom of the jukebox and strident babble of the customers. Not ten minutes after that, the man surreptitiously gave him an envelope containing a thousand pesos and a scrap of paper with a phone number on it. Gave it to him with the understanding that Arturo was to call him at that number on this particular morning as soon as Belmonte departed the house. And with the further understanding that if he failed to call at exactly that time, Arturo would see him again and regret it. Arturo promised he would call and the man laughed and clapped him on the shoulder in the manner of an old pal, telling him to take care of himself, then vanished into the night.

A thousand pesos. For telling the fellow something that anyone on the street could have seen for himself. Who can say he has done anything wrong? It was not wrong.

Then stop thinking about it, he tells himself.

Peering through a telescope from a third-floor window of the rented house two blocks from the Belmonte residence, a Jaguaro lookout phones the ops center and says, They're on their way. Yellow Caddy sedan. Black BMW Coupe. Drivers only, but can't tell who's in which car. Nobody following.

24 — CHATO

Parked at the end of a side street abutting the lightly trafficked two-lane junction road at the perimeter of Belmonte's neighborhood, flat-nosed Chato waits in the gray van, engine idling, wipers beating. He wears a waterproof jacket and a black San Francisco Giants cap.

The Cadillac comes around a corner six blocks away, and then the BMW. Chato closely watches the road behind them, the adjoining streets they pass by. No other vehicle appears behind them. He waits for both cars to go by, and then wheels onto the junction road and follows them.

He keeps checking his mirrors all the way to the entrance ramp to the beltway, then taps a finger on his phone and puts the phone to his ear.

We're getting on the belt, he says. Nobody behind us.

Very good, Espanto says. Let me know when Sosa starts back from the bank.

"Muy bien," Chato says.

Even in this miserable weather, the Monday traffic is as dense and swift as always, but Chato has no problem staying one or two cars behind the BMW. In the opposing lanes the lines of vehicles have slowed considerably as they pass a clutch of flashing lights of police cars and ambulances attending to a multicar accident. A few miles farther on, the Cadillac eases over to an exit lane and Chato does the same. He knows that Sosa's bank is the closer one to the Belmonte home and only five blocks beyond the coming exit. Belmonte's bank is near the heart of town.

At the Banco de Indio Tierra, Sosa turns in at the main entrance of the parking lot, but Chato keeps going to the end of the block and there waits for the traffic light to let him turn into a street flanking the bank. He drives halfway down the street and enters the lot of a small eatery named Tonto's Taquería across from the bank and parks in a space under a row of dripping trees. Through the rain-streaked windshield he can see the yellow form of the Cadillac parked in the rear lot and close to the bank's back doors, which Chato knows are kept locked and are for use only by employees or in an emergency. He knows, too, that a guard stands just inside the door at its little window. Sosa is already on the walkway leading around to the front of the bank, hunched into his coat, one hand holding an umbrella and the other clutching the folded gym bags tucked under his arm.

Chato switches off the van's motor and turns down the radio, then moves his seat back for greater comfort during what will probably be a long wait.

25 — MATEO AND RAYO

In a dark blue Ram pickup with dark-tinted glass, parked in the front lot of the Banco de Indio Tierra, Mateo and Rayo see the yellow Cadillac enter the lot and vanish past the end of the building as it heads for the rear lot. Presently a man comes around on the walkway. Mateo clicks the wipers on for one swipe to get a good look at him, and they recognize Sosa from his photos. He pauses at the front door to collapse his umbrella, then goes in the bank.

Mateo phones Rigo and informs him of Sosa's arrival.

He listens, then says, Yes, he did. Pair of bags, just like she said. He looks sidewise at Rayo, who looks away but cannot suppress her smile of pride.

We'll move around to the side where we can keep an eye on the car, Mateo tells Rigo. Odds on they'll let him out the back way with that bag of cash. . . . All right, then, he says, and ends the call.

They've been parked alongside the bank for an hour, Rayo a little chilly now despite her sweatshirt and Windbreaker, when she sees a man in a black baseball cap get out of the driver's side of a van parked near a taco café across the side street and go into the place. He's out again in minutes with a sack of takeout food and a paper cup of coffee and gets back in the van. She points to it, saying, That gray van over there—

I know, he says.

You've noticed? she says. What do you think? It's been there about half an hour.

It was there when we parked here.

It *was*? You think he might be—

I think that if he is, he could be wondering about *us*.

Mateo cranks up the engine and drives around the front of the bank and to its other end, out of sight of the van. He stops and tells Rayo to get out and position herself where she can watch the Cadillac in the rear lot without being seen by the van guy.

I doubt Sosa will come out for a good while yet, but call me if he does, Mateo says.

Before she can ask what he's doing, he wheels around and drives out of the lot's main entrance, in view of the van. At the first corner he turns right and then into the lot of a small shopping plaza and parks and phones Rigo.

In twenty minutes a Jaguaro operative who looks to be in his teens pulls up beside him in a black Dodge Charger, and they get out of their vehicles.

They said you wanted black glass, the kid says, but there wasn't anything available with it and they said you wanted a car *right now*. Hope this'll do.

It will have to, Mateo says, irked at the lack of black glass.

He gets in the Charger and goes back to the bank, driving around to the side where Rayo is keeping lookout on the yellow Caddy. As he parks and cuts off the motor, she sees it's him and comes over and gets in.

From here they can watch the Cadillac without being seen by the van. If the van follows Sosa when he leaves, they'll know it's a tail, and the van guy will then either lead them to Jessica or they'll grab him if he doesn't. Already the Jaguaros' chief interrogator has been summoned and told to stand by.

26 — BELMONTE AND SOSA

As Mr. X had deemed likely, the withdrawals at both banks prove lengthy. Belmonte and Sosa explain the perilous situation to their respective bank managers, who then must summon other key officers who must also be informed of the kidnapping and in turn must ask and have answered the same questions as the managers'. Belmonte and Sosa each explain that he will take full responsibility for his bank's cooperation. Each man also makes it understood that if the bank should inform the police of this matter—and even if his children are safely recovered—he will close all of his accounts at the bank and urge his friends and business partners to do the same. In addition, he will apprise the news media of the bank's callous disregard for the hostages' safety. The managers at both institutions hasten to pledge their full and confidential compliance with their valued client's wishes.

As it happens, however—and also as Mr. X had thought might prove the case—neither bank has on hand the requisite amount of American cash, and both banks must send urgent calls to other branches for an expedited transfer of dollars. The manager at each bank apologizes profusely to his client and assures him that, notwithstanding the requisite paperwork for the transfer of the American cash, it will come very soon.

The money arrives at the Banco de Indio Tierra just before noon, and very soon afterward Sosa is bid farewell and Godspeed at the rear door, where the bank manager pats him on the back and says his prayers are with him and with his children and asks that he please let him know as soon as they are safely retrieved.

Yes, yes, Sosa says with some asperity, gesturing at the guard, who gets a nod from the manager and opens the door to let Sosa exit into the rain, brandishing his umbrella, gym bags hung on each shoulder.

Not twenty minutes later, Belmonte departs the Banco Rosemonte with his hand and shoulders similarly occupied.

27 — CHATO

Eating his takeout tacos in the van, Chato is glad to see the blue Ram pickup depart. He had trained his minibinoculars on it at first notice and seen that it contained two persons, though he could not make out distinct features. Vehicles have been coming and going all morning, but the blue truck had stayed in place for over an hour and Chato's suspicions had grown almost keen enough to prompt a call to Espanto. But then the truck left. Whatever those two were up to, it obviously had nothing to do with Sosa. Who *still* hasn't come out. Jesus Christ. Anybody in a hurry to get his cash out of a bank would do better to just rob the fucking place.

The minutes pass. The rain again comes down harder for a short time before it again slackens. Then Sosa at last exits the bank's rear door and trudges out to the Cadillac.

Chato adjusts his seat and starts up the van and turns down the music. He calls Espanto and says, He's on the move with full bags.

Good, Espanto says. See him home, then join Chino till you hear from me.

The Caddy comes out of the lot and goes up the side street and stops at the red light. Chato waits for the light to turn green and the Caddy to make its turn before he wheels the van out to the street and then around the same corner.

Sosa is three cars ahead and Chato leaves it that way.

And is unaware of the black Dodge Charger three cars behind him.

28 — RUDY AND CHARLIE

From our window table of a restaurant across a four-lane street, Charlie and I keep watch on the Banco Rosemonte. The bank's off to our left a little but the rain's angled away from the window, and between the passing vehicles we have a good view of the bank's glass front doors, which aren't due to open for another fifteen minutes. Charlie's turned off the little lamp on our table to make it harder for anyone outside to see us very well. The bank is fronted by a small courtyard under a spacious canopy where people take refuge from the rain while they wait for the doors to open or their bus to arrive at the corner stop farther to our left.

We came here early rather than stick around the suite, feeling useless. We're in the heart of town, where parking is at a premium and the bank lacks its own lot, so we had to leave our car at the nearest public parking square, two blocks away. Belmonte's going to have to park there too. Rigo had said it would be pretty funny if on his way back to the car Belmonte was robbed of one or both gym bags by some street rat.

Sitting on one of the bank's courtyard benches is Duarte, a Jaguaro lookout Mateo assigned to us. Suit and tie, an attaché case at his side, a folded newspaper on his lap, a phone line in his ear—a typical businessman waiting to conduct some bank transaction. His phone is on open connection to the one plugged in Charlie's ear, but they haven't had much to say to each other.

For almost an hour now we've been watching a pickpocket working the crowd across the street. A kid ten or eleven years old, wearing a school uniform or what's meant to look like one. White shirt and tie, dark suit, flat cap to match, a big schoolbag strapped across his chest. He stays near the front of the canopy so he can be the first to see when a bus is coming and then ambles toward the stop on the corner, using a folded newspaper as a makeshift umbrella. As a knot of people start coming up behind him to board the bus, he turns around and makes his way back through them and each time snags a wallet. The first time, I wasn't really sure I'd seen what I thought I had. I pointed him out to Charlie, and about ten minutes later when another bus pulled in we watched closely and saw him pluck a wallet from a passing coat and transfer it to his book bag, slick as a magic trick. Twenty minutes after that we saw him take a wallet from an ass pocket. Following each grab, he goes to a covered trash bin at the nearer end of the street and rummages through his bag like he's looking for something, then takes out a wadded handful of notebook paper and shoves it in the little flap door of the bin. The wallet's in the wad of paper, of course, and he's stripped it of cash and maybe credit cards while poking around in the bag. We've known a few pickpockets and most of them work in pairs, but this kid's a solo act and is very damn good. We've seen him score five wallets so far, all from expensively dressed men. When I said the little dude had a real future in politics, Charlie smiled for the first time in a while.

Now it's less than ten minutes till the bank opens and I'm still watching the kid at work when Charlie says, "Lookee there. The Chinaman."

I see who he means. An Oriental guy now among the crowd under the canopy and standing near the bank doors, furling his umbrella then flicking water off his red baseball cap. Crew cut. Thin mustache. Wearing jeans and a canvas jacket.

"Rayo said when Huerta met with the spiky-hair guy and the other one, those two were chauffeured away by an Asian-looking guy."

"She did say that, yeah," I say. "And you know how many Asians there must be in this town?"

"I know. But I only see one standing at that bank."

"Orientals probably do bank business now and then. And I'll bet they sometimes take the bus."

"Yeah, but look at Chong there," Charlie says. "No briefcase, backpack, nothing. Just an umbrella. He ain't on bank business. Look, here comes a bus. . . . Look how everybody's checking to see which one it is, but not him. He doesn't care because he's not waiting for any bus. It was the same with the bus before. I was watching. He didn't give it a look."

"Maybe his bus isn't due for a while, so what's to check?"

"Listen, there was a Chinaman driving the spike-hair guy and *that's* him. I *know* it, Rudy. I've got the vibe."

"*Maybe* it's him," I say. "Vibe or not, man, we don't know it's—"

Charlie raises a hand to cut me off. He's listening to Duarte.

"Belmonte's here," he says to me.

We look over and see Duarte on his feet and craning his head to look past the canopy crowd like he's trying to see if the bus coming down the street is his.

From our left, Belmonte walks into view on the sidewalk across the street, his umbrella swaying a little in the breeze. He's got the gym bags tucked under an arm. He takes shelter beneath the canopy, folds the umbrella, and looks at his watch. The Asian guy might or might not be looking at him, hard to say. He moves off into the crowd as Belmonte goes to the doors, where others are waiting for them to open.

Our man Duarte is keeping his eye on Belmonte but seems oblivious to the Asian guy. Hard to believe he hasn't seen him or, if he has, that he hasn't recalled the Asian in the spider report Rayo brought us. But Mateo was so unimpressed with it he may not have bothered to pass it on to his guys.

Now the Asian guy notices Duarte watching Belmonte.

Chong's on him, Charlie says. Then opens his line to Duarte and says, You have to leave, man, now. Get on that bus just pulled in.

Duarte hesitates, giving Belmonte another glance. He puts a hand to his mouth.

No, don't *talk*, God damn it, just go, Charlie says in a tight whisper. *Go!*

Duarte heads for the bus and is the last to board before the doors close. The Asian watches him all the way and doesn't take his eyes off the bus until it drives off.

A bank employee appears on the other side of the doors and works the lock and pulls a door open to let the customers enter.

The Asian guy watches Belmonte go in. Then he takes a phone from a side pocket of his jacket and makes a call. Very short, just a few seconds. He pockets the phone and goes to a bench and sits down and picks up a discarded newspaper.

"If that's not our Chink I'll eat this table," Charlie says. "We've caught a break, cuz. He just let somebody know the man's here for the money. Ten to one he calls them again when Belmonte comes out."

I watch the Asian reposition himself on the bench so that he can see the bank doors over his newspaper—and I can feel it. Charlie's right.

"He's shadowing Belmonte," Charlie says. "Sosa's sure to have a shadow too, and I'll wager Mateo spots him. They follow the dads to the banks, make sure they come out with the loot, make sure they get it home."

"Maybe the business about calling at four is bullshit. Maybe they mean to grab the bags on the way back to the house."

"No," Charlie says. "I thought about that. But why strong-arm it and take risks you don't have to? One of the dads could phone an alarm before they can stop him, or raise a hell of a holler in the street. Attract all kinds of attention. Maybe force them to shoot and have to make a fast getaway, maybe get in a smashup at the scene. They don't need to risk any of that. Rigo was right, these guys aren't cowboys. They've got it figured for slick and quiet and they'll stick to it. They're just being careful, using tails on the dads."

He drums his fingers on the table, intently watching Chong. Now he's got me calling him that. "Okay," he says. "Here's what we do."

He lays out plan A. If Chong follows Belmonte when he comes out of the bank, we'll follow *him*. He's got a car for sure and may or may not have a confederate waiting in it, but either way, we'll follow him in hope that after he sees Belmonte get home with the money he'll lead us to where they might be holding Jess. If he does, we'll call Rigo for assistance. If he doesn't follow Belmonte, plan B is for Charlie to tail Chong while I stick with Belmonte and see if he goes home with the cash. When Chong gets to wherever he goes, Charlie will call me, I'll join him, and we'll decide our next move. If neither of these plans work out, plan C is to grab Chong and have a chat with him.

The big risk is that Chong might catch on he's being shadowed and phone the news to his fellows. Even if he just suspects it, he might call them. Which could make the situation worse for Jessie. What we have to do is render him phoneless. But it's a good bet his guys are expecting him to let them know when Belmonte leaves the bank with the money and that everything is cool. If they don't get that call, they'll go on red alert, no question. Again, bad for Jess.

We have to wait till after he calls in again, and *then* part him from his phone. Plus, we have to do it without his knowing it, so he doesn't panic about its loss before he leads us to Jessie. It's a hell of a long shot, since he might want to make a call for any number of reasons, and he might have another phone in the car, and he might . . . well, the odds aren't real good he'd stay ignorant of the missing phone for long. Still, we have to do what we can to cut him off from his guys.

And the best way is with pro help.

I go down to the far end of the street before crossing over. It's gotten colder out here. I wait under my umbrella until the kid comes over to the trash bin with another wallet to dispose of surreptitiously, and I say, "Oye, muchacho," and let him see the folded Yankee fifty in my palm. People are passing by us with their faces down against the blowing rain.

I tell him in low voice I'm not a homo or a cop and the fifty is his if he follows me to the restaurant to talk about a chance for him to make some good money. He'll get another fifty dollars just for listening.

He looks around and steps closer, wagging his fingers for the money, then snatches the bill from my hand and steps back, ready to run.

I shrug. Then cross the street again and go back to the restaurant. He follows me.

We don't ask his name and he doesn't ask ours and it doesn't take long to make a deal. Charlie tells him he has to keep an eye on two men, the Asian guy on the bench over there, and a man who will be coming out of the bank. When I start describing Belmonte, the kid interrupts to say he knows who I mean. He'd marked him going in and had intended to take his wallet when he came back out. He says he will not now carry out that intention. He'll wait under the canopy for as long as it takes for Belmonte to come out, and when Belmonte does, the kid will wait to see if Chong makes a call. If he does, the kid will take the phone after Chong puts it back in his jacket. If he doesn't make a call, the kid will take the phone when Chong starts to leave. Either way, Charlie tells him, for his time and service we'll pay him another fifty dollars now and another fifty afterward. He jacks us to another hundred bucks up front and one fifty after. His only condition is that after I slip him the hundred advance we go to the cashier and have her hold the other 150 dollars for him. We do that, and find out she's his cousin. He then makes a quick trip to the men's room and goes back across the street to keep an eye on Chong and wait for Belmonte's exit.

We stay at our table to do the same.

An hour crawls by. Then another. The kid's sitting on a bench and fooling around with an iPad or whatever it is. I never once catch him looking at Chong, who's had time to read every word in the newspaper twice and is now applying a clipper to his fingernails. The waitress stops by our table every few minutes to see if we want more coffee and we say no thanks and give her a big tip to keep her from pestering us any more. The quirky rain continues to alternate between stretches of light sprinkling and short-lived windy downpours.

It's past noon when we see Belmonte approaching the glass doors, the fat gym bags under his arms and strapped to his shoulders. The crowd outside is bigger than before, but the kid and Chong have spotted him too and are on their feet. The kid shuffles out to the sidewalk as Chong eases a little way into the crowd and gets out his phone and puts it to his ear. Charlie heads outside to make sure we don't lose sight of Chong after he makes his call, and I keep watching from the window to see if the kid does his job.

Belmonte goes by Chong, who slips the phone into his side pocket and starts after him. The kid heads toward Chong and they jostle past each other in the crowd and I catch the flicker of the kid's hand plucking the phone.

I hustle outside and jog across the street as the kid angles out of the crowd and bumps my arm and passes me the phone with an underhand move. We hadn't told him to give us the phone, and I'm so surprised I almost drop it, then stick it in my pocket and keep on chasing after Charlie. Up ahead of us, Chong's trailing Belmonte. All of us with umbrellas, adding to the bobbing sidewalk stream of them.

29 — THE BETA HOUSE

The five hostages are now all in the slightly warmer of the two bedrooms, the lights of the Beta house still on against the day's dark cast and still sporadically flickering, when Barbarosa gets a call from Espanto, wanting to know if the locksmith was able to open the basement door. It's been an hour since he said the smith was on his way.

Locksmith, my ass, Barbarosa says. The joke's over, prick. You wanted a big laugh and you got it and now you—

Hey, hey, hold on, Espanto says. You telling me he *isn't* there? I talked to him not twenty minutes ago. Took longer than expected for the mechanic to change the belt, but the smith was back on the road and on his way. He should've been—

Oh bullshit! Barbarosa says. Go fuck yourself. And I'll tell you something else. . . . *What?* . . . I'm on the phone here, God damn it!

Someone is addressing Barbarosa but Espanto can't make out what he's saying. What's going on? he asks.

Locksmith's here, Barbarosa mumbles—and severs the connection before he can hear Espanto's laughter.

A short, stout man carrying a toolbox, his Windbreaker beaded with rainwater, his fedora brim dripping, the locksmith introduces himself as Anuncio and begs their forgiveness for his tardiness but says it couldn't be helped. There are no signs on most of the streets around here and very few buildings have numbers, and in the rain it's been an effort to find the house by way of nothing more than Espanto's description of it.

He listens patiently as Barbarosa berates him anyway and expounds at length about the stink. Anuncio sniffs the air with a face of disgust and nods in sympathetic understanding. Then asks to be shown the troublesome lock.

Barbarosa says he doesn't know why they should bother trying to find the cause of the smell at this point, but leads Anuncio to the kitchen and the landing of the basement stairwell.

Woo, the locksmith says as he descends into the greater stench.

Yeah, says Barbarosa, stopping midway down the stairs. Like something dead rotting in an unflushed toilet.

The stairwell is very dim, the only light from the kitchen door. Anuncio coughs a few times, takes a handkerchief from his back pocket and wipes his eyes and nose, then gets a flashlight out of his toolbox. He turns the padlock this way and that, examining it closely. He fingers the small section of exposed shackle and purses his lips as if forming a silent whistle. I don't have anything with me that can cut this, he says to

Barbarosa. There's a certain grinder that could probably do the job, but I'd have to rent it from a place back in the city.

Jesus Christ, by then we'll be out of here, Barbarosa says. Fuck it. We've put up with it this long.

I'd sure like to know what that stink *is*, Flaco says from the top of the short staircase.

I may be able to pick it, Anuncio says.

A lock that hard to cut sure as hell can't be picked, Barbarosa says.

That's not always true, the smith says. I'd like to try.

Do what you want, man, Barbarosa says, going up the stairs. I gotta go out and get some fresh air, rain or no rain.

Flaco follows after him.

The locksmith endures another coughing fit, then folds his handkerchief and ties it around the lower half of his face like a bandit. He takes a ring of keys from his toolbox and finds three keys that will enter the lock face. He inserts one and bumps the lock lightly and repeatedly on the door, simultaneously trying to turn the key with each bump. He tries this with each key unsuccessfully. It would have been too easy had this technique worked, but you never know. He again resorts to his toolbox and extracts a small metal case containing an array of instruments. He selects one shaped like a little saw blade and one that looks like an ice pick with a curved tip, both of them very flexible. Then he once more sets to work.

Again and again he curses softly as he feels the tumbler pins' sly evasions of his probing. At times he feels the instruments touch exactly where they should, but each time, one or the other slips off its mark before he can execute the requisite manipulation. He pauses occasionally to work the stiffness out of his cold fingers and ease his frustration even as he admires the lock's interior design. From time to time, one or another of the men comes to the top of the stairs to watch him work, then goes away without comment.

Anuncio has been laboring at the lock for more than half an hour when Flaco shows up again and sits on the top step to observe him. When Barbarosa appears at the doorway, Flaco gestures at the locksmith and says he's never seen anyone so determined.

Barbarosa scoffs. "So crazy," you mean. He watches for a minute, then shakes his head and starts to turn away.

And there's the unmistakable *snick* of the shackle uncoupling.

Holy Mother, Flaco says.

Anuncio expels a long breath and pulls down his mask, removes the huge lock, and with a victorious grin at them raises it high like a trophy.

Barbarosa pushes the basement door open to almost total darkness and an even more powerful concentration of the stench. The men cough and cover their mouths and noses with their hands and stand fast just inside the threshold, reluctant to enter any farther for fear of what they might step on. A decomposed body or a bunch of rats rotting in traps, or as Flaco has suggested, a litter of starved cats after they pissed and shat in every corner of the place. Barbarosa now detects something vaguely familiar about the stink, yet can't quite place it. He runs his hand over the wall to one side of the door and says, Where's the light switch?

The locksmith feels about on the other side. "Aquí 'sta," he says, and clicks the switch.

The basement comes alight from a pair of shaded lamps to either side of the room and a naked high-watt bulb dangling on a frayed cord from the center of the ceiling. Tables line three sides of the room, covered with glassware and opened and unopened crates, with car batteries, plastic jugs of antifreeze, hot plates, rolls of plastic tubing, boxes of coffee filters and plastic baggies. The walls are stacked almost to the ceiling with propane tanks, cans of lye and paint solvents, acetone, lighter fluid, drain cleaners, kerosene, ammonia.

The lights flicker, cut out for a few seconds, plunging the room into darkness, and come back on again in a tremoring cast. Then the room again goes black and this time stays that way.

"Chingada!" Barbarosa says. Work the switch, man.

The locksmith clicks the switch up and down a number of times before the room's lights come back on but continue to flicker.

Terrible wiring, the smith says.

And now Barbarosa sees that the far corner of the room is piled almost to the ceiling with cartons of cold medicine. The floor is littered with torn and empty blister packs and small plastic medicine bottles, with flattened cardboard boxes.

The overhead electric cord starts to sizzle and a wisp of black smoke issues from the tattered insulation just above the bulb.

Oh Jesus, says Flaco, and takes a step back toward the door.

That's when Barbarosa remembers the laboratory in Jalapa where last year he and the lately murdered-by-his-girlfriend Chisto delivered a truckload of equipment—and just as the word "anfetamina" enters his mind, the overhead cord crackles and sheds bright blue sparks and the room detonates in a white blaze.

The stone-walled basement compresses the force of the explosion and directs it upward in a fiery eruption through the floor that sunders the house and everyone in it and propels wreckage as far as the next block. Chunks of concrete smash through neighboring windows. Burning pieces of woodwork clatter on adjacent roofs. The Beta house occupants who had been above the basement now litter the street, smoking and disfigured beyond recognition, all of them missing at least one limb, two of them headless. Body parts are strewn into weed lots and shrubbery and will be discovered and fed on by crows and dogs and rats. Of those who were in the basement no remnant will be found larger than a ham or other than charred black.

The neighbors pour out into the mizzling rain to gawk at the fiery remains of the Beta house and the smoking roofs of flanking homes whose residents stand huddled and crying in the muddy street. A few people with phones call the fire department, some the police, but it will be most of an hour before the cops or the water-tank trucks arrive and by then the rain will have dampened the fires to steaming embers.

The blast was heard at the perimeters of the slum but did not carry into the central city's tenacious clamor, and the smoke of its fires is hardly distinguishable in the overcast sky and perpetual haze encircling the Federal District. Still, word of the explosion reaches the city's news centers, and though the misfortunes of the slums are rarely deemed newsworthy, it has been a slow day marked principally by its miserable weather, and two television stations dispatch camera crews to the scene in hope of footage they might fashion into a local drama for the afternoon broadcast.

30 — CHATO

Chato follows Sosa from the bank into the beltway's teeming traffic, the chains of headlights and taillights streaking through the heavy grayness, but the yellow Cadillac is easy enough to keep in view. Even though Galán told the two fathers they would be followed to and from the banks, you don't want them to spot you. You want to keep them apprehensive with the knowledge that you see them but they don't see you. Chato maintains a buffer of one or two vehicles between himself and the Caddy, a tactic requiring deftness, as Sosa is staying in the rightmost lane and holding to the speed limit. Behind Chato, vehicles pull out to pass at the first opportunity, horns blaring and shadowy drivers making rude gestures as they go by. Chato pays them no mind. The radio is tuned to a rock station and he taps his hands on the steering wheel in time to the music.

A carpet store truck follows Sosa onto the exit ramp, preserving the shield between Chato and the Caddy. As he comes down the curving exit, Chato checks his mirrors and sees a pink-and-white station wagon directly in back of him and glimpses a blue car and a black one behind the wagon. Sosa makes a right turn onto the two-lane junction road, on which the traffic is heavier than it was this morning. The carpet truck makes the same turn and Chato stays behind the truck. Six blocks farther on, Sosa turns off the road and Chato makes the same turn and in the rearview sees the next cars and the station wagon pass on by, their tires raising small rooster tails of water. There's no one behind Chato now and only Sosa up ahead as they follow the winding street to Belmonte's house.

Chato imagines himself forcing the Cadillac to the curb, taking the money from it, absconding to some distant haven of the world to live in luxury for the rest of his life. It's a mere fancy, of course. Because he wouldn't be robbing only Los Doce, but Los Zetas, too, who are expecting a one-million-dollar membership fee from the ransom. Nobody to fool with, those boys. They would find him wherever he went, and what they left of him could be buried in a shoebox.

The Belmonte estate comes in view. The Caddy slows as it approaches the entrance to the driveway, and the attendant opens the gate. Passing by, Chato gives him a glance—Arturo, he recalls, whom he recently enriched by a thousand pesos.

Going through the next intersection, he sees a black car at the stop sign to his left, only the driver in it. Then in the rearview sees the car cross the street and vanish. A two-door.

He exits the Chapultepec district and before long is on a secluded narrow road winding through a rolling expanse of pastoral properties whose residences are set far off the road and unseen in the woods. He's thinking of the kid enchiladas he will soon be enjoying at Cuates Locos, a café at a shoddy little plaza a few miles the other side of these mini ranches. The plaza is on the way to both of the hold houses, except that two blocks west of the plaza you must turn south to go to the Alpha house, and north to go to the Beta. Chino will be at the café too. That's where they are to await Espanto's call to action.

The hills are higher here than in the Chapultepec neighborhoods, and more closely together. The road curves and dips and rises as it follows their contours, the muddy shoulder at times only a few feet from a rocky upsweep on one side and, on the other, a verdant sloping drop-off. The radio begins to pick up static. He pushes buttons until he finds another rock station with better reception. Then glances in the mirror and sees a dark car appear out of the curve. About forty or fifty yards behind him. He loses sight of it when he goes into the next bend.

The curve ends in a straightaway, and when the car reappears in his mirrors it is still at the same distance. From up ahead comes a pickup truck with a large load of old tires. It goes by the van with a high splash of road water and then Chato is into the next curve and both the truck and car go out of view.

As the road again straightens, Chato reduces his speed, and when the car again shows in his mirror it's only about twenty yards back—but it abruptly slows down to hold to that distance. A black two-door. There are of course many thousands of black two-doors in this town, but he recalls the one he saw on Belmonte's street. That one contained only a driver, and this one looks like it has two persons in it. It's hard to be sure at this distance, in this overcast. Even if it's the same car, that doesn't mean it's a tail. Could be it stopped to pick up somebody and just happens to be going the same way as himself. Besides, who would be tailing him except cops, and the only way cops could come into this is through the parents, who would not risk their children's lives by going to the police. Or would they? You can't count on people to act in their own best interest.

He and Chino have been instructed not to initiate further phone contact with Espanto after notifying him of the fathers' departures from the banks unless there's a justified need to call—as in the event that either Belmonte or Sosa did not take the money to the Belmonte house, or if he or Chino should spot a tail on either man. The question right now is whether the black car is following *him*. Considering the way it slowed down to keep its distance, Chato thinks it is. Which constitutes a justified need to call Espanto.

The upcoming curve is a wide one bearing right, the hill sloping upward on that side and dropping away on the left. As he enters the bend, Chato takes out his phone and brings it close to his face so he can better watch the road as he thumbs up the directory and scrolls for Espanto's name. Then he looks in the mirror and sees the black car closing on him at furious speed, a realization so startling he doesn't notice the old tire lying in the road ahead until he's almost on it.

He drops the phone and swerves to the right and misses the tire but goes off the road and across the shoulder and the van leans leftward as it angles up the stony rise, rocks rattling on the undercarriage. He cuts the wheel and the van swivels downward and back across the road and onto the other shoulder and he's fighting the wheel and working the brakes as the van skids through stony mud at the edge of the drop-off. Then the tires dig in and he swings back onto the road and gets the van under control for a moment before it's struck from behind in a crash of metal and glass, snapping his head back, and the van grinds across the left shoulder again and the world tilts in the windshield.

31— MATEO AND RAYO

The pickup with the load of tires swooshes past in a raised splash that thumps their windows. They're still not sure if the van guy has paid them any notice until they come out of the next curve and see the van only half as far ahead as it had been. There is no other traffic in either direction.

Mateo slows down to hold their distance at about twenty yards. He's checking us out, he says.

Why would he think we're following him? Rayo says. He has no reason.

Nature of the beast. If he suspects us, he'll call somebody and some of his pals will be waiting for us at the end of this road.

She sees the van driver raise a phone to his face and says, Oh shit.

Hold on, Mateo says, and the Charger leaps forward like it's been let off a leash. As they speed toward the van it veers to the right and goes off the road, spraying mud and partly climbing the rise and they see the tire it almost hit. "Águila!" Rayo shouts.

Mateo taps the brake and skirts the tire as the van comes off the rise and across the road and slews along the other shoulder. Rayo's sure it's going to go over but it somehow regains the road for a moment—and then Mateo deliberately rams it into a skid back off the pavement and into a fishtailing slide along the shoulder and it keels over it and is gone.

They slow down and pull over, see no other vehicle on the road, then slowly back up to where the van went out of sight. They put on baseball caps to keep the rain out of their eyes and get out and cross the road to the rim of the slope.

The van lies halfway down the incline, about fifty feet below, on its right side, its underside facing uphill, the two upside wheels still turning.

Steam rises off the engine compartment into the cold rain. The upturned doors are shut.

Think he's dead? she asks.

Could be. Or just hurt. Or might've got out.

Can't be hurt too bad if he got out so fast, she says.

He checks the empty road and draws his Beretta. Let's go down and see what we've got.

She unholsters a Ruger 9 and ensures there's a round in the chamber. She has never shot at anyone but is prepared to do it if necessary. One of the first things she'd been asked when she sought to become a Jaguaro was if she believed she could kill. She'd said yes with stronger conviction than she'd actually felt, but she knew the face to show her questioner, the tone to use.

He tells her to go around to the right of the van, he'll go to the left. Let's hope he's in there and alive but not able to make a fight of it, he says. If you spot him outside, let me know where and take cover and leave him to me. But if you think you have to shoot, shoot.

Charged with adrenaline, gripping the Ruger in both hands, she makes her cautious way over the tricky footing down through the dripping trees and brush, water running off the brim of her cap. She listens hard for any sound from the van, but all she hears is the patter of the rain, a passing vehicle on the road above. She's lost sight of Mateo.

Nearing the van, she smells gasoline. She's afraid and won't deny it. She was taught as a child there's no bravery in pretense of fearlessness, only a dangerous self-deception.

When she gets to the rear of the van's exposed underside she's uncertain how to proceed. Mateo didn't say. Should she climb up on the upturned side and take a look in the driver's window? She both wants to and she doesn't. The smell of gasoline is now very strong. She's heard of capsized cars whose spilled fuel spread to an ignition wire and *boom*.

She eases past the front wheels and scouts the area beyond the van. And there's Mateo. Partly showing himself among the trees, his position fore of the van but downhill of it and farther away than she'd expected.

He's seen her, too, and gestures for her to circle back to the other end of van. She raises a fist shoulder-high in acknowledgment, and he starts moving to another cluster of trees.

She backtracks to the end of the van and starts around it—and flinches to a halt at the blasts of several gunshots from its immediate other side. There follow three pistol reports from somewhere downhill, all three bullets striking the van. Then two more louder, closer shots.

Then silence but for the rain in the trees.

She stands immobilized. Scared. Then thinks, *Move, bitch!*

She steps around the end of the van, two-handing the Ruger straight out in front of her, wincing at the crunch of loose rock underfoot.

Standing by the front bumper is a man turning toward her with a pistol, and all in an instant she sees his face in stark clarity under his black Giants cap—young brown flat nosed, his wide eyes *seeing* her more intensely than she's ever felt herself seen—and as fast as she can pull the trigger she fires four rounds into him, knocking him back in a sprawl.

She keeps the Ruger pointed at him, her heart and lungs heaving, and eases up to where he lies with legs in awkward splay, arms outflung, cap askew, open eyes overrunning with rainwater. There's a red wound at the base of his neck and three others in a tight group over the heart.

She assesses her sensations, her feelings, and finds neither shock nor regret among them. She has grown up among men who have killed but speak of it only in serious timbre when they speak of it at all, and perhaps such familiarity and outlook have prepared her for this moment more than she could have known. She picks up the man's Glock. It's a fine weapon, and that it might have killed her had she been a second slower doesn't alter its worth. She tucks it in her pants.

She hears a car pass by up above, and then another behind it. She looks to where Mateo had been but doesn't see him. She calls out for him.

"Acá 'stoy. Por acá!" The response sounds strained, his voice odd, coming from off to the right of where she'd last seen him. Over here! he calls again.

She scrambles down through the trees and scrub and finds him lying on his side, one hand pointing his Beretta at her, the other pressed to his bloody stomach. He sees it's her and lowers the gun. He's also been shot in the thigh, his pant leg soaked with blood, and has already tied his belt as a tourniquet just above the wound.

He asks if she put the guy down for good and she says yes, holstering the Ruger. She hurriedly takes off her Windbreaker and the holster and her sweatshirt and balls up the sweatshirt and places it against his stomach wound. He groans and lays the pistol aside and holds the sweatshirt to himself with both hands, still on his side. Before permitting her to tend him further, he tells her to call Jaguaro operations and tells her what to say. She does it. Then she takes off her T-shirt and rips it into a long strip that she uses to bind his leg wound. She's shivering, goosefleshed, feels her nipples chilled rigid under the flimsy bra. He's closed his eyes. When she's bandaged him, she puts the Windbreaker back on.

They'll be right here, she says. Won't be long.

He nods, eyes still closed. Then his arms slacken and the sweatshirt falls free of his belly.

She says, Oh God, and puts her fingertips to his neck. He's still alive. She eases him onto his back and replaces the balled sweatshirt on the wound and holds it there.

Keep breathing, she says, just keep breathing, that's all you have to do and you'll be all right. Keep breathing.

She hears another car go by and wonders if the passing traffic has had any curiosity at all about the unattended car at the roadside. She gives thought to binding the sweatshirt in place and then going up there and at gunpoint stopping the next vehicle to come along and commandeering it to get him to a hospital. But she doesn't think her belt will hold the shirt properly, and anyway cannot bring herself to leave his side for even a minute, fearful that if she should cease exhorting him to breathe he will cease to do it.

Jaguaros arrive. A pair of SUVs with three men in each, and they move with brisk efficiency. One team of three carries Mateo up to the road, pausing to peer over the berm to make sure no witnesses might be coming, then places him in the rear of one of the SUVs. Two of the men then speed off with him, followed by the other man and Rayo in the Charger, the guy driving.

The other three Jaguaros have taken cans of gasoline down to the van. They heave Chato's body up to the open door and drop it inside, then splash gas into and over the vehicle and set it afire. Flames rush at them along the gas-soaked ground and they leap back, whooping with laughter.

Minutes later they're making away in the SUV, a dense column of black smoke churning up through the hillside trees.

32 — RUDY AND CHARLIE

The rain's coming down a little harder again but there's almost no wind. We make our way through the sidewalk crowd, staying about thirty feet behind Chong, who's less than half that distance behind Belmonte, who's carrying the two bags with no apparent difficulty. More than a few of the people streaming past us on either side—tight-faced under their umbrellas, seeming oblivious to everything but their own foul-weather thoughts—would start killing each other on the spot to get those bags if they knew what was in them.

As we approach the intersection before the block containing the public parking square, Chong takes a look back, and then a few paces farther on, looks again.

Belmonte crosses the intersection—the traffic light's little green stick figure walking in place, the yellow numbers above him counting down the remaining seconds before the light change. But Chong remains at the curb on this side and looks all around like maybe he's unsure of an address or something. He looks our way again. Charlie stops at a newspaper kiosk and I sidle over to browse at a shoe store window.

Chong waits at the curb until the light countdown flashes down to 1, then sprints across the intersection as the light turns red and the four lanes of traffic start moving in both directions, cutting us off till the next green. The lead car in the far right lane has to brake sharply to keep from hitting Chong, and the driver gives him a long blast of the horn. Chong gives him the finger and melds into the crowd.

We stand at the curb and wait. I don't know if he made a suspicious note of us or was just pulling a routine tactic, but I admire his expertise.

"God damn it," Charlie says. "If we lose that bastard . . ."

He jams his umbrella in the corner trash barrel and I follow suit, preferring to get wet and have both hands free.

The light changes and we jog through the people up ahead, rousing curses as we push our way through. The parking lot is halfway down the street, situated between a pair of tall buildings. We slow to a walk as we reach the entrance.

It's a large open square spanning the width of the block, with more than a dozen long rows of metered spaces. The entrance is on this street, the exit at a traffic light on the flanking street. Vehicles are pulling in and out, people parking, people on foot cutting through the lot from one street to the other. We don't see Belmonte or Chong.

Get the car, Charlie says as he keeps scanning for them.

The six-year-old Jeep SUV that Rigo lent us is parked a couple of rows away, and as I'm heading for it I spy Belmonte's black BMW backing out of a space a few cars to my left. It comes down the lane toward me and I pause, looking this way and that, like I don't recall where I left my car. Behind the swishing wipers, Belmonte's aspect is grim as he goes by. He turns at the end of the row and heads for the exit where a short line of cars is waiting at a red light.

I look back at Charlie and he nods that he's seen him too.

A nearby car horn emits a long resounding blare. It's coming from a dark green Focus one row over from me.

Chong's at the wheel.

He's behind an unmoving panel truck barring his way. The driver's on the phone and seems to be in a heated argument. He responds to another blast of Chong's horn with a two-finger "up yours" gesture into the side-view mirror. The exit light turns green and Belmonte drives away.

Chong gives the truck the horn again, an even longer honk this time, and the driver jabs the fingers up and down with greater vigor even as he's shouting at someone on the phone. Chong takes a hand off the wheel and I wonder if he's going to pull a gun on the dumbshit. Then his face goes funny and I realize he's searching himself for something he can't find. His phone.

He looks over and catches me staring at him. Then looks past me at Charlie.

He's pegged us.

The Focus starts backing up fast, and Charlie yells something I don't catch.

Chong's almost reached the end of the lane when a pink car turns into it. The Focus brakes and comes to a stop with a hard bang into the pink car's bumper—and then Chong's out and running, splashing through puddles, hightailing for the street on the exit side of the lot.

We go tearing after him, plans A and B shot to hell.

We race around the corner of the building and it takes me a second to see him, well up ahead and weaving through the thicket of pedestrians. Now he's in sight, now not, now giving us a look back, now vanished again.

There's a big intersection ahead, on a busy six-lane avenue, and we've lost him when we get to it. The light's red against crossing straight ahead, and while I scan the other side of the avenue for any sign of Chong, Charlie's searching the sidewalk crowd to our left and right.

"*There!*" he says, looking right, and runs into the throng. I stay behind him, letting him plow the way through this street's heavier press of people, our shouldering eliciting maledictions and threats.

Chong's getting into a taxi at the corner up ahead. We're still twenty feet from it as it pulls away into the passing traffic, his impassive face staring at us through the watery rear window. It's one of the thousands of green-and-white Volkswagen taxis working the city's streets, but this one's flying a Blue Cross soccer team pennant on its radio antenna. It cuts over into the center lane and stops a block away in a waiting line at a red light. We'd never reach it before the lights turns, and there we'd be, on foot in the middle of traffic.

"*Damn* it!" Charlie says.

We're looking around for a taxi when a microbus pulls up to the curb beside us, exactly like the one that outslicked Rigo's driver on the way in from the airport. As riders disembark from the rear door, Charlie and I cram in behind other boarders at the front door, each of them dropping pesos into the cash box next to the driver, who looks all of fifteen or sixteen years old under a Diablos Rojos baseball cap and is commanding the standees to press farther back. Charlie digs a fold of American cash out of his pocket and peels a few bills off it. He holds them fanned open under the kid's nose—five or six fifty-dollar bills—and points ahead and tells him if he keeps us in sight of the taxi with the Blue Cross pennant until it gets where it's going, the money's his. The kid's eyes widen at the wad and he looks out at the taxi, which now starts moving again with the green light. I'm standing braced at the open front door, barring a handful of pissed-off people who want to crowd aboard. In my shirt, the kid says.

Charlie stuffs the money in the kid's shirt pocket, saying, You lose him, I take it back.

The micro jerks out into traffic, raising outcries and causing wet skiddings. We're lightly bumped from the rear and there's a concentrated outbreak of car horns, but we're okay, off and running.

"Tell Rigo what's up," Charlie says.

I get out my phone and thumb his number and he answers on the first ring. I fill him in fast, speaking in English, and tell him where Chong's car is, in case there's anything in it that might be of use. He says he's got guys homing on our GPS and to leave my phone on. "Will do," I say, and zip it into my jacket pocket.

The taxi's now more than a block ahead but our kid's a whiz at the wheel. He works us into the center of the three lanes and nimbly wedges the micro into one flanking lane or the other in order to pass, and little by little we're gaining on the cab. The kid's ignoring all his stops and the waiting people flapping their arms at him as we speed past, and he's deaf to the cries of passengers demanding to be let off, cursing at him, though some of the riders nearest to me are grinning like lunatics, having caught on that a chase is in force and loving it. Charlie yells for everybody to stay put and not touch their phones. He takes out another fifty and hands it to a husky guy standing near him who's plainly enjoying the adventure and tells him to keep an eye out for anybody who tries to use a phone. You bet I will, chief! the guys says. He glowers all around and says, I see a fucking phone I'll make you eat it!

We're only five or six vehicles behind the taxi when it goes through an intersection in the last seconds of a yellow light. Go, *go!* the kid urges the cars in front of us, and most of them do, two of them after the light turns red. But the orange sedan directly ahead us brakes for the light as vehicles start into the intersection from our left and right. Without slowing, the kid whips the micro around the sedan and just ahead of a braking bus in the adjacent lane and we barrel into the intersection cross traffic.

As if he's done it a hundred times before, the kid zigzags us left-right-left-right through the moving cross traffic, the micro swaying with each swerve and almost losing traction, and on one sharp zig to the left I nearly get slung out the open door. I see cars coming at us and skidding off to our rear and to certain smashups but I don't hear any of them for all the passengers' screaming and bellowed prayers and, so help me, God, *laughter.*

And just like that, we're clear of the intersection and still moving along. With a strong odor of piss added to the micro's air.

The cab's now making some moves of its own. Whether the driver said something to Chong about the goings-on in the rearview mirror or Chong looked back and witnessed our reckless passage through the intersection, there's no doubt he knows we're in the micro.

"If the cabbie's got a phone," I say, "Chong's calling for help."

"Duh," Charlie says without looking at me.

The taxi's cutting from lane to lane, its size giving it definite advantage over us in maneuverability, but we've got a higher vantage point plus the miracle kid at the wheel. There's no letup in the micro's tumult of frightened weeping and enraged imprecations as we alternately gain on the taxi and lose ground to it, but it stays on this thoroughfare and its forest of camouflaging traffic, and sometimes we have the cab in view, sometimes we don't. It would have lost us easily enough but for that telltale pennant flapping above its roof.

We're coming up fast on a roundabout intersection circling a huge fountain with a statue in the center. We're four cars behind Chong as we enter the circle, and we're both in the center lane. Then the clever bastard cuts over in front of a full-size metro bus in the right lane and we lose sight of him. We have no choice but to get in the right lane too, a couple of vehicles behind the bus, because the lane offers drivers the option of exiting onto an upcoming turnoff or staying in the circle, and we have to be ready for whichever option Chong chooses. Not till the bus goes beyond the exit can we see that the taxi's turned off onto it and is whizzing toward a busy four-lane road. Then we're exiting too, passengers still screaming to be let off and some demanding to know where the hell we are, some telling each other to shut up or to fuck themselves, some still asking what's going on.

The taxi speeds down the road and then takes the first right, skidding partway into the opposing lane and forcing an oncoming car off the road and into a low ditch. Our kid makes the turn and now we're on a two-lane road running through a business zone of small stores and warehouses and garages. It's a straight road with no traffic light in sight and we're gaining on them. The kid asks in a shout what we intend to do when we catch up to it and Charlie yells back, We're gonna run his ass off the road! The kid purses his lips and arches his brow and Charlie digs out another pair of bills and tucks them in the kid's shirt pocket and the kid grins and says, goddamn right we are! Then glances in his side mirror and says, Oh mother, look behind.

We can't see out the rear window for the jam of standing passengers, so I angle over and look in the right-side mirror.

"SUVs," I tell Charlie. "Pair of them. Black. Way back but coming fast."

"Como?" says the kid, frowning at our English, his eyes fixed on the taxi.

"Cops, you think?"

"In *two* SUVs?" I say. "After us for *what?* Careless driving? Chong made a call, man."

"Como?" says the kid.

Catch the fucker! Charlie yells at him.

We're fifteen yards behind the taxi when it enters an intersection at the same time that a silver pickup truck barrels through a right-side stop sign and rams into its rear, sending the cab's bumper flying and knocking the car spinning off into the muddy lot of a lumberyard as the truck veers left and bounces over the corner curb and smashes to a stop against the side of a small grocery store, bringing down its plate glass window in a shower of shards.

The kid nimbly wheels the micro to a stop on the shoulder just past the intersection, and Charlie and I jump out and run across the road to the taxi, hands to our guns under our jackets.

The taxi driver's slumped over the steering wheel, dead or out cold. Chong's pulling himself off the floor and onto the backseat, looking stunned, one hand fumbling under his jacket. Charlie reaches in and grabs him by the collar and yanks him face-first into the door post. Chong groans and goes slack. Charlie opens the door and lets him fall out, then reaches into Chong's jacket and pulls out a Glock.

People are coming out to have a look, but at the sight of the pistol in Charlie's hand they stop short and keep their distance and some move back close to the doors.

Charlie squats beside Chong and puts the Glock muzzle to his forehead and says, Where are they?

Chong coughs, spits blood to the side, and says, Where's *who?*

The cabbie revives with a gasp and for a second gapes at me in fearful, wide-eyed confusion. Except for a knot over one eye he seems to be all right. I tell him to give me his phone and he says it was stolen while he was gassing up at a filling station this morning. If you're lying to me . . . I start to say, and he says yeah, yeah, he knows, the Chink made the same threat.

The black SUVs—Acadias with black glass—pull up behind the microbus. Charlie stands up and says in low voice, "Left one's yours." We both hold our weapon behind our leg, ready. I can't help thinking this could be it.

Two guys step out of each SUV, all of them in baseball caps, rain jackets, dungarees, dark glasses despite the overcast. But they're empty-handed except for one, who's holding a wallet. He flicks it open and raises it high for everybody around to see. "Policía Federal!" he shouts. "Quítanse de la calle! Váyanse!"

They all do as ordered and get off the street, but many of them go to the nearest window to keep watching the show.

The man comes over to us with the open wallet held out and we see a driver's license. He looks at it and says in English, "Oh shit, it's almost expired." He puts the wallet away and comes a little closer and says, "Somos Jaguaros. Tracked you on the phone GPS. I'm Tumaro." He glances at Chong, and in Spanish says, The chief told us to take him back. The interrogator's already there.

That's just wasting time, Charlie says. I can make him talk right here.

Tell you what, Tumaro tells Charlie. You question him on the way in. We got a tool kit under the seat. Pliers, box cutter, corkscrew, all kinds of persuasive stuff. He tells you anything you want to act on, we'll stop and let you have one of these vehicles and you can go your own way. How's that? No waste of time. Now let's move.

To argue the point with this guy would be futile and we know it.

Chong's eyes are *this* big after hearing about the tool kit—and maybe, too, the name "Jaguaros." Tumaro pulls him to his feet and runs a pair of flex-cuffs under his belt buckle and fastens them on his wrists, then hauls him over to one of the SUVs and puts him in the backseat. Charlie gets in with him, and Tumaro and another guy get in the front.

The other guys and I head for the other vehicle. The kid's no longer at the wheel of the micro, but the windows are jammed with faces. One of them brings a phone up to his ear and I scowl and point my forefinger at him, my thumb cocked like a pistol hammer, and he ducks below the window. The other faces look down at him and laugh.

As we head back up the road, we pass the kid driver, walking backward along the muddy shoulder with his collar turned up and his thumb out. His pockets packed with Yankee dollars. His microbus-driving career done with.

We're halfway back to the Wolfe building when the Jaguaro riding shotgun gets a phone call. He listens a minute, then says, "Muy bien, jefe," and puts up the phone. He tells the other Jaguaro and me that the call was from Tumaro up ahead, who said he'd just received a report that Mateo's been shot and is in emergency surgery. He and "la muchacha," as the Jaguaro refers to Rayo, got into a gunfight with the guy tailing Sosa. The tail's dead. Rigo's at the hospital and will join us at the Jiménez building as soon as he can.

Is the girl all right? I ask.

The Jaguaro shrugs and says, He didn't say.

33 — JESSIE

She'd meant to wait about half an hour before returning to the bathroom, but now isn't sure if it's been that long yet or much longer.

She's been picturing the bathroom window. Studying its structure in her head. Imagining how she might work her way out of it feetfirst. She can do it, she knows she can. *If* the sash can bear her weight.

Another worry is that Cabrito or Gallo might draw open the drapes. Anyone at those windows who looks to the left would be able to see her going out. But except for now and then parting the drapes just enough to check the weather, they've left them closed. Probably on the theory that the more confused their prisoners are about what time of day it is, the more tractable they are.

Her whole body aches, but to hell with it. Pain is only pain. A short while ago Luz had gently waked her from her feigned doze and asked if she was hungry. She was ravenous but didn't eat much—half a cheese sandwich, part of a small bag of corn chips, a few sips of orange soda. She feels stronger for having eaten the small bit she did, but didn't want to burden her stomach for the work ahead. Cabrito had shaken Aldo by the shoulder and asked if he wanted to eat, but Aldo only groaned and Cabrito flapped a dismissive hand at him. Luz now seems almost as downcast as Susi, and Jessie's glad of their disinclination to converse.

The food had been brought up by the dark bony woman she had seen at the kitchen door last night. After setting the sandwiches on the high table at the wall and the sodas in the Styrofoam cooler, the woman went over to the men at their card game and said something to Gallo. He made a face of irritation and went out into the hall with her, taking his hand of cards with him. As soon as Gallo was out of the room, Cabrito sneaked a look at the next few cards at the top of deck. He saw Jessie watching him and winked at her and she looked away. Then Gallo came back in and they resumed the game.

With your permission, Jessie says to Gallo in a small voice and with a look of affliction. I really have to use the toilet again. I shouldn't have eaten anything.

That reminds me of a joke, Cabrito says. There was this American woman who went into a Mexican restaurant and asked—

Never mind that, Gallo says to him, and tells Jessie to go ahead.

When the bathroom door shuts, Gallo says he'll be right back and heads for the hallway, taking his cards with him. Cabrito calls after him, Remember it's *my* play. As soon as Gallo's gone, he again peeks at the upper cards in the remaining deck and selects two of them and places them at the top. In less than a minute Gallo returns and sits down and Cabrito asks what's going on. Nothing, Gallo says, make your play. Oh, I see, Cabrito says . . . big fucking secret. Well, that's fine with me. He casts away two cards, takes two off the top of the deck and slips them into his fanned hand, says, "Woo-hoo!" and lays down the cards in a spread. Gallo says, "Carajo!" and tosses in his hand. He turns to Luz and Susi and asks them if Cabrito rearranged the deck while he was gone. The women say they weren't watching.

His face stiff with injured dignity, Cabrito says, How can you think such a thing? We're *partners,* man.

Jessie moves fast. She opens the sash and chins herself up onto the sill as before and looks out and sees that the trash bin remains in place directly below. The rain's still a drizzle but the air's colder now. She braces herself with her left arm and reaches up with her right to grip the top of the sash near its outward end, praying for the solidity of its hinges and the firmness of its wood. She pulls down hard on it, testing it. The top hinge makes a wee creak but holds.

Pulling on the sash, she raises herself a little higher, then whips her left arm up to grab the top of the window frame, a narrow projection of maybe two inches but enough for a strong fingerhold. She moves her feet up the wall, one over the other, her upper body leaning farther back and her knees bending until they're pressed to her chest and her feet are almost at the sill and she's balled up tight but for her outstretched arms holding her in place, her aching fingers clutching the top of the window frame.

She eases one foot and then the other through the window until the backs of her knees are on the sill, then works her thighs forward, her legs dangling in the cold rain, then wriggles her butt up onto the sill. It's a close fit but there's enough clearance. She moves both hands to the right side of the window frame and grips it tight, and bit by bit, with a series of grunting jerking twists, turns rightward, her hips bumping and scraping the sides of the window frame, her legs bobbing in a sidewise dangle that pains her lower back. Then her trousers snag on some rough projection of the upper frame, holding her in place, and she has a moment of panic in which she pictures the bastards coming in and finding her stuck like this and laughing at her. She keeps jerking to her right until the khaki slips loose and she's able to wrestle herself onto her abdomen, shifting her hands to either side of her waist on the sill. The sill presses hard into her belly and she has an impulse to throw up but fights it back. Her legs now hang straight down and her toes bump the wall. As she wriggles farther out the window, she feels the heavier pull of her legs. She grits her teeth as her ribs grate over the sill, and then her breasts feel like they're being skinned by it as the sweatshirt bunches up above them. Then the bunched shirt slips off the sill and for a terrifying instant she's falling—then jolts to a halt. Hanging by her arms outside the window in the misty rain.

Yes!

She puts her feet to the wall and pushes herself outward on them so she can look down between her legs and see the bin below. Even though she's closer to it now, it looks farther away than before.

Do it! she thinks—and lets go of the sill.

Her heart and stomach rise as she drops, legs together and arms straight up in effort to not hit them on the edge of the bin. Her feet drive though the mushy cardboard and the instinct of her dance training keeps her knees half-loose and she hits the bottom of the bin with a momentum that compresses her to a squat and rebounds her against the side of the bin with the bad wheel, and the bin tips over.

For a moment she lies there, burrowed in the soggy cardboard, inhaling the stink of the bin. Then she carefully tests her legs and arms and marvels that she's unhurt.

You're *out* of there! Move!

She shoves at the enveloping cardboard and crawls out of the bin, almost laughing aloud in her elation. She grins up into the gentle patter of cold rain, then gets to her feet and looks over at the back door and sees Rubio standing there, smiling at her, his hands crossed in front of him, a pistol in one.

The dark bony woman is looking at her over his shoulder. At her hip are the kids who moved the bin.

Oh God *damn*, Jessie thinks.

I would have made a very large bet that you'd break your ass and we'd have to carry you in, Rubio says. Gag you to keep the screams from irritating us too much. Go ahead and run and let's see if I can shoot you in the leg. I'm such a bad shot, though, I might hit you in the back instead. Maybe the head.

She gives a thought to running for it, but stands fast. He grins and beckons her. Slips the gun into his pants. Steps aside for her to enter.

The door is to the kitchen. As Jessie goes in, the dark woman and the kids back away. With Rubio behind her, she passes into the adjoining dining room where the squint-eyed girl sits before a bowl of pared and cored apples, seasoning them with sugar and cinnamon and watching a telenovela on the old black-and-white TV. She gives Jessie a commiserative glance.

Standing by the table is the Apache.

Well, look who's here, my favorite sweetie, he says, showing his wrecked grin. He grabs his crotch, just below the Glock tucked in his pants, and says, Would you like some more, my love?

The sight of him infuses her with such terrified hatred that her only thought is to distract and strike, as Charlie taught her. She looks off to the side of him as if at someone behind him and tilts her head at Apache, and as he starts to turn to see who's there, she steps forward and kicks at his balls with all the force she can muster.

Her unshod foot catches him only partly on the mark, and the Apache yells, *Bitch!* and grabs her by the neck with both hands and slams her down on the table, the squint-eyed girl shrieking and jumping away. He leans his weight down hard on Jessie's throat, throttling her, and she's bucking and kicking, her eyes feeling about to burst, his hands like stone under her frenzied clawings. The television and bowl of apples crash to the floor. Then Rubio has one arm around the Apache's neck and the other around his chest and is tugging him back, shouting for him to let her go, and she's dragged halfway off the table by the hands locked at her neck. When the Apache hunches forward to try to get free of Rubio, she thrusts a thumb into his eye and he screams and releases her and she slumps to the floor as he backpedals and rams Rubio into a wall, bringing down a cascade of glassware from a shelf and breaking free of his hold. The Apache stumbles forward and pulls his pistol as he turns, but Rubio pulls his sooner and fires two shuddering blasts, spattering handfuls of the man's head on the wall. The Apache falls onto the table and crumples to the floor.

Jessie pulls herself up onto a chair, breathing as though unpracticed at it, unable to swallow. The Apache lies supine, a puddle of blood widening under his head, one eye ruined by her thumb, the other obliterated by a bullet. There's a small black hole in one cheek. The girl and the woman and the two kids are gone.

Jesus Christ, someone says, and she turns to see Gallo standing there, gun in hand, staring down at Apache.

"Se volvío loco," Rubio says, and tells him what happened.

Oh, man, Gallo says. What's Espanto gonna say?

What the hell *can* he say except it's a good thing I killed this lunatic before he killed me or . . . this one here. He gestures toward Jessie without looking at her.

Lunatic, Jessie thinks. Right. And you, you bastard, *you* let that lunatic . . . do what he did.

As if he's heard her thoughts, Rubio turns and meets her eyes for a second and then looks away. He picks up the Apache's gun.

Gonna call him? Gallo asks.

Espanto? What for? He'll know soon enough.

What if *he* calls?

Yeah, sure, Rubio says. If he calls, I'll tell him.

Gallo shrugs and puts away his pistol and takes out his phone. Cabrito's holding a gun on them up there, he says, ready to shoot them. We thought maybe it was a rescue try. He touches a phone key, listens, then says, Everything's all right. . . I'll tell you when I go back up.

Well, whatever Espanto might want to do with him, Rubio says, let's have him wrapped up.

He tells Jessie that if she moves from the chair, he'll hurt her, and asks if she understands.

Yes, she says.

Say it.

I understand, she says. It pains her throat to speak, and though she can swallow again, each effort feels like a gulp of broken glass.

Fifteen minutes later the Apache's body, rolled up in a blanket and secured tightly with cord, lies neatly at the base of a living room wall, only his shod feet exposed. As she watched them roll him up, her chief feeling was regret that she wasn't the one who shot him. The squint-eyed girl and the bony woman, having returned from wherever they'd fled, are cleaning the kitchen floor. The broken TV has been removed.

Rubio takes Jessie back upstairs. Cabrito gives her a small smile and says, The daredevil, once again. Never surrender, eh?

José lies on his side, looking at her, but shuts his eyes when she looks back. There's an odor of urine and she suspects the boy has wet himself rather than ask to go to the bathroom and have somebody hold his dick.

Luz and Susi gawk at her as if she's a stranger.

IV

34 — RUDY AND CHARLIE

When we get to the Wolfe building's garage and Charlie pulls him out of the Acadia, Chong is distinctly worse for wear than when he was put in it. His bloody grimace shows a gap where his two top front teeth had been, a segment of one yet rooted to the gum. His hands are still cuffed to his belt, but now one thumb's swollen purple and visibly out of joint, and he walks in the manner of a man with acute testicular distress. Charlie's not one for torture, so it speaks to the size of his desperation about Jessie that he was able to do this to the guy.

Before I can ask, Charlie tells me there's been no further word about Mateo. Tumaro's still in the car and on the phone, trying to get an update on him, and the other three Jaguaros are off to the side, smoking and chatting. We hold Chong between us while we wait for Tumaro at the basement elevator. Charlie tells me he's been extremely forthcoming. His name is Benito Yuan but his fellows call him—big surprise—Chino. Besides ratifying what we already knew, he's told Charlie that the kidnappers are a small gang named Los Doce and that Mr. X is a guy called Galán, the only name Chino knows him by. Tumaro and the other Jaguaro in the Acadia had never heard of either Los Doce or Galán. According to Chino, Huerta was the only one of the security crew who was in on the snatch, but right after the snatch the gang got rid of him and all seven of his company's agents. I raise my brow at that, and Charlie nods and says, "That's right, cuz. Huerta could identify this Mr. X Galán guy, who didn't trust him. And even though the other security agents weren't in on the job, they found out that Huerta was, so . . . pop-pop-pop, problem disposed of. These dudes may be small time, Rudy Max, but they are not fucking around."

After shadowing Belmonte to the bank and then back to his estate, Chino was going to meet up with the Sosa tail—somebody named Chato—at a café in a little plaza on the route to the ransom sites. A few minutes after four, Galán's segundo, a guy called Espanto, is supposed to call Chino to let him know Belmonte's on his way to the first hold house with the money. When Belmonte passes by the plaza, Chino is to shadow him over there, keeping an eye out for other tails. Espanto will be at the hold house to receive the money and will then call Sosa and tell him where to take the other half of the ransom. Then he'll call Chato to get ready to tail Sosa there.

"Saddened this old boy," Charlie says, patting Chino on the shoulder, "when Tumaro told us the Chato guy was no longer among the living."

Chino has sworn, however, that he doesn't know where either of the hold houses is, and that neither did the Chato guy. He knows that both places are somewhere in the west-side slums and that the plaza is on the way to both of them, but he wouldn't know where Belmonte was taking the money until Belmonte led him there. It's the way Galán wanted it. He figured that the guys tailing the ransom carriers were the ones most liable to be caught if the cops got involved, and you can't tell the cops what you don't know. Chino claims he and Chato don't even have a phone connection with anybody else in the gang except Espanto, and they're under order not to call him except in an emergency.

Charlie thinks he's lying but I don't. I can't believe the dude would choose to undergo the sort of interrogation he knows he's in for rather than tell us the truth. The guy's a bandit, not some idealistic revolutionary or freedom fighter willing to suffer for cause and comrades. Still, Charlie's calling the shots.

Tumaro finishes with his call and comes over and says Mateo's still critical and Rigo will be here soon.

And Rayo? I ask, trying to keep it casual, but he catches something in my tone and fixes me with a look. *Rayo?* he says. The *girl?* The girl is unharmed. In fact, buddy, she's the one who killed the Sosa tail. You better be real careful about making a move on *her*, man. He and Charlie trade a grin, then laugh when I give them the old hand-to-bicep "fuck you" gesture.

Tumaro uses a card key to open the elevator door and we ride down to a huge basement. Its walls are stacked with crates and cartons, the ceiling's lined with pipes and ducts.

We go to a room at the far end. Waiting for us in there is the interrogator—a dwarf whom Tumaro introduces as Rosaldo. He's puffing a cigar and returns our nods of greeting. This is the first dwarf I've ever seen close up, and in contrast to the rest of him his normal-sized head looks enormous. His features are grimly Indian. He's taken off his suit jacket and rolled his sleeves and wears a black plastic garbage bag in poncho fashion, with holes cut in it for his head and his runty arms. He's got those bag things on his feet like hospital workers wear. A neat operator. Doesn't want blood or whatever else on his clothes or shoes. Besides a coat rack and a couple of foldout chairs next to it, the only other pieces of furniture are a narrow metal table like the kind used for embalming—except this one's equipped with hold-down straps for arms and legs and head—and the table-side platform on which the dwarf is standing, plus an elevated side table holding an open satchel whose top tray holds an array of gleaming metal instruments, some spear shaped, some curved, some corkscrewed. All very sharp looking.

The dwarf flicks ashes on the floor and blows on the cigar's lit end, inspiring a bright glow. He gives Chino a smile devoid of everything a smile is supposed to convey. Prepare him, he says, his voice deep. I'd be lying if I said the son of a bitch didn't scare *me* a little.

Two guys hold Chino tight and Tumaro starts stripping him.

I told you the *truuuth!* Chino screeches, addressing Charlie, the dwarf, everybody. I *swear* it, for the love of God! I *swear* on my mother's head!

They strap him naked to the table. He's screaming he doesn't know where the captives are, that he'd tell us if he knew.

"This is bullshit," I tell Charlie. "I'm outta here."

He doesn't look at me as I leave.

I know how he feels. If there's any chance at all the guy knows where Jessie is, Charlie has to use whatever means necessary to get it out of him. If I thought there was the slightest possibility Chino was lying, I'd be in favor of siccing the dwarf on him too. But I don't believe anybody can fake the kind of terror I saw in his eyes. Charlie would see that too if he wasn't half-crazed with his own fear for Jessie.

I go back up to the elevator bank in the garage and see Chino's green Focus parked close by. A guy's leaning on the front fender and leafing through what looks like an oversized comic book. He tells me they tossed the car and didn't find a thing of interest—no phone, no receipts, notes, nothing. Except for the book, he says, which I see is a graphic novel about Pancho Villa.

I'd hoped Rigo would be there by now but the suite's deserted when I get up there. I pour coffee and sit on the couch and watch the pulsing map colors on the soundless TV weather show. The bright emerald green of rain still dominates the screen. I take out my phone, thinking of calling Rayo, but find the battery's just about totally drained.

Not ten minutes later Charlie comes in, looking a touch hangdog, not a face you'll often see on him. He sits down and tells me he put a stop to it before the dwarf could get started. Chino's still down there but the dwarf's gone.

"You were right," he says. "He doesn't know where the hold houses are. He would've said so. He would've done anything to stop what the dwarf was about to do. You wouldn't believe what he was about to do."

"Yeah, I would," I say, and check my watch. "Tick tock, man. What are *we* gonna do?"

Our fallback hope has been that Rigo's supposition is correct, and even if we can't get to Jessie before the ransom's paid, the snatchers will let everyone go when they get the money. If that happens, we'll be glad to feel like fools for all our frantic and failed effort. But I know Charlie's thinking the same thing I am. This bunch has already killed eight guys—one of them a partner—to reduce the odds of being identified. That doesn't bode real well for the captives' release. No matter how we cut it, we now know we're not going to find Jessie before the first payoff. We don't know where the hold houses are and she could be at either one. Even if they plan to kill the captives, though, it's a fairly safe bet they'll keep the first group alive as security until the second ransom's made, and then do them all at once. All we can do is follow Belmonte to the first hold house and find out if Jessie's there. If she is, we try to get her out while the second payoff's on its way. If she's not at the first place, then the Jaguaro who tails Sosa to the second hold house can give us directions as he's on the way and we'll go there too—with no idea if we can get there ahead of the money or, even if we do, what the hell we'll do then.

"There's another hitch," Charlie says. "Chino's guys are going to call him when Belmonte heads out with the money and tell him to get ready to tail. When they do, they either won't get a response or our schoolboy pal will answer the phone. Christ, they might've already called Chino for some reason, and if they have, they're spooked. They'll have to assume that somebody's on to them, and so they'll want to keep the whereabouts of the hostages secret. They'll have Belmonte take the money somewhere else. We'll be tailing a dead end."

As he's telling me all this, I remember Chino's phone. I take it out and check a couple of items on it, then pass it to Charlie. "Courtesy of our schoolboy pal."

"*This* the phone the kid took?"

"The very one. Slipped it to me when we took off after Chino."

He grins at it. "You know what? We should've hired the little bastard. Take him back to Texas."

I tell him there's nothing on its phone mail. I just checked. And no calls on the log since Belmonte left the bank. A half dozen calls before that, all outgoing, all to the same number. No calls that could've spooked them.

"Unless they've tried to call the other one, the Chato guy," Charlie says.

I think about that a second. "No, they haven't called him, either," I say. "If they had and didn't get an answer, they would've—"

"Called Chino, you're right," he says. "But his phone doesn't show a record of it. We're cool there. So far, anyway."

We figure the thing to do is take Chino to the café with us and have him answer the phone when his guy calls. Play it like all is well, keep the Doce guys from spooking—if they haven't been spooked by something else by then. When Belmonte comes by the plaza, we tail him in the Focus. Chino's guys probably know the car, and that might give us an edge of some kind. Or not.

It's a sorry-ass plan and we know it, but the hour's late and the clock's ticking and it's the best we can come up with.

We've just decided all this when Rigo and Rayo arrive. Rigo tells us Mateo's in critical condition but in an excellent hospital endowed by the Wolfe family. There's blood on Rayo's jacket and she sees me staring at it and says it's Mateo's. In her quick but thorough way she recounts the chase out on the hills and the gunfight that put two bullets in Mateo's stomach and one in his leg. When she tells of shooting the guy and then tending Mateo as well as she could until help came, her expression is much like the one she had after backflipping off the palm tree trunk. There's a certain pride in it. I guess my own face is showing more than I realize, because when she looks at me she cuts her eyes away and it's the first hint of blush I've ever seen on her.

Charlie and Rigo either don't catch it or choose to ignore it.

Charlie gives them a summary account of our capture of Chino and what we've learned from him. Rigo agrees the only thing we can do is tail Belmonte, and he approves of how we intend to do it. But because Galán just might, for whatever reason, have Belmonte take the money somewhere else or have him go to the hold house by a different route, Rigo will have somebody follow Belmonte as soon as he leaves his house.

If Belmonte goes a different way than the plaza route, the tail can let us know and put us on to him.

I'll do it, Rayo says. Then gives Rigo an abashed look and says, I mean . . . I'd like to have the job, Uncle, if you think I can handle it.

For a few long seconds, Rigo just stares at her. I have to think he's considering how she's proved herself today. Maybe saved his little brother's life.

Very well, he says. And you'll do *exactly* as these two tell you.

She lights up. "Yes, of course," she says. "Claro que sí."

Rigo also wants to have a crew of Jaguaros in another vehicle tracking us on a GPS and a parallel route, but Charlie nixes the idea.

"We'll have two vehicles tailing and that's enough," Charlie says. "Any more than that just increases the odds of getting spotted. Chino said there's four guys at the hold house, plus the Espanto guy who's going to collect the money. Rudy and I"—he cuts a look at Rayo—"the three of us can handle five."

Rigo doesn't like it. He says Charlie's being foolish not using more men.

"Look, cousin," Charlie says. "If it goes to hell and . . . they kill her, I don't want to be blaming you guys for any part of it."

"Charlie, for Christ's sake," Rigo says.

"It has to be on *us*," Charlie says.

"And me," Rayo says. "She's my sister."

We look at her.

"Practically," she says.

Rigo expels a hard breath and flicks up his hands in resignation. "Okay, Charlie, whatever you wish," he says. "Jessica's from your side of the house. It's your decision."

By twenty after three, we're at a back table in the Cuates Locos Café, Chino seated between me and Charlie and carefully spooning tepid chicken soup into his broken-toothed mouth, his grip on the spoon awkward for his busted thumb. His phone is on the table. The Focus is parked out front, a roll of duct tape in the console between the front seats, Chino's Glock under the driver's seat. Never hurts to have a spare weapon.

We've instructed Chino in his responses to questions he thinks he might get asked when the call comes, and have impressed on him the necessity of keeping cool. Charlie has promised him that if he botches things in any way, the last person he'll see in this world is the dwarf.

At a small park two blocks over from Belmonte's street, Rayo's in the brown Jeep SUV Charlie and I used earlier, waiting for the surveillance guys to let her know when Belmonte leaves the house.

35 — ESPANTO

On this afternoon of persistent drizzle, there are but a handful of other patrons in the Casa Toltec, all of them seated at a distance from him. It will get dark very early. That the day has passed so slowly and seemed almost boring is testament, Espanto reflects, to how well everything has proceeded. He has received no calls from Chato or Chino since their reports that the money had left the banks, and no calls of concern or complaint from either of the hold houses since the locksmith's arrival at the Beta site. He had thought to call Barbarosa to see what they'd found out about the stink, but decided against it. Whatever it was, it was sure to be something that could not be remedied today, and there was no need to aggravate Barbarosa with another call about it.

Just a short while ago he spoke with El Galán, who was pleased that the phones have been so idle all afternoon. In less than an hour Belmonte will call Galán to get his instructions for making the first ransom delivery, and the operation will accelerate into its final phase. Three hours from now the whole business will be done with and Los Doce will be celebrating their biggest payday ever and by far—and raising their glasses to their imminent admission to the Zeta organization. Until a few weeks ago Espanto had never envisioned himself rising so high. Not bad, he thinks, for a kid from the east-side barrios.

It's nearly time to depart for the Alpha house. When Belmonte gets there with the first payoff, Espanto will dismiss Rubio and Cabrito to go join Galán at El Nido. Gallo and Apache will remain with Belmonte and the Alpha captives while Espanto goes to the Beta house to await Sosa's delivery of the rest of the money. Once he gets it, he will call Gallo and they will cuff and blindfold both groups, drive them both to the Alameda park, help them out of the vehicles, and leave them to the assistance of the first passersby inclined to offer it.

And that, as they say, will be that.

He has paid his bill and as always tipped Betina liberally, and she winks at him from her stool at the kitchen entrance where she and another waitress are watching the TV news. He puts the audio receiver/recorder and the ear buds in the laptop's carrying satchel, then turns off the laptop and closes it and puts it in the satchel too. His phone goes into his inside jacket pocket, opposite the shoulder-holstered Glock. As he gets up and hangs the satchel on his shoulder, Betina says, Oh, my dear God. She's staring at the TV, on which a small crowd of onlookers is standing aside to give the camera a clear shot of a blackened ragged corpse in a muddy street. The camera then moves past a police car and a pair of fire department water tankers and pans up and down the block, showing damaged roofs and vehicles.

He recognizes the neighborhood.

That poor barrio, Betina says to no one in particular.

Espanto moves closer to better hear the audio. The camera is now on a young woman reporter questioning a uniformed police officer. A razed structure is visible behind them, its smoldering ruins reduced to the foundation but for a small low portion of wall. Espanto comprehends that he's looking at what's left of the Beta house.

The cop is saying that the cause of the explosion appears to have been a drug laboratory operated by a gang of young thugs who, according to neighbors, came and went at all hours. No, he says, there were no survivors. He doubts any of the remains can be identified, but who cares? Punks are punks, he says, all of them the same. The curse of Mexico.

The camera moves in for a close-up of the reporter as she solemnly intones that it's one more tragic instance of young criminals trying to get rich fast but only making a fast trip to a pauper's grave.

Espanto hastens out to the Sierra pickup in the rear parking lot and calls Barbarosa. A recording informs him that the subscriber is no longer on the network. He calls Flaco and gets the same message, and then the same thing for Cisco's number. He had hoped at least one of them might have been out of the house when it blew up, although if that had been so, the survivor would have called him by now. So would anybody else in Los Doce who'd heard about this. Should he call Chino? Chato? What for? It would only distract them for no purpose. First see what Galán wants to do.

36 — GALÁN AND ESPANTO AND RUBIO

Business is also scant at El Nido on this somber afternoon. Other than Galán at his table at the rear of the room, the only patrons are an old man at the counter, nearly asleep over his coffee, and a young couple with eyes and ears for only each other at a table across the room.

Galán has just finished reading a magazine article about Baja California, replete with stunning photographs of the beauty of both of its coasts. He has never been there but is enthralled with the region. All that he's heard about it, all the pictures he's seen, the travel programs on television, have made him believe it may be the place for him. Exceptionally attractive to him is the area around Loreto, on the Gulf side of the peninsula. He has decided to fly there next week, rent a car, drive around for a few days, and see what he thinks. Talk to some realtors.

He's surprised by the phone's quiver in his jacket. Belmonte is not due to call him for about forty minutes yet, a call he intends to receive in the privacy of the silver Cherokee in the parking lot. He sees that the caller is Espanto, with whom he spoke not an hour ago.

"Dígame," he says into the phone. Then says, No, I have not. Tell me.

As he listens, he glances at the television mounted on the opposite wall, its screen dark. It is rarely turned on except for soccer and boxing matches.

When Espanto has told it all, Galán says, I see. Hold on a minute.

He considers the incalculable turns of fortune at play in the world—like a secret meth lab in the basement of your hold house blowing up and killing three of your men and half of your hostages. It's the stuff of endless platitudes reminding us that you can't plan for everything, anything can happen, you never know, blah-blah-blah. But as another saying has it, what's done is done, and he turns his mind to the immediate problem.... When Belmonte and Sosa don't receive the Beta captives, they'll assume the worst and go to the police. They'll no longer have reason not to. Given the families' social standing and the disappearance of five of the kidnap victims, the police will give greater attention and faster action to this case than they give to most. What's more, because the ransomed group of captives was held in a hold house in the western slums, the cops might wonder about the multiple deaths reported in an explosion on the same day in another slum on the same side of the city. They might perform forensic exams they would normally not trouble themselves with. They'll identify the missing captives and charge their abductors with their killing. Details of no import with regard to a kidnapping in which nobody's hurt can matter very much in a murder case. The Alpha group knows what they look like. It's possible they have overheard things that might be of help to the police. All of them would testify.

Unless they can't.

All right, listen, he tells Espanto. We'll proceed as planned, except that I'll call Belmonte and tell him to take the entire ransom to the Alpha house. I'll tell him everyone at both houses will be released on its delivery, though of course we can't do that, not now.

I agree, Espanto says. What of Sosa and the wives?

They know nothing of consequence. We can leave them to mourn.

Understood, Espanto says, and starts up the Sierra.

When I let you know Belmonte's on the way, have both Chino and Chato follow him, Galán says. Let Rubio know you're coming but don't tell him of the changes. You and I will attend to that.

You're going?

I won't place on you or the others the burden of what must be done. But I want everyone there when I arrive, so I'll wait along the route till Chino and Chato pass by and then fall in behind them.

Very well, chief, see you there, Espanto says, wheeling out of the parking lot.

Galán has no concern that the police might want to question Jorge Envordo, the owner of record of the Alpha house. Jorge Envordo does not exist. Galán bought the house for a pittance under that name expressly for use in this operation. And just in case they might have to do what now must be done.

Espanto phones Rubio to say he's en route, and asks if all is in order.

Rubio hesitates. Well . . .

What? says Espanto.

The Apache. He went crazy. Tried to strangle the American girl. I tried to stop him but he went for a gun and I had to shoot him. He's dead. We packed him up and he's ready for riddance wherever. And listen, man, before *that*, he pounded one of the wedding guys and he's practically in a coma. I'm telling you God's truth. The fucker went crazy. Gallo and Cabrito can tell you. He was—

All right, Espanto says, recalling his uneasy intuition about the Apache. I can believe it. You did what you had to. I'll be there soon.

Rubio is relieved. As well as a little puzzled.

Espanto did not ask if the girl had been hurt bad. Nor seemed upset about the unconscious guy.

What the hell. . . . Good.

37 — GALÁN

Galán is on the beltway when he phones Belmonte, whose fearful surprise at receiving the early call is evinced in his voice. But he is elated to learn that Mr. X is so pleased with how ably he and Sosa have carried out his instructions that he sees no need to prolong the process and has decided to accept the full ransom in a single payment and free all the captives on its receipt. Galán tells him to go to the payoff site alone and that he will be followed all the way there. He is to take the Cadillac, which will make him easier to keep in sight.

The instructions he gives Belmonte are few and simple, so too the directions to the hold house. Should you at any point get confused, Galán says, call me on the special phone.

Belmonte thanks him, but says the directions are not complicated and he's certain he will have no trouble finding the house.

Very good, Galán says. Go now, and drive carefully. It's getting dark.

He then calls Espanto to tell him Belmonte is on the way and gives him one further instruction.

38 — RUDY AND CHARLIE

Chino's phone buzzes on the table. The three of us swap looks. It's a little early for the call Chino expects.

Charlie gestures for him to answer it and says, Don't fuck up.

Chino holds the instrument so that Charlie can have his ear at it too. "Dígame," he says, and listens. Then says, Yes he is. He got here before me. He listens again, and says, Yes, sure, Espanto, I understand, me and Chato *both*. . . . Yes. Yes, we'll get ready right now. . . . What? . . . He gives Charlie a sidewise look and says, I sound like that because I've got a fucking cold. Been coming on since yesterday and now the damn thing—

He listens. Yes, all right, he says. See you there.

He presses the Off button and Charlie takes the phone from him and puts it in his pocket, saying, Well done, my little friend.

He tells me Belmonte's already on the way and that both Chino and Chato are to tail him, but the Espanto guy didn't explain why they had made that change in plan.

39 — JESSIE

She senses a higher tension among the captors, a keener excitement. Cabrito is now armed. He left the room for a few minutes and when he returned he was carrying a pistol in a shoulder holster, a Glock like his pals. Gallo is pacing along the windowed wall, periodically pushing a drape aside for a peek out.

They all hear the arrival of a vehicle in the alley below. Gallo parts the drape a little. "Aquí' 'stá Espanto," he says.

Espanto. Jessie recalls the name. He's the guy whose reaction to the Apache's death Gallo was concerned about. Must be the head man.

Is it the ransom? Luz asks.

Keep quiet, Gallo says.

José sits up and puts his feet on the floor but looks at no one.

Minutes pass. Jessie supposes the Espanto guy's getting an earful from Rubio about the Apache. Maybe about her, too.

Now there are footsteps in the hallway, and then the two men enter the room. The Espanto one carries himself like an athlete. Brush mustache, short-spiked hair. Hard-faced handsome.

He goes over to Aldo and tweaks his ear between his index finger and thumb. Aldo whines softly and his face pinches in pain but he doesn't awaken.

You see? Rubio says. That's how it's been. He reacts but he doesn't come to.

Espanto sniffs the air and looks at José. "Ay, chico," he says. Have you no shame?

The boy keeps his eyes on his own feet.

Espanto looks at the women. And holds his stare on Jessie. He goes to her cot and smiles down at her.

You are Jessica? he says, the *j* sounding almost like *y*.

Yes, she says. It's no surprise he knows her name but it unnerves her to hear him say it.

He gestures toward Rubio and says, My associate tells me you are an escape artist. Maybe we should call you Houdini. No . . . Houdina.

I don't think so, Jessie says. I'm obviously not as good as he was. Jesus, girl, she thinks, *shut up!*

Yes, well, maybe with more practice. Only, no more practice with us, eh?

No, she says.

He winks at her. Then says, Listen, everyone, your stay with us is almost over. Just be patient a little longer. Think of the many good things awaiting you in your lives. However, for the brief remainder of your time with us, you ladies must be handcuffed once again. I apologize for the discomfort.

Rubio produces flex-cuffs from his jacket and cuffs all three of the women, hands in front. Espanto goes to the door and gathers the men about him and speaks to them in a whisper. Then he and Rubio and Gallo depart, leaving Cabrito to watch the captives.

Cabrito seats himself by the lamp and takes his pistol from its holster and holds it on his lap.

You must stay on your cots, he says, or I must shoot you. Those are my orders.

He is not smiling.

40 — BELMONTE

He makes his way west through an expanse of mini ranch estates set in rolling hills. A light wind slings wispy rain across the road. He has not traveled this route before, and he marvels at this stretch of pastoral terrain so near the central city. Ahead of him on the winding road is a silver Porsche coupe, and at wide intervals behind him a couple of light-colored sedans and a dark sport utility vehicle of some sort. Though he was told he would be followed, he has no interest in which vehicle might be his shadow. He will very soon be trading the money in the car trunk for his sons and his nephew. Nothing else matters.

The road debouches from the hills into a dingy business district, merging with a broad westward avenue marked by traffic lights at every intersection. He comes to an intersection dominated by a cut-rate shopping plaza with a street-side billboard listing its resident businesses, including the Cuates Locos Café. Two lights beyond the plaza is a block of warehouses, and he circles it as Galán had instructed—an instruction whose purpose he did not understand but did not question, and that Galán had not explained was to make it simpler for the men following him to spot any other tails. Belmonte is unmindful of the green car that tracks him all the way around the block, or, on his return to the main avenue, of the brown Jeep SUV that pulls out of a corner gas station and melds into traffic behind the Focus. Two blocks farther on, he turns south on a four-lane road that will take him most of the remaining way to the neighborhood of the payoff site.

41 — GALÁN

Parked near an exit of a small lot fronting a row of weathered stores along the southbound road, Galán sees Belmonte's yellow Cadillac go by. And a few seconds later, Chino's green Focus.

With three men in it.

He catches only a glimpse of them but notes that two are in the front seats, one in the back. Gunning the Cherokee to the lot exit, he thinks that maybe it wasn't Chino's car, but as he idles at the exit in wait of a break in the passing traffic, he doesn't spot another green Focus. An opening presents itself and he wheels into the right lane.

Why a third guy? *Who?* If some exigency has required this change in plan, he's irked that Espanto hasn't apprised him of it. But maybe Espanto doesn't know about it either. Maybe Chino and Chato are acting on their own initiative for some good reason, and for some equally good reason haven't told Espanto yet. Maybe.

He gets out his phone but refrains from calling Espanto before he gets a closer look at the men in the Focus. He jockeys his way up the two southbound lanes. Luck is with him and he makes it through every green light the Focus does. He has caught up to Chino's car when they are both stopped by a red light, Galán in the right lane, the Focus in the left, and he puts on a pair of plain-glass spectacles, a simple but effective guise. There is yet enough light for him to distinguish between the three hatless men in the car. Chino is in the front passenger seat, bent forward as if tying a shoelace, but he doesn't straighten up and is obviously affixed in that position. Chato is not among them. The other two men are strangers to him. White guys. There are of course a great many Mexican Caucasians in the capital and on the city and federal police forces, but Galán is very familiar with Mexican cops and can spot one at a distance, and neither of these men has the manner or mien of them. They're Americans. The bearded one in the back looks his way, but Galán is holding the phone to his ear and feigning anger, working his mouth as if in shouts and making broad hand gestures, a bespectacled businessman consumed with his own troubles and not in the least interested in the immediate world around him.

Gringo cops? he wonders. Private operatives? Why would they . . . ?

The American girl . . . why else? Her rich relatives here in the capital. Family named Wolfe. He recalls file information—American lineage, society people, philanthropists, financial interests in all sorts of ventures. How would they know she'd been taken? . . . Sosa? The rich trust nobody, especially each other. Maybe Sosa didn't trust the Americans to reimburse him for their girl's ransom after the fact. Maybe he told them of the snatch and demanded her half-million-dollar share beforehand, and maybe they paid him—why would they not?—but maybe, too, somebody among them decided to send these hirelings to do whatever they could to retrieve her, and while they were at it, maybe recover their money too. Could they be that stupid? Maybe so.

Maybe, maybe, maybe . . . what does *maybe* matter? They're here.

The light turns green. He keeps to the right lane, letting the Focus get a few cars ahead as he phones Espanto and advises him of the gringos and tells him what to do. Then places the phone in the console.

As the last of the twilight fades, the road narrows to two lanes of inferior grade, and then there are no more stoplights. There are two vehicles between him and the Focus—the forward one a small brown SUV, the other an old sedan emitting so much exhaust smoke that Galán can catch only sporadic glimpses of the vehicles ahead of it. Still, the heap is maintaining a constant distance from the others, so there is no need to pass it and risk attracting the gringos' notice.

His rearview vision, on the other hand, is quite clear. There's no one on the dark road behind him. Only a looming black sky.

42 — JESSIE

Rubio comes into the room, aspect intense.

You, he says, pointing at Jessie. Come with me.

She exchanges fearful glances with Luz and Susi, catches José's morose stare.

"Ándale, muchacha!" Rubio says, beckoning her sharply.

She goes to him and he takes her by the arm and steers her out into the hall and down the stairs.

Espanto is seated at the near end of the dining table. Rubio seats her at the other end, next to the kitchen door, leaving the flex-cuffs on her, then nods at Espanto and goes out the front door. Gallo is not present. Except for the blanket-wrapped Apache on the living room floor, there is no one else down here.

Why am I—she starts to ask, but Espanto silences her with a finger to his lips.

He consults his watch. He examines his fingernails. He hums a tune unfamiliar to her. Each time he looks at her, she cannot stop herself from turning away.

In the deep shadows of the building across the street, standing behind a chest-high stack of empty produce crates, shivering in the cold and watching for Chino's Focus and the two gringos Espanto said are in it, Gallo sees Rubio come out of the house and hide himself between the Durango and the Suburban parked end to end at the front edge of the yard.

43 — BELMONTE

Where the southbound road begins curving to the east, there is a connecting westward road on his right, and he turns onto it as Galán directed. A truck that has been trailing him makes the turn too, visible only as a pair of headlights in the risen night. That's my follower, he thinks. The rain wafts across the road in misty webs. The westward sky ahead reflects a low orange glow that on this gloomy eve can only be from one of the garbage pits Belmonte has read about. Where the fires are said never to cease burning, not even in the rain.

It is a narrow road of fractured asphalt running through low woodland and alongside a rail track flanked by abandoned warehouses and collapsed loading platforms. Here and there, junction lanes lead to clusters of small buildings visible among the trees in the glow of trash-barrel fires. He enters a wide curve and is halfway into it when a scattering of hazy streetlights comes in view not a mile ahead. The hold house neighborhood.

The road becomes the neighborhood main street, a narrow thoroughfare badly pocked and rutted, and he is forced to go slower. The street is flanked by long blocks of buckled sidewalks and run-down two-story buildings, some of their windows showing dim light. At random intervals stand decayed houses fronted with ragged trees and dirt yards. Decrepit vehicles are parked along the sidewalks, in weedy lots, in the alleys. There are few people in sight, and most of them disappear into doorways or alley shadows at his approach. He's been paying little heed to his mirrors and is surprised when he sees the pickup no longer there. Not his follower, after all.

He goes several more blocks before he sees the vaporous green lights of Chula's cantina to his right at the intersection ahead. Exactly as Mr. X described. The next street is the one—long and weakly illuminated by a far corner streetlight haloed in amber. He crosses the intersection and slows even more. Halfway down the block and on the left, an SUV and a Suburban are parked one behind the other at the side of the street. A man steps out from between the vehicles, one hand hidden behind his leg, and indicates for Belmonte to turn into the short driveway next to the SUV. As his headlights sweep over to the driveway, Belmonte sees that the man is fair-haired and clean-shaven, that junk cars jam the yard.

Adhering to Mr. X's instructions, Belmonte opens the trunk with the interior switch and turns off the engine, then gets out and hurries around to the rear of the car, the light rain cold on his face. The blond man is already there and hanging a bag of money on each shoulder. Belmonte takes up the other two bags and the man shuts the trunk and shoves him toward the dark front porch, saying, Inside, *go!*

44 — RUDY AND CHARLIE

The old pickup between us and Belmonte follows him west off the southbound road, twenty-five or thirty yards behind him. We're staying the same distance from the truck, and Rayo's about half that far behind us. We're keeping open-phone contact with her, and she reports that there are two vehicles fifty or sixty yards back of her. Some old junker trailing a cloud of heavy smoke just ahead of something larger. There's no traffic at all coming from the other way.

We've got Chino cuffed to the seat frame, which forces him to sit bent way forward and a little to his left. Now Charlie gags and blindfolds him with duct tape. Not real comfy for the dude but it works for us.

We're a block behind the pickup and two behind the Caddy when we enter the derelict neighborhood. The truck soon turns off, but we hold our distance from Belmonte. Rayo moves up closer to us and reports that the smoky car is three blocks back of her. Here and there we spot a lone car or truck plodding along, but otherwise there's an eerie dearth of traffic, even for a rainy night.

A few streets farther on, Belmonte passes a corner place with a sign bordered in misty green lights and he slows down on the next street. We're still more than a block from the green-sign intersection when we see a guy step out into Belmonte's headlights, and the Caddy stops. Then it turns off the street and out of our sight.

"That's it!" Charlie says. "Hang a left *here*."

I do it, and Rayo follows us down a darker beat-up street, the buildings here smaller and set even closer to each other. Charlie has me take a right at the first corner and then go right again at the next one, which brings us back toward the intersection with the green-sign place. I switch off the headlights and slow down. Charlie figures they'll have a lookout posted, so we'll leave the cars at the corner up ahead and go down the hold house street on foot. Sneak our way up to wherever the Caddy is, try to spot the lookout before he spots us, take him out quiet. If he sees us first, well . . . we'll play it as it comes.

It seems awfully catch-as-catch-can to me. But that's pretty much been our planning style and I don't have anything better to suggest.

As we advance slowly toward the corner, we spot an alleyway on our left and Charlie says, "Stop!" I hit the brakes and Chino bonks his head on the dash and the Jeep's tires scrunch behind us as Rayo stops just short of hitting us.

"Jesus, guys!" she says, her voice coming from Charlie's phone in the console.

A white late-model pickup with a camper shell mounted on the bed is parked halfway down the alley in the hazy glow of a distant lamppost. One of those big GMC Sierras.

"In this neighborhood, it's gotta be theirs," I say.

"And *that's* the house, right there," Charlie says. "One-two-three-four, fifth one down."

He has me move up closer to the corner and next to the building and shut off the engine, then takes up the phone and tells Rayo to park the Jeep in the alley to block the Sierra, then position herself back here on the street.

"Got it," she says, and wheels into the alleyway.

She's back in a jiff and gets behind the end of the alley wall. "Now what?" she says out of Charlie's phone.

"We're going around to the front, you're covering the rear," Charlie tells her. "Stay out here and stay low. Anybody but us or Jess comes out the back, be ready to pop them."

"Okay," she says.

Up at the intersection, the smoky clunker that had been behind her makes a right turn and heads away from us, lost in its own smoke. Then a silver Cherokee crosses to the hold house block.

"Another one, you think?" I say.

"Maybe the guy who's come to collect," Charlie says. "The Espanto dude." He continues staring at the intersection, and I know what he's thinking. We're *here*, and hope Jessie is, too. But if they intend to let her go, then we're doing the worst thing possible. Then again, we're here because we don't trust them to let her go. We have to act. And if it goes to hell . . . we'll have to live with it.

"Let's do it," Charlie says.

I pat Chino on the head and say, Don't go anywhere, buddy, you hear?

We get out of the car and check the Berettas for chamber rounds, then head up to the corner in the murky drizzle, moving fast and keeping to the deeper shadows. It's gotten colder.

45 — JESSIE

She still has no notion of why they've brought her down here, and her dread enlarges by the minute.

There's the sound of a car pulling into the driveway and a brief flash of its lights against the living room window drape. A moment later, Belmonte and Rubio come rushing through the front door, large bulging bags hung on their shoulders. Espanto directs them to put them on the dining table.

Belmonte gawks at her in recognition. They have spoken only once, for maybe a minute, when Luz introduced them at the wedding rehearsal. He looks as if he wants to say something to her but has no idea what. His attempt at a smile is pathetic.

Stand over there, Espanto tells him, indicating the hallway entrance.

Belmonte does it. If he's noticed the carpet-wrapped body in the living room, he shows no sign of it. I have brought all of the ransom as Mr. X said to do, he says. I have done everything exactly as—

Be silent, sir, Espanto says.

All the ransom? Jessie's puzzled. Luz said Rubio told them half the money would be paid here and the rest at the other hold house.

Espanto unzips a bag and digs a hand into it, pulls out a packet of bills and riffles them, then replaces the money. Rubio zips up the bag and shoulders it while Espanto checks another one, then Rubio picks up that one too and goes through the kitchen and out the back door while Espanto checks the last two bags. Then Rubio comes back and gets them and takes them out too.

Espanto checks his watch and smiles at Belmonte. You are no doubt eager to see your people, he says.

Yes, yes, Belmonte says. Please.

They are upstairs in fine spirits and will be delighted to see you, Espanto says. Needless to say, they are quite ready to leave. We'll go to them in a minute.

Jessie can't suppress her excitement. Does he mean it? Are they all going to be released?

A vehicle door slams shut in the alley and Rubio returns and stands at the kitchen entrance, within easy reach of her.

This way, sir, Espanto says to Belmonte, gesturing for him to precede him into the hallway. As Espanto starts to follow, Jessie sees him take something out of his coat pocket and hold it behind his leg. A blade appears from it like magic.

They go in the hall and she hears a grunt. A low groan. A heavy thump.

Her fear returns like a hand at her throat.

Espanto comes back from the hall, adjusting his jacket. There's the sound of another vehicle arriving in front of the house.

Rubio takes out his pistol and goes to the window next to the door. He fingers the curtain aside a bit. "Ya llegó Galán," he says.

The vehicle's engine shuts off. Rubio opens the door and stands aside and a man in a pristine white suit and fedora enters. He is tall, of resolute aspect, and Jessie knows that *here's* the chief of the bunch.

He peers into the hallway, then looks at Espanto and says, Did he bring it all?

He did, Espanto says with a smile. Four full bags. It's in the backseat of the Sierra.

Galán nods. Then he gestures at the body on the floor. "Quién es?"

The Apache, Espanto says. He tried to kill the blonde here, but Rubio stepped in and that's the result. My fault. He was a crazy bastard and I should've seen it and shouldn't have hired him.

Galán gives Jessie an appraising stare, then looks at Rubio, who turns up his palms and says, He gave me no choice, chief.

The fault is mine, Galán says. I should not have approved the hire. Gallo on lookout?

Yes, Espanto says. He hasn't seen the gringos or he'd have called me.

The *gringos?* Jessie thinks. . . . *Charlie?* She begins to understand why she's down here. Why she's been set apart.

They may have turned off before this street. I couldn't see, Galán says. But it's just the two of them. Maybe they lost Belmonte and are searching for his car. Maybe they're going around the block to come from the other end of the street, try to outfox the lookout.

He glances into the hallway again. But first things first, he says. Then goes into the hall, Espanto following.

She knows without question what they're going to do, but she cannot find the voice to remonstrate. To plead for them, beg for them. For Luz and Susi, Aldo, José. She can only think, *Oh, dear Jesus, no, please no.*

Rubio leans on the wall and studies the palm of his hand.

In less than a minute comes the first gun blast. Followed by incipient screams cut off by more shots, very close together. Then four more, evenly spaced, and the house goes quiet again.

She feels hollowed, incapable of coherent thought.

There's a burst of gunfire somewhere out in front of the house. Rubio draws his pistol and rushes to the window, squats beside it as feet come thumping down the stairs. He carefully pushes the curtain open a few inches to take a peek—and a gunshot pops a glass pane and the rear portion of his head disintegrates in a red spray and he falls back wide-eyed dead with a small black hole above an eyebrow. Jessie slides off the chair and huddles on the floor.

Galán and Espanto and Cabrito run in from the hallway, crouched low. Espanto yanks out the cord of the crookneck lamp, dimming the room to the candlelight of the shrine and the glow from the kitchen door.

Hold them till we honk for you, Galán says to Cabrito, then come running.

"Bueno, jefe!" Cabrito says, and positions himself behind the end of the sofa and facing the front door.

Galán pulls Jessie up by the hair and shoves her into the kitchen ahead of him, Espanto already at the back door, easing it open. The Sierra stands not four feet away. With an arm around her from behind, Galán holds Jessie tightly to him, his pistol to her head, and presses her forward to the threshold.

A brown Jeep SUV stands a few feet behind the pickup. It looks unattended but he can't be sure.

"Oye, gringos!" he calls out. You see who I have? You shoot at us, I shoot her!

There's a smash of glass in the other room and a volley of gunfire and he says to Espanto, *Go!*

Espanto bolts to the Sierra and scrabbles into it. Galán sticks the pistol in his waistband and propels Jessie toward the truck by the back of her sweatshirt and the seat of her pants and heaves her into the cab and clambers in after her. As Espanto revs the engine and starts blaring the horn, Galán makes sure the back door is unlocked for Cabrito and grins at the bags of money on the seat.

Cabrito staggers to the kitchen doorway, his gun dangling in his hand, his face bloody and distorted—and two pistol shots knock him into the jamb.

Galán yells, Go! and the Sierra roars away as Cabrito hits the floor.

Galán tells Espanto to take a left at the third alley ahead. It's a narrow turn and Espanto has to brake hard. The Sierra scrapes the alley wall and loses the right side mirror, and they're speeding on.

Before making the turn, Espanto caught a side-mirror look at two men getting into the Jeep. They're coming, he says.

Good, says Galán. Because I know where they're going.

46 — RAYO

She watches Charlie and Rudy slip around the corner to the hold house street, then gives her attention to the alley. As soon as she ran back after putting the Jeep in there, she realized she had made a mistake, but couldn't bring herself to tell Charlie. She should have parked a little farther back from the camper shell Sierra. Where the Jeep stands, it blocks her view of the back door.

It now comes to mind that the bastards might come out of there with hostages for protection. Charlie didn't say what to do in that case. What if JJ's one? What if they take them in the Sierra and haul ass? Got this end of the alley blocked with the Jeep, yeah, and it's a cul-de-sac at the far end, but when she parked in there she saw cross alleys up ahead. They can cut out through one of those. The Jeep's in good position to give chase, but on a night like this, all you'll see of them is their taillights. They get into heavy traffic, you can easily lose them, and JJ. Unless . . .

She looks around, sees no one, and dashes up to the Jeep. The drapes are closed on the upper-story windows, but somebody might open them at any time and see her, so she has to be quick about this. She peeks around the front of the Jeep at the closed back door—which she's sure opens to a kitchen as in most of these old houses—then scoots over to the Sierra, which she now sees is equipped with black glass. She has an impulse to try the driver's door, see what the cab might be holding. The *keys* maybe? But what if there's an alarm? Forget it. Standing near the back end of the camper shell, hidden from the doorway, she takes out the Ruger and with a clout of the barrel breaks the truck's left taillight cover. Then brushes the red plastic shards under the truck with her foot. Won't be as hard to tail them in traffic now, if it comes to that.

She's scanning the alley for a position with a clear view of the back door when there's a pistol shot upstairs, followed by screams cut off almost immediately by several shots fired in rapid sequence, and then four distinct reports.

She stands rooted. There's a short clatter of pistol fire on the other side of the house.

What to do? Stay here? Run around to the street to help Rudy and Charlie?

There's a single gunshot out front. Then silence again.

She can't leave. What if the fuckers come out this way?

She squats low among the trash bins on the driver's side of the Sierra, prepared to shoot whoever comes around to get behind the wheel.

A voice calls out from the back door for the gringos to see who he's got, and if they shoot at him he'll shoot her.

He's addressing gringos, so *her* must be JJ, Rayo thinks . . . and God damn it, they *are* taking her . . . and if you shoot the driver when he comes around, they'll kill—

There's a sound of breaking glass in the house and a barrage of gunfire and somebody yells, *Go!*

She's holding the Ruger ready and hoping the driver doesn't see her so she doesn't have to shoot. Then the truck starts up and the horn starts blaring and she realizes they all got in on the other side and they're about to take JJ away.

Do something! she thinks.

She jams the pistol in her jeans and scoots in a crouch to the rear of the Sierra and gets on the recess in the middle of the step bumper, grabbing tight with both hands to the tailgate latch just below the camper shell's back window. At which moment two shots sound in the kitchen and the Sierra lunges forward with a roar.

Speeding away, she sees a body lying in the door . . . and then Charlie and Rudy are there, gaping at her with their guns pointed, then sprinting to the Jeep.

The Sierra skids into an alley, grinding against a stone wall, almost jolting her from her perch.

47 — RUDY AND CHARLIE

We've had excellent shadow cover all the way up the street and have heard nothing other than distant barkings and the rustlings of leaves in the chill breeze. Not a soul to be seen. Not a window showing light. Places like this know when danger's afoot, when to lay low. We're almost to the yard of the house where Belmonte turned in—an SUV and Suburban parked in front, the Caddy in a short driveway, the porch and windows dark—when Charlie grabs my arm and we freeze. He very slowly guides me a few feet over to the deepest shadow of a large tree alongside the broken sidewalk, then puts his mouth right at my ear and whispers, Building across the street. Far corner.

It's dark over there, too, but there's just enough glow from the lamppost at the far end of the block so that if you look hard you can begin to distinguish shapes and discern movement, as I do after a half minute of intent searching. Somebody's standing at that corner of the building, the uppermost part of him slightly moving above some sort of barrier. The lookout. Shifting around a little, maybe trying to get more comfortable. I wouldn't have spotted him on my own, but Charlie's always had the night vision of an owl.

We're debating what to do, keeping our eyes on the lookout's indistinct form, when gunshots sound in the house, a bunch close together, then four measured ones. Coups de grâce is my guess.

"Mother*fuckers!*" Charlie hisses.

The guy across the street steps out from the edge of the building, maybe as surprised by the shots as we are, maybe thinking of heading for the house. Just one step out, but it gives us a partial silhouette and Charlie says, "Smoke him." We each fire three rounds and down he goes.

Paralyzed, staring at the lightless sky, the rain in his eyes, Gallo is astonished by the towering arrival of his death. If only I had known, he thinks. If I had only . . .

We hotfoot it to the Suburban and take cover behind it, ready to shoot whoever of them comes out of the house, but nobody does. But a lower corner of the porch window suddenly shows light as the drape moves aside slightly and then something blocks part of the light—a head taking a look—and I say, "Dibs," and shoot, and the head vanishes.

We run to the porch without drawing fire. I'm on one side of the door, Charlie's on the other, the side with the window. The knob's on his side, too, and he reaches out and tries it very gingerly and it turns. He eases the door inward the tiniest bit to keep the latch from closing. "Go low," he murmurs, and I get down on my belly right next to the door.

Standing clear of the window, he smashes one of its panes with a snappy flick of the Beretta barrel, and somebody inside starts shooting, the bullets punching the drape through the glass, and I push the door open and see a goat-bearded guy crouched at the other end of a sofa. In the second it takes for him to see me lying prone in the doorway, a car horn starts blowing behind the house and I shoot him twice in the face, taking off part of one cheek and a chunk of his chin—and I can't believe it when he swings his gun over and shoots back. I roll off to the side with bullets gouging the door sill and glancing off the concrete floor of the porch.

Charlie peeks through the window, then runs into the house, and I jump up and follow and see him stop at a doorway and shoot into it twice. We hear a vehicle pulling away in the alley and we dart to the back door and hop out over the goat-beard guy, our guns up and ready to shoot the tires, and we see Rayo huddled on the white truck's bumper. Looking back at us all big-eyed.

She wouldn't be there unless Jessie's in the truck.

"Come on!" I say, and we run to the Jeep. We were both given a key to it this morning and then Charlie gave his to Rayo but I've still got mine. The truck turns at a cross alley as I get us rolling, and Charlie says, "Dumbfuck cooze! Why didn't she get off and get in with us?"

It's a silly question I don't bother to answer. He knows why. Because she couldn't be sure we'd catch them, but as long as she's on the Sierra she's with Jessie.

I whip into the cross alley, banging a back fender on the stone wall, and we see them up ahead, one red taillight and one white. They're hauling ass pretty good.

"That busted light's *her* doing, man," I say. "Smart!" The tag light's out too but probably their deliberate doing.

We figure they took Jess because somebody made us when we drove through the neighborhood. Saw we were Yankees and so knew who we'd come for, who to hold the gun to. We also assume they saw us getting in the Jeep before they made the alley turn and know we're coming. I leave our headlights off anyway, just to make it tougher for them, not pinpoint ourselves.

We follow them this way and that, turning into other alleyways, other streets, zooming down long lightless lanes of mostly dark buildings, our wipers working at the drizzle. Intermittent vehicles go by in the other direction, and now and again we have to pass somebody that turns out in front of us from a side street and whose headlights give us a glimpse of Rayo before we cut ahead of them and can't see her anymore. I have to wonder what those drivers make of a girl crouched on a rear bumper. Or of us running without lights. Probably nothing. Not around here.

48 — THE NEIGHBORS

Within minutes of the last gunfire, of the sounds of vehicles speeding away in the alley, the boldest of the young street rats converge on the scene, moving in warily. Then the word goes out that the place is deserted but for the dead, and the neighbors descend on it with their tool kits and looting sacks. They make swift work of stripping the vehicles, ransacking the house. The vanguard rats acquire guns and phones, the cash and credit cards and driver licenses from the wallets of the four downstairs bodies, one of which they have to unwrap from a blanket. There is outrage on discovering nothing of value on the bodies upstairs but their shoes. Across the street, three young boys happen on Gallo, and while two of them fight over which of them will have his gun, the third runs off with his wallet and phone. The last looters to leave the house call the police and report a mass killing in the neighborhood and that two of the dead are federal policemen, an embellishment to ensure that the cops will respond and clear the bodies away before they stink up the neighborhood.

The police arrive in a half-dozen wailing, flashing vehicles, including a special tactics team in body armor and armed with automatic weapons, plus a night beat crime reporter who was at the station when the calls came in. The cops are both relieved to find no colleagues on the scene and furious to have come out here for any lesser reason than to assist their own. Their first inclination is to interpret the scene as a gangster dispute that for whatever reason included the obvious executions of the two males and two females upstairs. There are no purses to be found, and discarded wallets are without money or credit cards or other forms of identification—except for a body in the hallway, next to which are scattered several club membership cards.

Half an hour after their arrival at the Alpha house, the lead investigator and the reporter are on their way to deliver the terrible news to Mrs. Belmonte and ask what she knows about her husband's presence in that place.

49 — RUDY AND CHARLIE

We're soon out of the slum altogether and jarring over a muddy washboard road, moving through utter blackness except for the city's glow behind us and the Sierra's headlights on the road ahead, its red and white taillights, and a dull amber glow along the lower sky ahead. We'd seen the glow when we turned off the southbound road but didn't give it much thought, then lost sight of it in the slum. Now there it is again. We're on a gradual rise, moving into the foothills. Charlie can't believe she's been able to stay on that bumper.

"That latch isn't much to hold to," he says. "I was just waiting for that corduroy section back there to shake her loose."

"She's strong," I say. "And limber as a cat."

"Pretty cold wet cat about now."

If we turned on our lights we'd see her, but we might blind her too, maybe spook her by lighting her up, plus we'd be letting them know exactly where we are. Without ambient light, and the sky so black, they can't see us, can't know how close we are. All they know is we're back here somewhere. If she weren't on the bumper we could move up close enough to shoot out their tires, bring the bastards to a halt, have a parlay.

Tell them keep the money, take the Jeep, just give us Jess. They'd have nothing to lose and could go for it. That'd be just fine. We could track them down later and exact recompense.

But she *is* on that bumper. If we get too close and she falls off without us seeing it, we could run over her before we know it. There's nothing to do but keep our distance and tail them till they stop, then try to promote the deal before anybody pulls a trigger.

I don't now how far we've come or how much time has passed when they turn off onto a side trail, rutted and rocky and steeper yet. Wherever we are, it's way the hell outside the city. The glow across the lower sky is now directly ahead and seems to be redder.

"What *is* that?" Charlie says.

Their headlights swing left and right as they climb and we follow them a long way before the lights disappear, and we know they've cleared the hilltop.

Then we crest the hill, and Charlie says, "God *damn*."

The source of the red glow is spread before us like a sea of hell.

To the left, the Sierra's making away on the tableland bordering the pit—and in the hazy radiance of the fires, we can see Rayo's dark figure still hunched at the tailgate.

We give chase.

50 — JESSIE

Winding their way up the hillside, they talk as freely as if she weren't even there, jammed between them on the seat. Though they can't see it, they know they're still being followed by the Jeep with the two gringos—*Charlie*, Jessie's sure of it, him and somebody else of the family. As the Sierra wove through the lamplit alleys and streets of the slum, Espanto had caught glimpses of the Jeep in his side mirror, running with its lights off. Since entering the darkness of the countryside, he's lost sight of it, but neither he nor Galán doubts the gringos are still right behind them.

Galán plans to bushwhack them. They're heading for a shantytown he is familiar with, a place bordering a garbage fire pit. They'll follow the pit's perimeter to where both the road and the pit rim make a sharp turn leftward behind a rocky rise that will put them out of sight of the Jeep long enough to cut off their lights and pull over and get out, ready to shoot. When the Jeep comes around the curve, they'll be within ten feet of it and they'll fire as many rounds as they can into the windshield and front windows. The Jeep's momentum will carry it off the curve and onto the shoulder and probably into the pit, but if it doesn't quite make it, they'll push it over the rim. Once it sinks into that smoldering rot-sodden bottom it will be forever lost.

Galán sees it as a much wiser and neater way of getting rid of the gringos than if they had killed them back at the hold house. Three dead gringos on television and in the papers is a matter the federal police could not dismiss, and zealous federals on a mission are a distraction to every criminal enterprise in the capital, small and large. It would not be in our interest, Galán said, to be the cause of any distraction to the Zetas. Jessie has read about the Zetas, and the idea that these men are in some way associated with them deepens her dismay.

Three *absent* gringos, on the other hand, Galán had continued, is a much different matter. Who can say where they have gone or why or whether they even want to be found? Who can even say whether they are dead or alive? No bodies, no crime. No distractions from the federals. The Zetas will be appreciative of such care on our part.

Three dead gringos.

Jessie heard him clearly.

Three absent gringos.

Charlie and whoever's with him . . . and who else but her?

They talk, too, of the Beta house, which she comes to understand is the other hold house. *Was* the other house. There was an accident, an explosion in the basement. A drug laboratory they hadn't been aware of. It destroyed the place and everyone in it—their partners, and the other half of the wedding party. Galán tells Espanto to see to it that Spoto pays for that mistake.

As they say, however, Galán adds, there's nothing bad that happens that doesn't bring some kind of good with it.

Espanto glances past her to grin at him. More for *us,* he says.

Money is such a poor recompense for the loss of loved ones, Galán says. But we must carry on as staunchly as we can.

They both chuckle.

They're all gone, she thinks. *All* of them.

She cannot suppress a small sob.

They ignore her.

Now they're on a truck road overlooking a monstrous garbage pit to their right, its black surface mottled with countless patches of pit fires, red and steaming in the soft rain. She can tell there's a sort of slope all along its edge but has no idea how steep it might be. In the light of the dashboard, the men's faces are shadowy carvings. The speedometer reads a hair over seventy kph, which she knows is around forty-five miles an hour, very fast for a narrow muddy lane and seeming even faster in the encompassing darkness and the ghostly rain in the headlight beams. There's also a scattering of vaporous fires at a distance to their left, illuminating the shantytown dwellings in eerie geometric silhouettes. The roadside is littered with refuse of all sorts, much of it unidentifiable, though she notes a wheelless bicycle, a large headless doll, a birdcage, all of it passing in the flash of the headlights' side glow like fragments of a distraught dream.

She feels removed from her own reality. Abducted from herself.

By the glow of the garbage pit, Espanto can now make out the black shape of the unlit Jeep in his mirror. They're holding at about forty, forty-five yards, he says.

Good, Galán says. That's sufficient leeway for us to get set before they come around the curve. Dim the lights and be ready to move fast. It's coming up. Maybe a mile.

51 — RAYO

She's relieved to be able to see the Jeep's dark form behind them, to know they can now see her, if not very well. She's wet and shivering, rainwater running from her soaked hair down her neck and into her jacket and shirt like icy little snakes. The pit's smoky stench burns her throat, her nose, stings her eyes. Her fingers are almost numb from the cold drizzle and the effort of clinging to the small handhold of the gate latch. As the Sierra had come up the hill, the downward pull of her body strained her hands so that she thought her fingers would break, and her shoulders had hurt to their roots. She has at times almost lost her foothold to a hard bump, a jarring patch of road, a sharp turn. She cannot guess why these guys have come up here, or what Charlie and Rudy have in mind to do, but she knows she can't hold on much longer. It shames her that she can't, but it's the truth and she'd better deal with it, because if she tries to hang on like some kind of champ she's going to fall off and lose JJ. Once again, she has to *do* something. *Now*. She tightens her left hand's grip on the latch, gritting her teeth at the pain, then eases her right hand from the latch and grimaces at the ache of flexing those fingers to loosen them. She puts the hand to the Ruger in her jeans and makes certain she's got a sure grip on it before drawing it out. Then she leans down, hanging by her left arm, her right arm stretching below the bumper. She angles the Ruger slightly to the right and squeezes off a shot and blows the tire. The rear of the Sierra abruptly sags and yaws and detaches from her grip. She's briefly airborne and then tumbling over the muddy ground, still holding the Ruger, then crawling fast to the meager cover of a mud knoll and crouches there, knocking mud out of the pistol muzzle.

52 — RUDY AND CHARLIE

Her dark form moves, shifts on the bumper.

"What's she doing?" says Charlie.

Then *bam*, we see the muzzle flash and the Sierra tilts and sways and she's flung off as the thing skids and does a one-eighty and comes to a stop facing us, off the road and only a few yards from the edge of the pit.

I pump the brakes, trying to keep from skidding in the mud, and we fishtail a little as we slow down and stop about fifty feet shy of them.

Their headlights just sit there, the seconds ticking by, and I wonder how Charlie proposes to broach them about a deal. I can't find Rayo. "You see her?" I say.

"Hit the lights."

I switch on our headlights and we see the front passenger door wide open and somebody standing behind it—and then their lights flare brighter, huge and blinding, and *bam*, they're shooting.

We duck behind the dashboard with bullets popping through the windshield and whanging on the engine block. Charlie squeezes between the front seats and into the back, and I'm right behind him. We yank down the backseats to get to the swing door and open it and he gives a loud grunt and we tumble out. I pull my gun and huddle behind the wheels . . . and God almighty, the stink!

They've shot out our headlights and now the motor quits. The shooting stops for a moment, and then there are two more shots, a second apart, and their headlights are out, too, and the only illumination on us is our taillights. Charlie breaks the one on his side and I bust the other, and we're in the blessed dark.

"Guys? You okay? *Guys*, over here!"

Rayo! She shot their lights.

We peek around the Jeep and see the Sierra standing darkly against the back glow of its taillights, both front doors open, Rayo's vague silhouette moving toward it.

"They ran off!" she calls.

We hustle over to the truck as she looks in the driver's door, saying, "JJ?" and then opens the cab back door and asks again, and then we're all at the rear of the camper, which is slanted to the right, the blown tire's wheel mired in the mud. She lifts up the shell window as I lower the bed gate and we see by the taillights' glow that Jessie's not there either.

"They went off that way," Rayo says, pointing up ahead. "I couldn't see clearly. They had these bags, the money, I guess, I don't know. I couldn't see if she was with them, but she must be! God *damn* it!" She starts sidling in the direction the way they went. "We can catch them. Come on!"

"We *can* catch them," I say to Charlie. "They don't know if our vehicle's dead and they have to reckon we'll drive up the road, so they'll stay way off it, close to the pit. But with Jessie and those bags, they ain't gonna set any foot-speed record, wherever they're going."

Rayo's still moving away. "Come *on!*"

"You guys do the chase," Charlie says. "I'll hoof it up the road in case they try to cut over to the shantytown."

There's something in his voice besides the urgency of the moment, and he's pressing a hand to his left side and just above his belt, the side away from me. I sidestep for a better look and see a stain under his hand. "Hey man—"

"Yeah, yeah," he says in a lowered voice, glancing past me at Rayo. "Don't announce it. Can't run, but I can walk up the road." Then loudly says, "Get going, *go!*"

"What is it?" Rayo says. Maybe she caught the thing in his voice too.

"Go!" Charlie snaps.

We do.

A second later, the taillights go out. I hadn't thought of the silhouettes we made against them. But Charlie did.

53 — JESSIE

Galán is pulling her along by the handcuffs, holding her to the bag hung on his shoulder, Espanto beside them. When they opened fire on the Jeep, she was sure they were going to shoot her, but here she still is, and the only reason she can think of is they still see her as a bargaining chip.

The men cannot believe their tire was shot from a moving vehicle some forty yards behind them and running without headlights, but there's no other explanation and in any event it doesn't matter how it happened. They keep glancing back at the Sierra's taillights, the vague silhouettes moving about them. Then the lights vanish and the darkness is mitigated only by the pit's orange glow from their right and the ground before them is absolute blackness. The rain is in steady drizzle once again and their footing is unsure. They stumble on rocks, their feet suck through mud. Jessie's socks are sogged around her ankles and the pain of her feet is now worse. The bags weigh heavily on the men, and the engulfing fetor adds to the labor of breathing. Up ahead are what look like low black hills, their crests rosy with fire glow.

Speaking in huffing breaths, Espanto says he's sure they killed the Jeep's engine, and just as sure the gringos are coming behind them on foot. But *they're* not weighed down and are sure to catch up.

Not before we get . . . into the Mounts, Galán says, panting. We ambush them . . . throw them in the pit. . . . In the morning when . . . the trucks come . . . we ride back in one.

The Mounts! That's what she sees ahead. Hills of a sort, yes. She's seen them before, on a midsummer day during her research trip, and had been told that's what the mounds of garbage in this region of the pit are called—Los Montes—and as bad as the stink is now, it had been far worse in the summer heat, the storm of flies like some biblical plague. Along here, the rim slants slightly into the pit, and it's too dangerous for the garbage trucks to back up close enough to dump their contents into it, so they unload the garbage on the flanking ground. The daily mounds accumulate, and once a week bulldozers equipped with extrawide tracks and blades on extendable long arms are trucked up here to shove it all in.

They're almost to the nearest mound when Espanto looks back and says, Here they come! Keep going and . . . I'll slow them down.

Jessie sees them. A pair of vague forms in the smoky light. When Espanto stops and turns toward them, they drop to the darker ground. He fires shots in their direction, then hurries to catch up.

Then they're into the mounds, moving through firelight and shadows, weaving around heap after heap of garbage, clanking through tin cans, crunching on Styrofoam, their feet squishing in mud and who knows what else, Jessie again fearful of gashing or puncturing a foot. They catch periodic flashes of the fire pit, its profound stink undiminished by the rain. She hears the skitterings of rats in the rubbish, the low growlings of dogs in the deeper shadows.

They arrive at a small clearing and there's the fire pit, directly before them, their view of it framed by opposing pairs of mounds near the rim. Galán tells Espanto to position himself on the rim side of the mound to the right and he'll set up on the inward side of the one to the left. Their chasers will most likely turn left just before the left-side mound, stepping into Galán's line of fire and giving Espanto a clear shot at their backs. If they come up to the pit to search the rim side of the mounds, they'll be presenting their backs to Galán. Either way, they'll have them in a crossfire.

"Muy bien," Espanto whispers, and hurries off.

Galán takes Jessie with him.

54 — RUDY AND RAYO

One of the guys stops and turns and we drop to the mud on our bellies just as he opens fire, muzzle flashing. Then he's off again, following the other guy, and we're up and running too. With those bulky bags hanging on them, they're large shapeless forms and we can't tell which one's got Jessie and we can't risk shooting her. They disappear into what Rayo says is a bunch of garbage hills. In the pit's glow they look a little like black buttes with ember-covered crests.

We enter the hills of garbage and stop to look around, listen hard. Through the low patter of the rain, we hear a clatter of cans and head in that direction. We sprint from one mound to the next, pausing to keep a fix on the sounds of their movement, then hustling on, following their winding route. Then we come around a mound and see the fire pit right in front of us, the rim maybe forty feet away. It's a clearing of sorts, maybe a turnaround point for the garbage trucks, flanked by two mounds to either side.

It's unlikely but not out of the question that they'd lie low in the warmth of the rim until daylight. Best to check out the rim sides of both mounds. If they're there, though, they'll be facing the gap between the two mounds, ready for whoever might come to the rim for a look. I put my mouth to Rayo's ear and tell her I'm going to circle around the dark side of the mound on the right and check out the rim. She's to stay right where she is and watch both mounds.

"Got it," she whispers.

55 — ESPANTO

It's not much of a rim. Maybe six feet wide, slight downward slope covered with gravel. Some garbage trucker risked his ass to dump a load this close. Same goes for the mound opposite. Maybe a bet between drivers, a pissing contest. He keeps the bags on his shoulders, imagining the horror of setting even one of them down and then accidentally bumping it and sending it sliding into the pit. He's crouched low, facing the opposing mound across the gap. His line of sight extends only a few feet past the inward side of the opposite slope, but that's enough to see anybody who turns in there. Excellent crossfire setup. Smart man, Galán.

56 — RUDY

It's awful dark on this side of the mound, and slow going over uncertain ground. The putrid breeze coming off the pit is a mix of warm and cold. I truly doubt there's anyone on the rim and feel like a dope for having chosen to waste time checking it out. These guys are running, not looking for a fight. If they would just let Jessie go, the whole thing would be done with. Which the assholes would've found out if they hadn't been so quick to start shooting.

I'm holding the Beretta muzzle up by my shoulder as I come around the mound and step out onto the rim and I don't see the guy until he's coming up from his crouch and whirling around toward me. If it weren't for the heavy bags hanging on him he might've had me, but the bags slow him enough for me to pop him three times, center mass, staggering him rearward, and he squeezes off a wild one as he steps back off the rim and drops out of sight.

I get on hands and knees and carefully ease up to the edge of the rim and look down at the smoking red-black talus twenty feet below. No sign of him or either bag.

There's a sound to my left and I jerk back and whip the Beretta up . . . and there's Rayo, pistol pointed at me.

We both lower our guns and grin big.

57 — JESSIE AND GALÁN

Rather than position himself at the mound opposite Espanto's, Galán goes past it and then passes two others before crossing a fire-lit patch of ground and posting himself in the deep shadows just beyond it. This is a better spot to lay for them. If they go to the rim, Espanto will still have the edge on them. If they come this way, they will be open targets when they step into that lighted ground. If they go some other way? Fine. He'll stay here until the trucks come in the morning. Before then, Espanto will come looking and find him. And the girl will be in the pit.

He unshoulders one bag with a grunt, then tucks the pistol into his pants and switches his grip on her cuffs to his free hand and lets the other bag slide off his shoulder.

She flinches at the pistol reports—four of them, fairly close by, though she isn't sure of the direction they came from. Galán pulls his gun and grabs her to him, holding her face to his chest and rasping to her to stay quiet.

The last gunshot was from a Glock, he's sure of that, and it may have been Espanto's, though half the world now carries a Glock.

She smells his sweat and feels his heart beating under her cheek. Her cuffed hands, pressed to the side pocket of his jacket, touch on an object it holds. She knows what it is. Recalls the one Espanto used on Belmonte at the Alpha house.

Hey you! Listen! . . . Your partner's dead!

Rudy! she thinks. Galán's hold tightens, nearly smothering her. She eases her hands into the jacket pocket.

You hear me? . . . Let's make a deal!

Galán believes that Espanto is dead, but he knows the sort of deal they have in mind. Give us the money and the girl and we'll give you a bullet in the head. No, thanks, fuckhead, not today.

If I see you, Galán yells, *if I hear you coming . . . I kill her!*

He hears a faint *snick*, and before he can react she twists sideways and drives the blade into his stomach with both hands. In instinctive reaction, he clubs at her with the pistol, but holding her pressed to him as he is, the blow is clumsy and only partially catches her ear. *Shoot her!* he thinks. But she lets go of the knife and grabs the pistol barrel, pushing the muzzle away from her. They slip and fall in the mud, fighting for possession of the gun, she with both hands, he with one, his other arm still holding her to him. They writhe and gasp like possessed lovers and she feels the gun slipping from her grip and clamps her teeth onto his hand, biting hard on the bones of it, tasting muddy blood. He snarls and the gun slips free of them both. His bitten hand searches for it as his other holds tight to her sweatshirt, but she's able to heave herself up over him and drive her forehead hard into his mouth—then pull free and roll away, and she's on her feet and running.

Breathless with pain, he sits up, sees her fading into the deeper darkness, his hand finding the gun, but now she's gone. The switchblade is buried in him to the haft. He takes hold of it with his left hand and yanks it out, breath hissing, eyes flooding.

She's calling for someone.

You're all right, he tells himself, wiping his eyes. It's not bad, it's not bad. Doesn't feel like there's much blood. Get it cleaned, sewn up, cauterized, whatever, you'll be fine. It's only pain. Now think, man. *Think.*

Phone. His phone's in the Cherokee. But even if he had it, who could he call? Who's left? There even any reception out here? Fuck it. You don't need help. Never have. You can handle this. He spits a mouthful of blood. Runs his tongue over his mashed lips.

Should have killed the bitch as soon as we were clear of the house.

Now other voices. Briefly, then silent. The gringos.

She knows he has the money. She'll tell them.

Bracing himself with the hand holding the pistol, his other hand at his wound, he manages to get to his knees in the mud, then stand, and tucks the gun into the side of his waistband. He drags the bags over to the near mound and kneels at its base and digs into the garbage with his hands, digs into the rot and stink and filth of it, digs until there's room for one bag, then for two. Then covers them over with the excavated garbage.

Wheezing with the effort, choking on the horrid stench, he throws up, nearly fainting at the twisting agony in his stomach.

He wipes at his eyes again, at the snot streaming from his nose. There, he thinks. That's better. You're all right.

He listens for sounds of their approach but hears nothing other than his own pained breath. He stands up and stumbles over to the adjoining mound and sits down, facing directly at where he put the money. It's right there, he tells himself. That's all you have to remember.

Sweet Mother Mary, just *look* at this suit.

There's a darkness on his shirt and the front of his pants where the blood has spread. He takes off his jacket and balls it up and presses it tight to his stomach with one hand and holds the Glock in the other. They show themselves, you kill them. If they don't . . . fuck them. Just sit here till the garbage trucks or the flatbeds come in the morning. Won't be long. You pull the bags out and give a driver money and ride into town with him, then give him more money and direct him to Mago's. Mago will fix you up. Done it before. . . .

58 — RUDY

If I see you, the guy hollers, *if I hear you coming . . . I kill her!*

"That motherfucker!" Rayo hisses. "I swear to God, Rudy, I *swear to God. . . .*"

"Hush," I say. "Listen."

We're standing in the little clearing in front of the pit rim. It's hard to place where the guy's voice came from. Rayo's waiting for me to say what we're going to do, and I don't know. We stand still, listening hard. Waiting . . . waiting.

"*Charlie! . . . Charlie!*"

We turn toward Jessie's call and Rayo's about to yell something but I say low voiced, "Don't answer! He might be with her."

We listen and listen.

"*Charlie!*"

She runs out from behind a mound less than fifteen feet away, just her, and Rayo calls, "JJ! Over here, baby!" At the same time I yell, "Jessie, this way!"

She stops and stares at us as we come running.

And then we've got her, and I cut off the cuffs.

The cloud cover has broken somewhat, and although there's still sporadic sprinkle, bits of moonlight are coming through. Jessie's limping, rubbing her chafed wrists, Rayo holding her close. I'm bringing up the rear, continually checking behind us. Jess said she left the Galán guy with a switchblade in his gut, so there's not much chance he's going to come up and nail us from behind. I keep a close eye anyway. If you're not sure they're down for good, you assume they're not. Basic rule.

We spy Charlie up ahead, sitting in the road. He sees us, too, and gets up slowly, dropping the hand from his side and tucking his pistol in his pants.

Jessie slips out from under Rayo's arm and hobble-runs to him. I flinch when she throws herself on him and he swings her around. He sets her down with a slight cringe and she realizes he's hurt. She puts his arm around her shoulder as if she might support him, insisting he lean on her, and he's grimacing and laughing.

We move off into the shadows and Charlie tries Chino's phone and it's as dead as mine, but Rayo's still has a charge and he gets reception. He calls Rigo and tells him where we are and says yeah, we're all okay except he got nicked in the side and Jess is pretty beat-up and her feet need attention. He listens for a time before saying, "Yeah, I think so, too. That's how we'll do it. . . . All right, we'll be waiting."

Charlie tells us somebody in the hold house neighborhood called the police and they found Belmonte's body there, and his wife and the

Sosas have told them all about the kidnapping. Tumaro and his guys are coming for us and will take us to a private medical center where he and Jessie can get patched up. Rigo thinks it's better to let the cops know Jessie's alive rather than let them think she's dead and later find out she's not. Charlie agrees. She'll have to talk to them, though. Routine stuff, but some Wolfe lawyers are going to talk to her first. Also, Mateo is no longer critical.

Charlie then calls Harry Mack. "Hello sir, it's Charlie.... Yes sir, we have her. She's all right.... No, sir, no, we're all okay." He listens, clears his throat, and says, "Thank you, sir. I appreciate it." He listens some more. "Yessir, I understand.... Yes sir." He hands the phone back to Rayo but doesn't say anything about the call.

We go back down to where the two vehicles are and wait in the Jeep, Rayo and I in the front seat, Jessie with Charlie in the back. While we wait, she tells us the whole thing.

Almost the whole thing. She purposely leaves something out. Over the years I've interrogated a lot of people and listened to a lot of explanations and versions of one thing or another, and I've gotten pretty good at sensing when something's being deliberately omitted. Maybe Charlie and Rayo picked up on it too. Whatever she's skipping, though, it's not something that would endanger any of us for not knowing it, or she would not have left it out.

"He's still got the money," Jessie adds. "Half of it, anyway."

For a minute nobody says anything. Then Charlie finally says, "The money's not our business. They didn't take it off anybody in our house. We got what we came for."

Nobody argues the point. Jessie falls asleep against his chest and doesn't wake till Tumaro and his Jaguaro crew show up in the two Acadias, plus a tow truck to take the Jeep back.

Tumaro asks if any of us is in shape to drive one of the Acadias, then tosses me the keys and says to follow the other one, and he and the other Jaguaros get in it. Having caught a whiff of us, they'd rather ride back in a crowded vehicle than in one with any of us in it.

59 — GALÁN

He does not immediately know what revives him or how long he's been out. It's very cold. The rain has stopped. The clouds have broken and there's a bright oval moon. Under the abiding stink of the pit, he can smell the sop of his own blood. His tongue tastes of copper. His swollen mouth is gummy.

There it is . . . the sound that roused him from his pain-hazed sleep.

Growling.

From near the mound to his right? He can't see the dogs but knows they're there. The pistol! *Where's the pistol?*

At his side where he dropped it.

All right, you sons of bitches . . .

He points the gun into the black shadows where the loudest growls are and squeezes the trigger—and the pistol, its barrel packed with mud in his struggle with the girl, blows apart and removes his thumb.

He screams and curses. Howls his agonized rage at the moon.

The dogs flee.

Then a short time later come back.

More of them this time. The growling is louder and seems to come from all sides.

The first of them materialize from the shadows like nightmare apparitions. Snarling. Craze-eyed. Insane with hunger. Drawn by his blood on the fetid air.

And then they're on him in a biting, tearing frenzy.

60 — RUDY

We follow Tumaro to a medical center in which the Mexican Wolfes are chief shareholders. Everyone recoils at our reek, and once Charlie and Jessie are put on gurneys and rolled away to be treated, Rayo and I give the staff a break by going outside to wait on a bench. The Jaguaros are out here too, but stay upwind of us. The sky is mostly clear now, with a gibbous moon to the west. It's cold out here but feels good.

A pair of criminal lawyers in the employ of Juan Jaguaro himself had been waiting when we arrived. They had a short private session with Jessie before she was rolled off for treatment, then they called the police. Rigo has already spoken to the head administrator, who in turn has instructed the staff in what and what not to say to the cops if they're questioned. Shortly, a trio of homicide detectives shows up and they and the lawyers repair to a private room to wait for Jessie.

For a while Rayo and I just sit there on the bench, not saying anything. It's been a hell of a day but it's been easy working with her. Yet for some reason I can't figure, and even though I'm older than she is and, if I say so myself, I've had a way with the ladies since I was a kid, I don't know what to say to her.

Which is when she tells me she'd like to go back to Texas with us to spend some time with Jessie. "I know she'll have the best of care," she says, "but it'll be a while before she can walk without pain. Plus, she might have a time of it for a while dealing with, you know, what's happened to Luz and the others. She might like it if I was around to lend a hand or, I don't know, just to talk to. What do you think? Should I ask her?"

"Oh hell yeah, you should ask her," I say. "I think it would make her really happy. She'd love to have you there while she heals up, she really would, really good of you. It's a great idea." It's a struggle to quit babbling.

She's smiling the greatest smile I've ever had smiled at me. "I'm glad you think so," she says.

Charlie had been afraid the bullet hit a kidney, but he proves lucky. Like Lila the barmaid says, he's not called Charlie Fortune for nothing. He walks out of the place on his own, stitched and bandaged, all cleaned up and in sweat pants and sweater. Rayo goes to him and hugs him gently and asks if he's in pain and he says not now, after the injection they gave him. Catching my "do not disturb" look, he excuses himself to go talk to the Jaguaros, and she comes back to the bench.

Jessie's no less lucky—a black-and-blue ear, a few stitches in her feet, a bunch of bruises and cuts but no real gashes. We're notified when she's brought out of the treatment room in a wheelchair and we go inside to see her. She's been cleaned up and makes a big show of holding her nose and waving us away. An attendant then wheels her to the room where the police are waiting and we go outside again.

As we later find out, she gave them a simplified version of events, omitting details that might naturally be missing in an account of a terrified and confused kidnap victim—which, as she has emphasized to us more than once, she damn well was. Mainly she wanted them to know what happened to the other five members of the wedding party. The cops had heard of the meth lab explosion—a not altogether uncommon occurrence in the slums—but would never have tied it to the missing kidnap victims if not for Jessie's information. One of them immediately relayed it to headquarters.

When she asked if Mrs. Belmonte or the Sosas had requested to speak with her, the cops seemed embarrassed to have to tell her they had already asked the surviving parents if they wished to see her, and they had all said they saw no reason to.

Who can blame them? Not us. They have ten members of their family to bury.

Ten.

Rigo and the other Wolfes want us to stay for as long as we'd like, at least a few days, but they understand that the Texas side of the house is anxious about Jessie and wants her home as soon as possible. She's now wearing a pair of thick sponge-soled sock slippers that are easy on her bandaged feet, and she can limp around with the help of a cane, though the doctors have advised her to stay off her feet as much as she can for the next two weeks. She jokes about comparing walking sticks with Aunt Cat when we get home.

While I get cleaned up at the Operation Center, Rayo Luna goes home to do the same.

We collect her on the way to the airport.

TUESDAY MORNING

61 — CHINO

He has been scraping and scraping the tape of his bound hands on the seat's metal frame, his shoulders and arms aching, blood seeping from his wrists, his broken thumb a swollen anguish. At last the tape severs. He sits up, groaning at the pain in his spine, then carefully works the tape off his eyes and mouth. His broken tooth is an agony. By his watch, it's 4:27. The rain has quit and there are glimmers of starlight. He reaches under the driver's seat and finds the Glock and eases out of the car. He makes sure there's a round in the chamber and that the magazine still holds ammunition, then slowly stretches and twists, grunting, sighing. He probes under the floor mat on the passenger side and finds his spare key. He goes around and gets behind the wheel and starts the Focus and backs up and looks into the empty alley. He had heard the shooting, the vehicles speeding away. Had some time later heard the sirens, the crackling car radios, had surmised the whole thing had gone to hell. He drives up to the intersection and passes through it slowly and sees the flashing light of a single remaining cop car in front of the Alpha house. Maybe some of them got away, he thinks. Maybe with some of the money. Nothing to do but go to a doctor, a dentist, then home. Wait to see what happens.

Anybody who made it will be calling soon, checking to see if *he's* still standing. And if after a while no call comes, well . . . there are other gangs.

62 — MELITÓN

The morning breaks bright and chilly and pretty. The sky an immaculate blue but for the wispy smoke at the far horizons of the greater city. Melitón's neighborhood lies refreshed, the streets gleaming, the green trees sunlit, the air clean and bracing. At a sidewalk table of a corner café, he reads about the kidnapping of an entire wedding party the night before last and its terrible outcome last night. The families have declined to speak to the media. The police say none of the perpetrators have been identified, but the investigation is ongoing.

He sighs. Then signals the young waitress through the plate glass. She comes out and refills his cup and remarks on the lovely weather, and he smiles and says it is indeed.

The pity, she says, is that it doesn't last.

Yes, he says, that is the pity.

63 —THE PIT

By midmorning the bulldozers have come off the flatbeds and are at their task, engines gnarling, the drivers wearing goggles and smog masks, wielding the extended blades, gouging smaller heaps out of the mounds and shoving them into the smoking pit, all the dross and refuse and bloated dead things, all the jetsam and junk and now worthless matter, including a pair of engorged blue gym bags and the muddy remnants of a white silk suit.